About t]

Tabatha Stirling is a published writer, poet, book cover artist and indie publisher living in Edinburgh, Scotland with her husband, two children and a depressed beagle, called The Beagle.

Her publishing credits include *LITRO, Spelk, Literary Orphans, Mslexia, Feminine Collective, Sick Lit Mag, Scottish PEN* and *The Magnolia Review.*

An extract of her addiction memoir is to be published in the *Wild and Precious Life* anthology edited by Lily Dunn and Zoe Gilbert.

When she's not writing, reading grimdark fiction or designing she enjoys watching dark, blood-splattered dramas like *The Walking Dead, Ray Donovan* and *Sons of Anarchy.* Tabby is absolutely ready for a zombie apocalypse.

BITTER LEAVES

BITTER LEAVES

TABATHA STIRLING

Unbound Digital

This edition first published in 2019

Unbound

6th Floor Mutual House, 70 Conduit Street, London W1S 2GF

www.unbound.com

© Tabatha Stirling, 2019

This book is a work of fiction and, except in the case of historical fact, any resemblance to actual persons, living or dead, is purely coincidental.

ISBN (eBook): 978-1-78965-021-1
ISBN (Paperback): 978-1-78965-020-4

Cover design by Mecob

Printed and bound in Great Britain by Clays Ltd, Elcograf S.p.A.

First and foremost, I dedicate this book to Clarita Dumadora Baer. My heart sister and great friend whom I based the character Lucilla on, and she was kind enough to let me use her mother's name for the character's name. Without her testimony and courage and the moving accounts from so many maids and helpers in Singapore – this book could never have been written.
Thank you, Clarie Bell, Mahal kita po. Xx

Acknowledgements

To my darling Bub and Boo – you have made me a better woman, person and mother. Your love is a blessing and gives me so much strength.

And my Papa Love – for being the first person to actually tell me to commit to my writing or just give it up – but make a choice. And I did.

To my mother, Diana, life will never be the same again. You've gone and I miss you every day. So much I want to share and can't, but your loss has helped me to produce some of my best work – so your influence still shines through.

And my father, Brod Brodhurst, in your words, 'a bit of a bastard but I do what I can'. I loved you anyway.

Robs, my brother – God! I miss you. I wish you'd see your worth and brilliance because I do.

Desiree and my darling Rory and Gabs. Don't see you much but know that I love you.

Ria and Auntie Colin. My BFFs. Probably wouldn't be here if it wasn't for you both. Constant love and support, worry and acceptance – you are both beautiful human beings. And to my Godsnorks, Louis, Ella-Jane and Elsie.

To my Muv and Farv – thank you for being so supportive of my endeavours and forgiving of my foibles. Best in-laws in the world – and Rachael, Abi, Owain, Corey and Stuart.

Johnny Coburn – because… well, you know. x

Authonomy friends – so much talent. Kate, Angelika, Big O, Mr Maitland, Bradley Darewood, Skippy, Di Dickson, Sebnem, Matteon, Katerina, Nutkin & Russell, my favourite 'reds'; Polly (if I only had half your talent); Ellie (first review on Authonomy, which snowballed because you are so respected – thank you); Tottie Limejuice … bonkers and glorious; Tee Tyson – so full of grace; Robarticus – also bonkers and glorious and a brilliant actor – take note Hollywood but hide your green plants! And all in our Facebook Write and Rant group.

Once upon a time there was an online writer platform called Authonomy. It was a complex and at times quite insane window into the minds and craft of writers. This was the first outing for *Bitter Leaves*, formerly *Blood on the Banana Leaf*, and it was a wild ride. I met some incredible friends and extraordinary talent and if I missed anyone please forgive me.

To all my Unbound author chums – Colgers, Sarah, Helen, Ian, Shona, Emily and the rest of the Unbound Social Club.

To the Society of Authors for the encouragement and safe harbour. Your ongoing support is just brilliant and generous grant was vital to my work.

To the ones I've lost. Judith Williamson: oh! darling Jude, how I miss you. So much more for you to have written – so much more to discover about each other. Swing on, sister x

To my editor Scott Pack, who found me on Twitter and put up with my Aeschlyean tragedy that was happening because 'writers are needy buggers', aren't they? To Mary Chesshyre – frankly my respect for copy editors has risen stratospherically because of her insight, ideas and thoughtfulness – thank you.

To Lesley Glaister, Jean Rhys, Lionel Shriver, Chimamanda Ngozi Adichie, Simone de Beauvoir, Maya Angelou, James Baldwin, Flannery O'Connor, Denise Mina: your contributions to literature and blinding talent have shaped me into the writer I am today. Thanks doesn't seem enough but you have mine. To Sylvia Plath for showing me how poetry should be written – authentic, brave, true.

To the first reviewers on The Pigeonhole, in particular Lesley and Pheadra. Incredible reviews that made my heart sing – *enorme merci*.

To everybody at my super-cute publisher, Unbound, for the support and for publishing my book; they have given writers a credible but unconventional route to traditional publishing.

Everybody who pledged for *Bitter Leaves* – this is your book too.

All the maids and helpers in Singapore and all over the world – I hope they see you now, brave women.

Dear Reader,

The book you are holding came about in a rather different way to most others. It was funded directly by readers through a new website: Unbound.

Unbound is the creation of three writers. We started the company because we believed there had to be a better deal for both writers and readers. On the Unbound website, authors share the ideas for the books they want to write directly with readers. If enough of you support the book by pledging for it in advance, we produce a beautifully bound special subscribers' edition and distribute a regular edition and e-book wherever books are sold, in shops and online.

This new way of publishing is actually a very old idea (Samuel Johnson funded his dictionary this way). We're just using the internet to build each writer a network of patrons. Here, at the back of this book, you'll find the names of all the people who made it happen.

Publishing in this way means readers are no longer just passive consumers of the books they buy, and authors are free to write the books they really want. They get a much fairer return too – half the profits their books generate, rather than a tiny percentage of the cover price.

If you're not yet a subscriber, we hope that you'll want to join our publishing revolution and have your name listed in one of our books in the future. To get you started, here is a £5 discount on your first pledge. Just visit unbound.com, make your pledge and type STIRLING19 in the promo code box when you check out.

Thank you for your support,

Dan, Justin and John
Founders, Unbound

Super Patrons

Kathryn Backhouse
Festive Barclay
Papa Big Beard
My darling Clarie Bell
John 'Brod' Brodhurst
Johnny Coburn
Claire Crowe
Susie Driver
Lesley Glaister
Clare Jenne
Emma Macaulay
Yvonne Marjot
Nick Matthews
Jock Hoots McCrivens
Hannah McGoran
Cass McMain
Evelyn Mitchell
Rachel Moore
Barbara Morgan
Kate Murdoch
Pat Murdoch
Nicole Nic
Matthew Ogborn
Diana Robinson
Maria Simpson
Michelle Simpson
Fiona Spence
Roslyn and Iain Stirling
Jill and David Wall

Sabre Green is a pseudonym for a genuine neighbourhood in the West Coast area of Singapore and the characters created and described are fictional. Most of their experiences, however, are not.

Singapore and related countries have a complex and quite ritualised system of Foreign Domestic Worker employment. The employers are called Ma'am and Sir and the employees are referred to as the maid or helper. Quite often these women's Christian names are changed for the convenience of their employers.

LUCILLA

19 Sabre Green

The black clouds gather in the distance over the South China Sea. The storm comes here soon; I can smell it in the steamy air and the over-heated frangipani in the garden. My throat chokes on homesickness. I miss the fresh air of the Leyte Mountains and the cool streams of the gorges there. I miss my mother and her smell of banana leaves and woodsmoke.

Ach! This missing will do nobody any good.

Here it comes. The rain. It bloody pours down, as my Ma'am would say. She is making bread and kneads the dough with a wistful expression. My Ma'am says it remind her of her mother who died five years ago and my Ma'am still misses her with much pain. Sometimes, I find her crying softly and I tell her, *mahal kita*, Ma'am, and she reply, *mahal din kita*, Lulubell. And I hug her and her perfume smells like Moh jasmine. She has black hair too and green eyes like mossy rocks in the river back home. And her smile is light up the world smile. And her heart is God filled.

Other days, she has the sad sickness and sometimes she stays in bed all day. She never closes her door though. Ma'am say she always wants her little boy to know she is there for him. Ma'am loves her child more than rain in a desert. She is like a Filipina in that respect. Not like the other expat ladies often drinking and having parties. And she has good figure not like other western Ma'ams. They look so old with their wrinkle skin, cloud-white hair and bones sticking out like hungry branches. My mother always exclaims, 'Who would choose to be thin when you have so much food available to you?' And I have no answer for her.

Asian woman are naturally slender. Our frames are small and our smiles are big. Some Sirs have an agreement with the maid and pay headache money to them. When the Ma'am has headache the maid keeps their Sir 'company'.

My Ma'am and Sir are very in love. They cuddle and kiss all time except when Ma'am has her sad sickness. Then Sir brushes the hair gently from her face and his face loses sun too and becomes dark like night. And he don't smile properly until Ma'am feels better and begins to smile again. I will know she is better because she will sing down the stairs and hug me and cry, good morning, Lulubell, and smile that big smile and hug me again and all the sparkle returns to the house in a blink. And she has energy to do her yoga or running.

But not today. Today Ma'am is in the grip of the sadness so I chop some fruit and arrange it prettily for her and make a cup of tea. Ma'am prefers strong black tea from the terraces that line the mountains in her homeland in Sri Lanka. My Sir met my Ma'am in London and they fell in love. But my Ma'am's father was very angry because he wanted his daughter to marry an older, wealthy man who had been chosen when my Ma'am was just a little girl. Her jadestone eyes and skin just a few shades darker than mine are much prized in her homeland.

But my Ma'am refused and eloped with my Sir and they married and had Rory. And this beautiful boy's grandfather was so in love with the baby that he forgive my Ma'am and welcomed Sir to the family too.

Sometimes my Ma'am shows me pictures of the big cities in Europe where some of the women look like me. Ma'am says that is because my ancestors were Aztec princesses. She sighs that my hair is like a midnight waterfall and my skin like *café con leche*. I think I look ordinary like all girls from my village but my Ma'am is right because I do have good hair. It is silky and shines in the sun. Western men like it very much and always want to touch. They see women like me as exotic butterflies. My friend says the *ang moh* like to capture butterflies and stick pins through their wings. I'm not going to let that happen. That's not love.

I let myself wander slowly round the house. It is not a big house but still takes some cleaning. With my beloved little boy, Rory, running here and there pulling the world's dirt behind him, like a baby elephant hard at play. Today I find myself in his bedroom and I let my fingers trail over his bed covers and smell his boy smell. Sweet and sour; delicious like mangosteen. And I love him like a bleeding heart. He has many toys and every Christmas time he chooses some to send to my village. And good ones too. This boy is full of spirit and God's love. He will grow into a man who respect women and do not fear them.

My Ma'am says that western men here see us as fresh starts. That most of them would never get a girlfriend back home unless they pay for it. She says they are disgusting and wrinkles her pretty nose. We were shopping last week on Orchard Road and we pass many old men with young young girls. The men are sweating with pride and the girls look pleased with themselves. Ma'am says that they should be ashamed, strutting around like peacocks, and that these men are no better than slave traders, buying girls with diamonds instead of shackles. I smile small at her because no *ang moh* can truly understand how poor we are. My village in Leyte is a bamboo-shack village. No electricity and no medicine. Some of the kids don't have slippers and walk to school barefoot. Barefoot is okay, but there are snakes and creatures that bite in the jungle. Sometimes a child steps on spider and it is a long time to the doctor on a moped.

Ma'am wants to visit the village but I keep making excuse because I am both ashamed and proud of my village. I don't want her to see our shabby clothes and the dirt. The cockroaches that run up and down the walls like drain water. The toilet is a hole in ground. But I am proud of the love and laughter. And that I am a fortunate daughter indeed to have Rodrigo and Mayella as my parents. My mother stiff-limbed but full of grace and my father, handsome still and proud of his family

My Ma'am cannot understand. Praise God! How could she? I look around my room which is much bigger than other maid rooms and I have a double bed with a soft mattress. I decorate the walls with stickers of free, pretty things. Butterflies, flowers and birds. My friends are so jealous. Let me work for your Ma'am, they cry, and sigh over the *maganda* leather shoes my Ma'am gives me for Christmas and tiny bottles of *pabango* from France.

My Ma'am gives me all her little creams. She calls them samples. I have Chanel and Lancôme and Guerlain. They smell so good. Most I send to my mother in the big boxes back to the Philippines to my village that smells of dirt and rain and banana leaves. Where hope dies for many. But not for me! I have hope. I'm not going to become *angmoh* weekend girlfriend. Or China man's mistress.

I have a boyfriend. He is China Malay. He is kind. Sometimes too jealous. He tries to read my texts on my phone and demands who that, and who this? It wears me down but it's so lonely here and worse if you are single. Sometimes, he takes me for seafood on the East Coast and we watch the shipping lanes and listen to the foghorns. When there is a sea fog the big container ships look like ghosts in a strange dance and we play a game guessing where each ship has come from and where it will go to next. But when I see the word Pinoy painted onto a hull homesickness haunts me for the rest of the evening. Sometimes my boyfriend is understanding but often his face sours like old durian and he lights another cigarette and sighs heavily between puffs.

Singapore is a city of glass and light but it isn't friendly to us. The Ma'ams stare us down like lions and work their maids too hard. The Indo and Myanmar girls get a much worse life than me and they are paid less. Like sad Shammi who lives next door. She is paid 350 dollar one month. But until her debt is paid off to her agency she won't get paid at all. Eight months, no day off, no wages. And now she looks like a *multo*, a pale, slow walker living between two worlds.

I see her washing that damn car at 5am every morning. What is the point of cleaning a car in Singapore? Bloody rains, lah! Every second. My Ma'am says it's about oppression. The employer make the maid clean the car simply because he have the power to. Ma'am's face darkens as the light leaves. Like when she grieves her mother. And she mutters about modern-day slavery and bloody Nazis. And she sigh very deep like it hurts. And I say, oh, Ma'am. And her clear eyes mist and she trudge upstairs as if her heart is broken.

And I so want to make her smile again so, like I say, I prepare the fruit the way she like it. I arrange the blueberries and strawberries like a flower, and cut up the cantaloupe into sweet wedges and perfect mouthfuls. And the longan that my Ma'am say are like delicious eyeballs. I've never eaten eyeballs and I'm too scared to ask Ma'am if she has really eaten one. If a person can eat an eyeball what else could they eat? I cross myself quickly and offer up a prayer to Jesus and St Jude and take the bowl up to my Ma'am. The bedroom is dark and breezy from the fan but she lie still and sad and I hover like a worried Mama until she gently ask me to leave.

Later, I move slowly up the stairs, sweeping gently. Ma'am has beautiful wooden stairs although it keeps dust too close like lovers who can't let go. But I find the sweeping a peaceful job. My Ma'am is not fussy and she never checks or runs finger over the furniture to look for dust like Chinese employer, and my face sours at the thought. Even the Singaporean taxi drivers complain about the China man, and their fists clench and their mouths screw up into a tiny ball like a baby wailing. The Uncles, they smash their fists onto the taxi steering wheel and whine like dogs. *Damn China man this* and *damn China man that*. And also *I have a friend who like pretty Filipina. You want give me your number? He very rich.*

They never say my friend is very nice or my friend work in an animal shelter on the weekend. Never, my friend will read you poetry while dusk settles or look after your family forever. Being wealthy is the prize to the China man more than beauty or happiness.

It is everything.
And it is nothing.
Ashes in mouth nothing.
Sour yam nothing.
Child cries nothing.

MA'AM LESLEY

35 Sabre Green

The left side of my face flares in pain whenever I eat or drink. It is a mass of bruised flesh. Although, as I now seem to have turned into a social leper and venturing outside is unappealing, I just sit and manage the pain. I have become a tired, obsolete object, and while I wait for the Xanax to start its miraculous, gentle rescue I feel the torpor in this city of steel and glass. That wrings me out and leaves me gasping. I feel old and crumpled. The tiny waist I had as a young woman is a wistful memory. I fear I'm now the very cliché of a middle-aged frump.

What makes me eat so much here and why is my gorging so secretive and anxious? I stuff chocolates into my mouth without tasting them and cower in the bathroom, running the taps to disguise the crackling sound of their wrappers. Devouring them, one by one, heedless of my fat and disgust, until the ornate Venetian mirror reminds me. I have such beautiful shoes and clothes but they mock me endlessly from the wardrobe, reminding me that I resemble a sow in Louboutins. Asian women are so thin and graceful. I've never felt so invisible as I do here. Only five years ago, when Ralph was offered a job in Zurich, I was having dreams of Toblerones and mountains in Lausanne. But he chose Singapore.

How I hate it here. I cannot settle or even have a reassuring drink because of my bloody hormones that dash about like manic horse flies. There are times when my body is a dynamo and times when I can't leave my bed. And meanwhile Ralph is uninterested, attracted only by the beauty of *things*. He tries, I suppose, but the talented, confident younger woman he married has aged. And he is exceptionally disappointed with the results.

The problem with Asia is that fat western women are an anomaly here. We don't shine and we can't resort to corsets and velvet drapery because it's too bloody hot. So I have started wearing shapeless blouses and sensible skirts just so I don't feel too obvious. I've bought some size twenty clothes back from the UK where the shop assistant didn't actually snigger or look embarrassed and for a moment I felt quite confident. Whereas the last time I tried clothes shopping here was a humiliating experience. I walked into Marks & Sparks in Wheelock Place and just browsed a bit, getting my courage up. When I approached one of the sales girls, a tiny Singaporean with false eyelashes and breasts, and asked if she had any larger sizes, she shook her head in a decisive way and stared pointedly, just above my head, until I realised that I was dismissed, and I left.

As I walked out of the store with their scornful laughter adding to my humiliation I decided I would never put myself through that again. Later at home as I sobbed into my towel I cursed those skinny little bitches. I was thin once. Thin and not bad-looking. Perhaps not the belle of the ball and in great demand, but not exactly a wallflower either. When did it all change and I become middle-aged with all the clichéd attachments?

I'm thankful that the invitations to the dreaded dinner parties have dried up and I don't have to make endless excuses. Feeling like paper cuts every predictable comparison with other women. I'm not even fat and jolly, just fat and sad. Very bloody sad and somewhere, 35,000 feet above the Bay of Bengal, I lost my sense of self and started to become a shadow.

And here I am creeping about trying to smuggle packets of Fox's biscuits into the house and secreting them in what I viewed as clever, silent places. But Jocelyn, our housekeeper, always finds them and enjoys making me feel guilty and humiliated. She is so capable and easy with her life. I hear her and Ralph laughing together sometimes in the evening and I suppose I should be thankful that he has someone who does manage to make him laugh in this house.

I must have failed him in many ways but by far my greatest betrayal, Ralph informs me, is that I can't give him a child. The golden baby that would have changed so much for us. He gave up trying two years ago. By that I mean he doesn't touch me at all. And anyway I have become a sweating piece of dough that has over-risen. Eventually the initial talk of adoption dried up. It must be embarrassing for him to have a barren wife. I should be grateful that he still bothers to live here with me.

But I wish heartily that Jocelyn did not. I would much rather attend to my own housekeeping. I find it very soothing and I'm good at it.

I like to handwash clothes and bedlinen, gently encouraging the suds, easing out the stains, making things look pristine again.

Sometimes, I daydream I am back in Bristol, maybe owning a modest dress shop. At night, after closing for the day, I would climb the stairs to my tiny kingdom and snuggle up with my cats. I would have two, but not haughty, distant things. Probably a couple of Norwegian Forest cats with coats that would make a Viking proud. They would wind their furriness around my legs and neck and make me feel safe. I would pop a nice ready-meal in the microwave. Maybe salmon and watercress, or something cheerful like that, and pour a glass of wine. Not the unfriendly, sour white wine that Ralph likes but something syrupy and unfashionable. And then I would read a book or watch forbidden television programmes, like *Bergerac* re-runs or *Midsomer Murders*.

And I would be happy.

Now I find myself pretending to love Ralph's life and its exhausting trimmings. His friends tolerate me but they are all ex-public school. Not one from a comprehensive, and sometimes I think they enjoy teasing me when they ask about whether I like Lambrusco or something similar. The fact is I do like it. It's cheap and sweet and I feel comfortable drinking it. I also like Babycham but haven't had that for years because it definitely is on the forbidden list. Along with toilet. I have to say 'loo' or 'bathroom'. Ralph really hates it when I forget. But I get so nervous and, naturally, begin to forget far more frequently. And then I have to deal with the consequences. Of course, Ralph is very apologetic about hitting me. Well, he used to be; not so much any more, but then he rarely acknowledges my existence at all these days.

I remember when I was free to cook and bake, but Jocelyn doesn't like me in the kitchen. She doesn't like me downstairs really, and moans that I bring down dust from upstairs into her clean space. She tells me that my area is upstairs and hers is downstairs and that it is better that way. Last time I tried to cook she became quite nasty. It's very hot in the kitchen because there's no fan and the air conditioning is ancient. I was reducing some stock in my risotto and wiping my red and steamy face with the edge of my sarong when I felt a spiteful hand grab my hair and wrench me back from the stove. The shock and pain buckled my knees and I sprawled onto the kitchen floor. A flurry of slaps stung my cheek and my ears as Jocelyn made her displeasure clear. And as she ranted about my weight, and countless other faults, I lay there and accepted it all like the useless lump I have become. I know that she wants me out of the way. I wonder how far she would go to achieve this. And do I even care any more?

Sometimes when I get lonely I wander downstairs making sure Jocelyn is out of sight. If I can hear the television from the *drawing room*, as Ralph insists it is called, then I tiptoe past and wait for one of Jocelyn's cackles to cover the sound of me quietly opening the front door. Once I ventured into the drawing room, or front room, as I call it, and found Jocelyn lying on the sofa, one hand holding a glass of champagne and the other plucking chocolates from a box of champagne truffles that I had received for Christmas but been banned from eating by Ralph. Honestly, I'm not that keen on champagne and don't understand the universal devotion to it. I stood in the doorway long enough for Jocelyn to notice me, and when she did, her teeth clicked in annoyance and her throat made a sound like an irritated thrush. What you want? she drawled. Jocelyn gave up calling me Ma'am a long time ago. I was never comfortable with it anyway. This is my time, she insisted, and waved me away with a dismissive hand. Her fingertips were brown and sticky, like they were covered in shit. It gave me a tiny thrill when she licked them clean. But as I stuttered an apology and backed out it occurred to me that she was only doing what deprived children do when they come into possession of things and spaces. I found it hard in that moment to be angry. She had had so little and I so much of life already.

Anyway, once I'm outside, I like to stand hidden by a pillar and watch the neighbourhood children play in the park across the green.

The cicadas start their chant early in the day here and the gnarled, canopied rain trees stand guardian over the patchy grass. The houses around Sabre Green are uniformly pleasant. But underneath the manicured surface lurks a pitchy darkness. Each house has an iron gate and grilles on the windows giving it the impression of an isolated fortress. The residents play at being sociable, but their attempts seem forced, as if they are reading a manual on how to do it properly. Just before dusk the play area starts to fill up with maids and children. Western, Indian, Chinese, Singaporean, Japanese and the odd Filipina. If I had a child we would play over there too, and I would refuse to let anyone do any tiny thing for him or her at all. I would celebrate my motherhood and swing from the stars with it.

I think Ralph mentioned that he would call his son Oliver when he still thought it was possible. I quite liked that. Although, Ralph would have forbidden any shortening of the name. It would have been formal and polite. Just like Ralph.

When my husband first told me that the blame lay firmly at my feet for not conceiving, I did ask to see the evidence. I wasn't able to smile for eleven days after that and my jaw still crunches badly. I only wanted to know, to see, if I could do something about it. Take a herbal remedy or seek a second opinion. But Ralph became enraged. I never asked a second time. As he stood over me he explained, very clearly, that the fact that I couldn't bear him a child was so deeply disappointing and hurtful that he never wanted to hear it mentioned, ever again.

I tried to understand his hurt, to share it. I thought that if we could comfort each other a bit and talk about options perhaps we could find a solution. But Ralph was adamant that Dr Liu had told him quite forcefully that I was infertile. The emphasis he put on that particular word made it seem that Dr Liu and the whole of the specialist fertility community in Asia were also deeply disappointed with me. He refused to discuss it and I was forbidden to contact the fertility specialist. I wanted to tell him that I was disappointed enough in myself and that I wore my failure like a winter cape, heavy and unyielding.

Soon after, Ralph stopped bringing visitors home, and I became frightened of leaving the house. It was odd that nobody rang and that when I tried picking up the handset I could never hear a dial tone. I presumed that this was an Asian constant and with all the naivety of a new resident gave it little further thought. Jocelyn and Ralph have their mobile phones and there are always flurries of activity around them, but Ralph has insisted that I don't need one. Who was I going to call anyway? I stared dumbly back, hoping that a name would spring to mind, but he was right. I couldn't think of a single person who might call me.

My family seem to have given up. Mum is very old now and the last communication I had from my sister, Linda, was when she put Mum in a residential home and could we spare some money for the fees? I had tentatively put this idea to Ralph and he had said, quite generously, that he would consider it, but I never asked again. And consequently, I never heard back from my sister. Now all their faces have become blurred and inconsistent like faulty memories and it is easier to let them fade away gently – a hopeful dementia.

What will happen to me if Ralph decides to move on? I promise I'd go quietly and gratefully back to suburbia but will it be enough for a man who eradicates all evidence of past mistakes? Even in the heat, anxiety squeezes my stomach so completely I have to run for the lavatory. How long am I safe for?

SHAMMI

20 Sabre Green

When I came here it was with big happiness in my heart. I knew I was doing a good thing, making my parents proud. The girls that go to Singapore and Arabia are spoken of with reverence and as good, dutiful girls.

Sawtoh, the skinny girl from my village, she married a western man and now they live in Singapore in a palace with beautiful children and swans. I hear her bed is made from gold and she has many servants. I wish her luck but I never liked her much. She was cruel to animals and the younger children. Would pull pigtails and tear clothes and kick the dogs around the village when the mood took her. My Ebu says the devil is inside her. I don't disagree with Ebu, but I think that Sawtoh is just very selfish. Most of the girls who marry western men are cunning but – until they have ring on their finger – they play it very sweet like *bubur candil*. Sawtoh must have been kicking many puppies but in private to mask her real self. I feel sorry for that western man. He went to the market and bought a duck but it turned out to be a fire ant.

It is very dark here at my Madam's house. I am expected to wash the car before the family wake up. As I stumble out with sleep still in my eyes and weary bones that sigh I see the other black shapes, other maids washing other cars. We might smile and nod but we never call out. The maids that wash cars know better than that. We are divided between the maids that speak and the maids that do not. I see the happy girls wander down the road carrying shopping and *chat chat* on their cellphones and I think how good do you have to be in the eyes of the Lord to deserve an employer like that? One that gives you free-dom and maybe one day off every month or even every week, like

13

Ebony Ma'am? And I steal a glance next door to reassure myself that she is still there.

The sun is rising and I think I am lucky to see such glory every day.

I haven't been to church for a long time. I think God must be very angry with me. But Madam does not believe in church and she say that I'm a heathen and no better than a dog. I ask for a few hours off to attend service but Madam says that is selfish of me. *Selfish! Selfish! Selfish!* And I get a slap with her hand each time she shouts the word. The children watch and their faces are full of bitter leaves.

If the dog barks after a certain time at night then it is my fault and money is added onto the agency bill. How am I to keep the dog quiet? Bind its mouth? Speak softly to it like I do with the piglets back home? The dog is excitable and hot tempered. It does not get enough exercise. I tell Madam at the beginning that I will walk the dog for hours. I would run the dog and laugh with the dog and we would take off with happiness and fly back on a cloud to my village. But Madam says *no!* Sometimes I think she say no so much that a yes might kill her.

Madam gets angry very quick and I learn not to speak, not to ask and not to be. I am forbidden to speak to anybody outside of the household and am only ever allowed to talk to Madam or Sir if I bow first or they ask me a question. My Madam is very particular and old-fashioned about such things. She is from a province in China but my Sir, he is from Singapore. Madam is very pale and she refuses to go out in the sun. I am expected to hold a parasol over her head when we go out in the day. I am also expected to walk slightly behind her. It is difficult and when I first arrived I would trip and stumble. But when we are out I can look at the world around me. I see the big houses and the even bigger office buildings. So much glass and light. Only sometimes does Madam take me into the city but when she does I study everything so I can't forget. I watch the sky the most and remember that my Ebu and I share the same sky every day to make me feel less lonely.

The kind woman next door is also brown-skinned and her skin is like honey-roses and she has green eyes like a watermelon rind that glow with health and sweetness. She is full of love and smiles at me when she sees my tired spirit. I call her Ebony Ma'am because she shines like the polished roots of the wood tree that grow near our village. After Ebony Ma'am caught my employer slapping my face Madam makes me do it to myself now. Ebony Ma'am was very cross with my Madam and shouted very fast and when she shout at my employer I heard *police*. So now Madam makes me take a shoe in my hand and hit my own face with it. If I don't hit hard enough she makes me do it again and again. At least it is a flat shoe. One of her spike heels that look like a spear would hurt much more.

I don't tell my parents about these sad things. It would only worry them and what would they do? Old people worry more, it is well known. My mother's health is no good. They need the money I send home. And I am happy that they can't see my teardrops and my blood drops. I am not allowed a phone so I could only make a call if Madam was out. But who would I phone? The village I come from doesn't have telephone lines or electricity. My Ebu and Bapa sleep on the floor on mats. There is more room now I have gone. But that is little comfort. And they are expected to grow hashish on their land. A man from the government came and shouted at them. My Bapa shouted back, why would we want to grow something we can't eat? And the man hit Bapa across the face and spat at his feet. He said he did not care that Ebu and Bapa would not eat. He did not care that they might die of hunger. And if the government man thinks that then that is what the big men in Jakarta must think.

Last time I saw my parents was two years ago. At least, I think it was. Sometimes, I forget things. I am so tired because five hours sleep is not enough for a person. Am I invisible? Dear Lord, please see me. Please, Jesus. Am I so low that even my God has turned away from me?

Late in the evening while I am sweeping the porch steps and feeding the koi fish that swarm to the side of the pool whenever my shadow darkens the water, I steal a little time leaning on my broom for a few seconds to gaze wearily through the fence at the family next door. What I see is like a picture from the tatty western book our Ebu used to read from at night. Even as little ones, my sisters and I never understood that what we were hearing might actually be real. The story was called *A Little Princess*. It was about a western girl who had

15

lost her Ebu but her Bapa loved her more than anything. She was sent away to a school, which to us sounded like a terrible punishment, but western ways are different and strange. Then her Bapa died and she was made to live upstairs in the attics. My youngest sister, Yuli, used to say that the house must have been a mountain to have so many floors and how was it a punishment that she had a bed for sleeping, and four walls and a fire and no cockroaches. Yuli is a spirit of the air. She likes to fly free. Then in the story the rajah who lived next door transformed the young girl's attic into a fairy cave where she ate and drank and took care of the other poor girls. Soon she was rescued and lived happily ever after. I used to believe in ever after and fairytales. Now, I believe even more in monsters.

Next door is like the good queen's kingdom. Ebony Ma'am wears her heart in her smile. Her helper is from the Philippines and laughs and hugs her and the little boy. I love that little boy. He looks like an angel from my Bible books. He has a tan skin but blonde hair like his Bapa and green eyes like his Ebu. Their helper, Lucilla, is very friendly to me but it is difficult because I am forbidden to speak to her. But she whispers that she can go out every night and every weekend. She has a lovely room with her own shower and her Ma'am gives her birthday day off and brings back presents from her travels. Every year the maid visits her parents and Ebony Ma'am pays for it.

Sometimes Lucilla will press an apple into my hand or hide some homemade sweetmeats in a hollow between the fences. Once they gave me a necklace for Christmas. It is the most beautiful thing I have ever seen and I keep it under my pillow.

I am not supposed to speak to her, but some days Ebony Ma'am will reach through the slats of the fence and hold my hand softly. She looks me in the eyes and says God bless you, *Babu*. She tries to speak my language and has stuck signs on the tall marble pillars in her garden that read 'We love you!' and 'Don't give up!' in Javanese.

Madam gets very angry when she sees them and wants to know what they say. I tell her I don't know what language they are speaking but smile secret and wrap my arms around my skinny chest keeping the memory of the words close. Madam can't do anything about the signs because they are not on her property. Ebony Ma'am knows this and laughs at her. Madam hates her very much. She spits in private about Indians knowing nothing and how they are just jumped-up chapatti workers. Through a clenched mouth she say that the immigrants in this country are bringing it down and it is time to stop tolerating the trash. She says the darker the skin the more animal is in you. She stares at me when she says this because I have dark skin. And black, downy hair on the sides of my face. Madam says I look like a monkey and laughs. Sometimes she says it in front of her friends that look like glass. They play cards for hours, slamming and slapping them onto the table.

Why are the Chinese so loud? It hurt my ears and head but I have to wait to the side of the table, staying still, and they play and talk about me while I stand there in full view. How lazy I am. How hairy. How dark.

The darkness is in *their* hearts. Not mine.

MADAM EUNICE

134 Sabre Green

Singapore is not what it used to be. And not just geographically, where it has changed out of all recognition, but demographically as well. I told Little Ping and Joyce that the dark-skinned maids and Indian man would soon swamp us for construction. And, praise Taisui, that they need to have their bottoms kicked.

My husband is a very well-respected man in the community and he says the Indian man is lazy to his bones and that he grumbles about everything. The wages, the lodgings and the long hours. No Hokkien man or woman would complain about having a job, and long hours are to be expected and embraced.

We have a good end-house so the chi can flow between buildings. It has five bedrooms and three bathrooms. We only use four of the bedrooms – for my mother, our two children and myself. Both our children, Philip and Bernard, are doing exceptionally well at their studies. They do many after-school activities at which they both excel. Philip is eight and already has won the science prize at his school. Bernard is younger and now speaks Mandarin, English and can do many maths problems. I tell them time and time again that to succeed you must work and practise hard. Childhood is short but life is long. Do you want to spend your time playing with toys, or preparing yourself for a successful adult life? They are both quiet children and very respectful to their parents. I approve of that. *Xiào* is the most important virtue in our culture. In English it would translate as 'filial piety', which means your parents are sacred and you should spend your life both inside and outside the home honouring their names and their lives. The adult offspring must work hard at their careers and be able to support their parents in financial need, always display courtesy, ensure male heirs, show sorrow after their parents have died and then manifest that sorrow in sacrifices.

This is our way.

I am proud to say that I have two obedient and hardworking sons and that I have done my duty. I feel both pity and contempt for my friends, Joyce and Little Ping. We call her Little Ping because she is very tiny. Under five foot and with small-girl hands and feet. Joyce has managed only girls and Little Ping cannot conceive. A sad but unforgivable thing for a woman. Surprisingly, her husband still loves her. My husband would have divorced me instantly and I would have bowed my head in understanding because having children is our duty.

Having boys is better.

Little Ping told us confidentially at our last Mahjong game that she'd been to an HDB – a Housing Development Board apartment block – on Serangoon Avenue last Friday night to visit a psychic her cousin's wife had recommended. The oracle had apparently told her cousin's wife that all her children would be male – to much rejoicing. Little Ping will not disclose what she herself was told by the oracle, but she seems lighter somehow, and I feel irritated by this. I am used to feeling superior, and her constant *tristesse* was reassuring. This change in her heart is frustrating. *Wah piang eh?* Is it not enough that her husband still loves and cares for her when she has failed so utterly in her duty? Who will look after them both when they are old and frail? She is fortunate indeed if she does not end up in Nightingale Nursing Home on Braddell Road, lah!

Our Mahjong battles happen on a weekly basis and are born of duty and social warfare. They are seemingly genteel but hiss just below the surface like a trapped rat; subterfuge and distrust join hands, in mutual loathing. We play with my great grandmother's set. The tiles are made of the finest ivory and the images, though faded, are painstakingly etched and coloured with what were the most expensive inks of the time. It is becoming very difficult to get ivory sets, with the elephant's numbers dwindling and with the western hysteria that surrounds the issue. Elephants do not need saving! They have tonnage to crush and tusks to pierce. I think they would be humiliated to be 'saved' in this way. At the university we had many robust discussions about 'saving the planet'. My stance was and always has been a practical one. When this world is done then it is time. There is no need to try holding back the world ending.

The western men come here, fat and wealthy, and you would think they would pick only the most vibrant blossom from the tree. But they choose ugly, ugly woman or woman with little virtue like Filipina or Indo. Mesmerised by whatever dark magic is woven between their legs and then thinking they are Bojing and Peacock emperors. Their own women so thin and bony with straw hair and washed-out eyes and skin that hates the sun and so it marks quickly.

And always interfering! Telling *us* how to treat *our* maids. I give the girl a roof over her head, a mattress to sleep on and food in her stomach. I expect her to work hard, I won't deny that, but I also work hard. And why does she need a day off? What is she going to do with it? Get a boyfriend and get pregnant, that's what, and then there is another mouth for her family to feed. These village girls are very lazy, lah! Any excuse they will sit down and dream.

My father used to say the stone cannot be polished without friction nor the man perfected without trials.

The western attitude towards Singaporeans is insulting, and what do they know about Asian ways? We are not Americans and do not expect the same culture as America. We are not *ang moh*. They come here for two, five years and suck what they can from Singapore and all the time they whine about the weather, the food and human rights.

There are no 'rights' in China but working together collectively makes things smoother like grease and cogs. I remember at a party, several years ago, being rendered almost speechless by the ignorance of a British woman on the subject of China. I asked her, what do we have a right to in this world? We have to make our way and take what we can, when we can. She and the other western women were outraged as I knew and hoped they would be, but their men regarded me differently. Some with admiration and one or two with sexual pique.

I'm a Tiger Mother and I roar with love and pride. My Bernard is a Pig so I have to continually keep him on track. He needs extra tuition in maths and English and so as I said he is enrolled in an after-school programme. Sometimes, he cries at night and I run to comfort him because he is still so small and in his pyjamas he looks such a little boy. My husband forbids it but I do it anyway. My one rebellion in such an obedient life. Sometimes, and I wouldn't dare tell his father, his sheets are damp in the morning. My husband would say it is a sign of weakness, and cane him. They sell short, spiteful Malacca canes in all the *yībān shāngdiàn*. It is the Asian way, though I myself was beaten very little because I excelled at being dutiful.

I will shout this in my head: *I will not beat my sons. Do you hear me? Not for honour, duty or the Chinese way.*

Privacy is a strange thing for the Chinese. We are used to living with big, extended families and one or two live-in maids. The maids are slipper quiet and, sometimes, I forget that Lisa is even here. That's not her real name but I can't pronounce her village name so Lisa is easier. My maid was quite vocal about it initially but she has learned her place now. It is a western name so she should love it, but the initial look of horror on her face! You would have thought I wanted to eat her children! Look, these maids clamour for western things all the time. Western clothes, food, phones and those 'rights'. So why is she so ungrateful about the name? Yesterday, I saw Lisa with an apple. I asked her where she got it. She said the maid next door had given it to her. Lies! And she knows that to take food without my express permission is forbidden. So, I gave it to the dog and made her watch. I think she understands. She gets three meals a day unless we are out and then she has to wait, but it is more than a lot of her village could count on.

I hear the doorbell and take one last look in the mirror to satisfy myself that when the maid opens the door to Little Ping and Joyce they will see only what I allow them to see.

A flawless sculpture carved from ice.

LUCILLA

19 Sabre Green

It is Saturday and the sun is shining very brightly today. I am luckier than most helpers as I have every Sunday off and all the evenings too. Many of my friends have no day off or only one day off a month. My Ma'am always puts her hand over her mouth when I remark on these things. Sometimes she talks about her adopted country, England, and describes the free medical care and schooling and as I listen my eyes widen. And on other occasions she speaks quietly about her birth country and how terrible the poverty is there. But then my Ma'am looks sad and says she wishes she could do more and that she feels so useless and hand-tied because she has no voice.

I look sympathetic but if you have never had a voice that has been heard what is there to miss? As a woman in a very poor Asian country you have tiny strangled voice, weak and brittle from lack of use. As a little girl the only voice I used was for shooing chickens or soothing the little ones. As a young woman the only voice I had was to say yes to leaving my village and my family. And here, in Singapore, my voice is kept in a big box at immigration. But my Ma'am has encouraged me to speak of painful and hurtful things past that are like a wood splinter digging deep into my skin.

And I say, Ma'am, I'm so lucky to be working here – my mother is so happy now and doesn't worry so much – thank you, Ma'am.

And my Ma'am, her eyes fill with tears and she say, no, Lucilla, I am the lucky one. You are my heart sister. And my Ma'am will take my hand and touch it to her forehead. This gesture shows great respect for me. I know of no other Ma'am that would do that. And I look at her deep into her green-that-sparkle-with-tears eyes and I think I *am* lucky, I am so very lucky.

Sir and Ma'am have nice friends too. The men are respectful and don't allow their gazes to linger too much although men can't help the looking, it is in their nature. But my Sir never does that. Sometime it seem that he is frightened of me. Like I might break easily and he keeps a great distance between us. Not like those Sirs I mentioned who have an agreement with the maid and pay headache money to them.

Many of the other helpers in our neighbourhood think that my Sir is very handsome because he has a good figure and fair skin and he runs everywhere for fitness. My Sir was born in Scotland and I hear him sighing how much he misses the mountains and the space to cycle for miles. In our village we are lucky to have a few battered cycles and maybe two mopeds. These mopeds are very old but the bus service is changeable. Like Leyte rain, sometimes it comes, sometimes it doesn't; it has no timetable. Just like the buses.

My Ma'am is also trying to keep fit. It shows as she is becoming thinner. Sir grabs her even more and rains love and honey down on her shoulders and lips. He has more love for her than even Dian Masalanta, our goddess of love. And my friends giggle and discuss and some of the other helpers who don't know me also discuss and say, yes, your Sir is very handsome. Very tall. I wouldn't mind him running after me. Then they giggle and put their hands over their mouths and I shout, don't be foolish, cha! Are you crazy? My Sir loves only my Ma'am. And the other girls raise eyebrows at me and sometimes they stare sour at me like bitter fruit is in their mouths.

My friend Marlene she tell me they complain. *That Lucilla, she boast too much. Just because she has good employer she think she better than everybody here.* I am not better but I *am* happier. My friend, Mimi, who works up north in Ang Mo Kio, she works for an okay western family but every year they forget her birthday. Each birthday she wake up and no card or present and no offer of a day off. She is very heavy-hearted and holds it against them. She doesn't make the extra effort and takes her time and does just what she can and no more. Always she is sad but that is because she misses her babies back home. She has two beautiful little girls, but her sadness has twisted her and she carries her missing like a Wakwak. It makes her a little less human every day. She stumbles like zombie through the park, the dog leading the way, and Mimi, she just follow like her mind is not her own. Sometimes she receive text and she bite her lip and soft tears fall. She wipes these away with anger. Always, she is angry. She is trapped in this country working for her babies.

This is why marriage to western man is such a prize. Compared to most Filipino men they are powerful and rich. Even my parents want me to marry western man. But I cannot marry for anything but love even though an *ang moh* can help Asian girl with money and status. If you have proper western boyfriend or husband then you are someone. The government has to treat you better. You can even get British passport if you are lucky. I've heard that with the British passport you can get into any country without a visa and they welcome you and treat you like a queen. Every country I go to I need a visa and most countries don't want to give visa to a Filipina because our voices are silent, our bodies weak and our value little.

I watch the black women here and they are expensively dressed and smell sweet. They have glossy, black skin the colour of molasses or earthy roots. And it glows like dark stars in coconut oil. They look free to me.

On Sundays I like to go up to Lucky Plaza on Orchard Road. On this day it bustles and hustles with many Filipinos sending money, trying to transfer employer, or just being social. Even the older helpers dress up in their best and make up their faces with bright lipsticks like sharp flowers from the garden. I usually meet up with Marlene, my best friend, and we giggle and swish our way through the crowds greeting the odd person we know.

Then Tagalog becomes the first language and the city exhales a sense of homeland. The foreigners have long lunches and sit drinking cold wine and beer from glasses, sagging with sweat. The women wear dark glasses so they can pretend not to notice when their man is looking at the sunbirds walking and flying past him. Sometimes there are groups of western men drinking late into dusk. They are preparing for the tea dances and clubs of Orchard Towers. Some sit with world-tired guides who are paid to take these men on sex adventure and they wear masks of shame and excitement. If they catch your eye they will smile lazily as if they are the most handsome men in the world. They should look in the mirror more. But Asian mirrors tell western men lies, they think because they have a pretty girlfriend they have suddenly become good-looking overnight. They haven't. They are still ugly and fat. I don't mean to sound harsh or bitter.

But I am.

I pray to St Jude for the health of my mother and father and to Jesus to guide me and keep me safe and I still believe in the fairy story but perhaps at my age I should know better.

I have been to many of the tea dances in Orchard Towers but they have become more pig market than dance and how the Bangla men swagger and writhe. Cha! The Bangla man is full of sex. I think he must dream about it and bathe in it. Ma'am told me a story about her massage place near Beach Road. The girls that work there are mostly Filipina and Thai. Very good massage and beauty treatments, Ma'am says. But they have panic buttons in the rooms now because China and Indian man have made 'unwanted advances' towards the therapists. Ma'am say they have a 'blacklist' now and escort men from the premises even if they are guests.

They are bad. Always *touch! touch! touch!* Hands linger and eyes promise violence. I have friends who have dated Indian man. Their boyfriends have become possessive very soon and sometimes they hit to make their point. And then those soft chocolate eyes become like chips of tar, mean and narrowed. And then the blood flows and the cries start.

I shrug and say, worse things can happen, Ma'am, as my past comes back to me like a punch to the brain and I have to grip the counter to steady myself. I think at least those women are protected, most of us are not. Ma'am is concerned because I look so pale and shaky and tells me to go and rest, feeling my forehead and making anxious noises.

And I go, grateful to be alone so when the fear and the guilt come I can fall to my knees in private clasping my hands so tightly in prayer that my fingers turn white. And that half-seen man's face shimmers just out of reach, bobbing and floating, but never completely there.

MA'AM LESLEY

35 Sabre Green

I am peering out the gates when one of the local Filipina helpers saunters by and nods at me. She is a typical Filipina beauty but much softer than Jocelyn. Her eyes are not glass-like but shine softly with warmth and humour. She startles me and I find myself laughing out loud in surprise, an unfamiliar sound. Instinctively, I cover my mouth with both my hands, unsure of myself. The woman reaches through the bars and gently pulls my hands away.

'I'm Lucilla, Ma'am. I live at number 19,' and she gestures vaguely across the green. Slowly and with a gravitas borrowed from the nineteenth century, she asks, 'Why you look so sad?'

It is a good question and a complicated one.

'Your helper she not nice.' The young woman screws up her perfectly smooth face. 'You should transfer her, lah. She lazy and say bad things about you.' I look down at the chipped paving on my driveway. None of this is news to me. I know that Jocelyn despises me. It streams out of her like poisonous tendrils. I shrug, and turn to go, but Lucilla reaches out again, and covers my hand with hers and says, 'Don't be sad! I see you.' Tears bulge and threaten like dark clouds. I muster a shaky smile and plod back to the front door.

Jocelyn is nowhere to be seen and I am poignantly aware how much of a stranger I am here. In my naive days, when I thought we might be friends, I gave her a choice of rooms in the main house. Her look of incredulous distaste at the thought of having to live with us was unmistakable and she has shunned my company from that day.

Frankly, Jocelyn intimidates me, and because of that I have never been in her room since she arrived. I have always treasured my own privacy and try to award that courtesy to others. True, I have heard rumours that some employers remove the door to the maid's room so they can monitor her, but I don't have the energy. Today, however, I find myself standing outside her door. There is an overwhelming desire to know my enemy and so I hold my breath and push the door gently.

The first thing I notice is two dresses of mine draped over the bed. They are Diana Von Furstenberg and I bought them when I was slender, engaged and felt my future was assured. Is it odd that I don't even feel remotely annoyed, rather oddly gratified that they are being used? I always feel pretty things should be displayed and not hidden away. I allow my eyes to wander around the room and notice a huge arrangement of red roses. There must be two dozen long-stemmed, crimson blooms, soft and velvety – they resemble a young woman's labia. These flowers are about lust, wildness and devotion. I pick up the card and read it quickly.

To my beloved, my fragrant lotus, Oh! Bid me with your joy rejoice til riotous longing rest in me. Devotedly, R.

So. There it is in black and white. My knees give way and I sink onto the bed, still holding the card. I recognise the quotation, not only as Rossetti, but because I received it early on, at the beginning of his courtship. Maybe he has others, I'm not sure, but I know this one. I was once totally overwhelmed by his gravitas and his education. He could weave words like spider's silk and I had thought him the cleverest man on the planet.

I am remembering again when we met. At a dinner party in London. There was nothing particularly romantic about the actual meeting. In fact, I remember it getting rather heated and politically strained. I was with a male friend and wasn't much interested in politics – or men, for that matter. I was studying to be a librarian and my attention was captured only by books. My love affair with fiction started with Beatrix Potter. Using a torch that I had stolen from my older brother's room I would burrow under the covers and read until I was caught or fell asleep.

My passion for the written word increased exponentially and by the time I was being coached for my scholarship exam to the local grammar school I had managed to convince my parents to provide me with an account at the local bookshop. I devoured authors, title by title, page by page. I plunged into Sartre and then discovered I liked De Beauvoir so much better. I blossomed under the visceral Maugham and felt inferior to Waugh's arrogant satire. Lawrence made me tingle and Maya Angelou made me proud and awed. I was a bluestocking, albeit a reasonably pretty one, and enjoyed the status that I was earning as a guardian of books. I suppose I should say I was ripe for the picking. I hadn't so much repressed my sexuality as found it irrelevant. Like a novice whose love for God had induced a radiance that makes her breathless, I was content to bask in my knowledge and devotion to the written word.

Librarians were going through a bit of an image revamp. Suddenly, they had become sexy, and to my surprise men who had never seemed to notice me before made clumsy advances. I enjoyed the attention for a while but it became tedious and some of my suitors became overtly sexual and I have always felt that to be vaguely insulting, as if they had become bored of the chase and decided it was time to stop mucking about.

Ralph was the opposite. On reflection, I believe that my naivety was a magnet and my constant adoration the most elaborate ego-stroking. The dinner party we attended, separately but together, was thick with the usual suspects. A couple of ambitious low-level politicians, a nauseating advertising exec, a model or something similar, and our hosts – very old friends of Ralph's, Mark and Philip, who owned a small but successful literary agency together and were partners in both senses of the word. I was very fond of Philip but found Mark a little acerbic. Bluntness in a person has always baffled and alarmed me. I suppose it is fashionable to be sarcastic and edgy but I have always thought it an excuse for acceptable bullying. I was out of my comfort zone and barely said a word. The usual jokes had already been guffawed at my expense about stockings, lesbians and nymphomaniacs and I had ignored them or been humiliated by turns.

Ralph was seated far down the table from me, and I had noticed him but was not at all aware that he had even registered my presence. Like all insecure, unworldly creatures I felt sure that the other guests would arrive at the conclusion very quickly that I was a fraud and that I would be escorted unceremoniously from the house with tuts and disapproval. I had studied Ralph a little but was given a hazy impression of a patrician type, distinguished rather than handsome but very charming. The model almost fell out of her dress on several occasions and she strove to impress Ralph in her own way. Meanwhile, I was in my cups, which was entirely unusual, but this wine was sweet and my preference has never been for bone-dry wine. I don't pretend to be an oenophile and I have certainly never had or wanted the ability to discern a hint of blackberry or mineral or anything else for that matter. As I have said, what I enjoy is a fairly sweet wine that doesn't challenge me. A supple, unfashionable tipple (another Ralph word) that wouldn't catch in the back of my throat or build reflux from early evening onwards. In those days, if I wanted to drink these blackballed bottles I could. Now, it would be impossible. Ralph has a delivery every month from a wine merchant along Orchard Road and however much he might be in raptures about them they will always be sour and unreachable. And, really, Ralph's wine has always disappointed me. The labels have such sonorous promise (Fleurie, Chablis, Nuit Saint Georges) but deliver piss and vinegar.

It was much later in the evening, when the guests could be found draped over the furniture and were becoming louche under the influence of heavy food and wine, that Ralph spoke to me for the first time. I was feeling uncomfortable and had headed for the bookshelves to self-medicate. Philip and Mark had an impressive collection of books and rather refreshingly were not at all put off by pulp fiction. Murdoch, Irving and the ubiquitous Amis, senior and junior, all held their place, but I was delighted to see *Lucky Jim* slightly askew on the shelf, being rebellious. Then I had just spotted their collection of Dumas, when a voice of honey and oatmeal drawled that Dumas, in its opinion, was one of the greatest storytellers of the millennium, and the Three Musketeers are iconic characters that attempt to capture the notion of the goodness of men.

I heard him first. And then I felt him. His velvet jacket sleeve constantly brushed my bare arm, which I found enormously arousing, and slowly I turned to look. Ralph stood quite close, puffing on a short, stubby Habana and smiling with the arrogance and self-belief only one class can every truly have.

From there it was a sandstorm. Dinners, holidays, thoughtful gifts, lines from sonnets, the traditional asking for my hand that sent my father into a fluster normally reserved for cake-baking ladies of a certain age. And I was blinded by it and allowed myself to be led through the chaos that disguised itself as infatuation.

The first time he hit me was just before the wedding. I had, in direct contrast to most brides, put on some weight with an enormous amount of comfort eating. Ralph commented that I had put on some pounds, and while he loved me, of course, it was just that it wasn't particularly attractive. I had giggled, being in the first throes of sexual awakening and feeling magnificent and powerful. And while I didn't love Ralph exactly, I felt a certain affection for him and a rather inappropriate schoolgirl crush. He backhanded me. No explanation, no warning. A short, flat slap that knocked me off my chair and left me speechless on the floor. I stopped eating that day and starved myself to the point that I almost fainted at the altar and I remember the look of quiet approval on Ralph's face.

And that's when I should have run.

SHAMMI

20 Sabre Green

Tonight, my Madam has a big party. I always fear these parties. It is so much extra work and not sleeping for almost a day and a night. There will be shouting and shoving, exclamations and excitement. And my Madam will turn into Rangda, demon queen of the Leyaks. She will glitter with nerves and bark instructions and become a *tap tap* of worry with overlong fingernails like small machetes. A huge drumming band will play for hours to encourage good luck. How I shrink from those drums that are joyless to me. They hurt my head and make my thinking like damp earth. And on a day like today I must be sharp and solid like cassava. I will fail today as I always do. And there will be punishment. Sometimes, when she pushes me or lets spitting oil peck my skin her eyes glow and her skin becomes flushed. I think she enjoys the hurting. She must do because she does it so much. And I will have to do all the cooking although Madam stands over me with wooden spoon and smacks my hand, arm or head when she thinks I'm doing it wrong.

I hate cooking Chinese food. Too much oil, too much fish sauce, too much sour. Too much of everything except goodness. At home in my village we have little food but it dances with life. My Ebu makes delicious *rotis*, stretching them thin so they are like lace and then baking them on stones in the fire that lifts them delicately in the heat and curls the ends slightly like a piglet's tail. If a goat has been slaughtered Ebu will make a thick stew, with cassava if the mealy worms have been kind, or rice, beans and chillies if we have them. Sometimes, it is so hot even Bapa has difficulty and he will laugh and choke and say his wife is fiery and good for him. And Ebu will look at him from under her eyes and smile a small but important smile. A smile just for him. And then I envy my mother and father so much for their love, for their faith in each other. I think that faith is as important as love.

Eating in the village is very different too. The evening meal is a reward for the hard work of the day. The family sits together, usually on the floor, crowded but safe, and share what is in front of them. But here, great dishes are prepared and the men and woman nibble at them like spoilt monkeys. And then they are thrown in the rubbish. Mounds of vegetables, meat, fruit and sauces. It makes me want to weep. My village could survive for days on the waste here. These parties are loud and raucous. Every guest seems to be competing for attention and each other and my Madam and Sir dress up like peacocks. Madam paints her face so pale she looks like ghost and her shoes are very high. She has three wardrobes of dresses and silk things. Some garments she has never worn and never will. I have two pair of trousers, six shirts, one skirt, three brassieres and six pair of underwear. There are holes in everything and they have been washed so much that the colours have faded to poor impersonations of each other.

But the one good part of tonight is that I will wear a proper maid's uniform. I am not allowed to keep it in my small chest of drawers. My Madam brings it out for these occasions. She keeps it locked up the rest of the time. But it is the nicest thing I have ever worn. The material is silky to the touch and the white apron is clean and fresh. I feel so proud in it and this strikes me as foolish because it is a symbol of my pain. But wear it I will because that is what my Madam expects and at least it is clean and fresh and new.

I have been busy since 5am and will stay up long after the party has finished. When Madam and Sir have gone to bed I will collect the debris, the dishes, the soiled napkins and the stinking ashtrays and will clear and wash and wipe and dry until every tiny thing is back in its place and when Madam comes downstairs in the morning, later than usual, because she'll drink too much, she will stretch and yawn and cast a keen eye over the spotless surfaces and somehow find fault. She will not thank me. Not once has she ever thanked me for the work I do. My very presence seems to make her angry.

My hair, which is long, but now falling out because I'm hungry all the time, is still more beautiful than her thinning, brittle, black reeds –

brushed and backcombed and sprayed with lacquer that is like a poison cloud. Her eyes are bug black and have a sly cast to them; her hate feels like a pillow over my face.

She is the type of person that gives the evil eye naturally. It would have come to her at birth. Born under the wrong star at the wrong time. My Ebu says that if that spirit is present when the baby is born it can swim through its little mouth and sink deep into the baby's soul. If it takes root that baby is cursed for the rest of its life unless the person can find a witch to trade with for it. The witch will draw it out of the person's soul and capture it in a jar and bury it deep underground. The cursed person is then free but if the jar is ever opened the evil can find its way back like a firefly to the moon. My Madam never found the witch to trade with so she carries the evil in her heart. This evil gets stronger as the person ages and darkness etches lines in her face and neck. And Madam looks like pale bark that is scored with sickness.

When I first arrived I offered to make Madam bread. I thought she might like to taste Ebu's bread from the village. But her face became hard with rage and her eyes were stone. She slapped me so hard that I fell to the floor, crying from shock. She shouted, why I want your shit country bread? Lah? Why you ask? I bring you here and put roof over your head and feed you out of my own pocket. Flecks of spittle appeared in the corner of her mouth. I pay you to insult me, you little bloody bitch? You bloody, dirty, hairy animal bitch. And she kicked me hard, poured herself a glass of water and left. And I lay and wondered what I had done that was so terribly wrong.

Afterwards, Madam gave me tiny, spiky nail scissors and forced me to cut the front lawn with them. It was late at night. By early morning I was so tired I had fallen asleep on the grass and when I woke up I find the kind Ebony Ma'am next door has seen that the gate is open and has come right in and put a cup of water to my lips. She brushes the hair from my face and whispers, poor *Babu*, and I gaze at her like she is a dark angel. When my Madam come out the Ebony Ma'am gets very cross and points a finger in her face. She mentions police. Prison. My Madam looks at her and says not one word.

And sometimes Ebony Ma'am comes even further into the garden and stares in at the kitchen while I cook and my Madam is leaning over me shouting instructions. And then they both glare at each other and my Madam snorts and leaves the kitchen to go upstairs. And the Ebony Ma'am reaches through the window and links her little finger through mine for a second before going in. And I hold onto that touch for weeks. I think about it at night when I'm cold, which I often am even with the humidity and the lack of air in the corridor.

My employers lock everything at night, even the windows. Huge metal grilles cover every window, big and small, and every door has a lock. The keys to these locks are on a huge ring that my Madam hangs on a hook in the doorway. They are labelled with letters of the alphabet – one for each lock. Why, you might ask yourself, would a Singaporean do this when they have such low crime? Would it surprise you if I say it is not to keep people out? It is to keep us, the maids, in.

My Madam accuses me of things in the future. She accuses me of terrible acts of filth that I might do if I am allowed out. It is a strange joke as I have no money to do anything. I have no friends because I am forbidden to speak to anyone and I have no phone to arrange these dark meetings. My Madam shouts about sex and having babies and that it's for my own protection because I am too stupid to know what is good for me and there are men everywhere that will take advantage of that stupidity.

And if I get pregnant then I will get sent back in shame.

No money, no reference.

Just a single, shamed girl, and another mouth to feed.

MADAM EUNICE

134 Sabre Green

A strange thing happened at Mahjong this week. The afternoon started out perfectly normally with the girls arriving full of gossip and wearing new outfits. Little Ping's nails were very long and freshly lacquered, 'Russian Red' she called it, and Joyce has a new Prada bag. Her husband has had a significant promotion recently and she talks about it at every opportunity, as she should.

My own husband is a politician and works for the government. He deals with many foreigners and my role is very social. There are cocktail parties, dinner parties and soirées. Women glitter like frost in a weak winter sun and talk rather too loudly. The men are unconcerned and generally use the occasions as an extension of the office. The older Singaporean man is very traditional whether he is Malay or Chinese by extract.

Our role in Chinese culture is complicated. The western press always latches on to the most negative of images. Bound feet, submission. Girls as unwanted burdens. It is true that girls were seen as a great weight on the family until they were married and in my grandmother's time, unless you were from a wealthy family, you would generally go from being an unpaid servant in your parents' house to being an unpaid servant in your husband's. The great change for us came during the Communist years. The distinctions between men and woman became so blurred that women for the first time were able to study and work alongside men. Mao even elevated women to positions of political power. It was very liberating. So Mao is still viewed with great affection by the older generation. The peasants mutter about him, of course, though they mutter about everything: there is a distinct divide between rural and urban Chinese. It is a vast country and westerners forget that. Even the indigenous people change rapidly from the Great Steppes near the Russian border, where the peasants are wind-whipped and sunburned, to the softer southerners near the coast. The Americans don't have these exact distinctions. They all look the same: big, fat, fair and greedy. I find it terribly ironic that they are ready to espouse so many causes; although they may be here for a while most of them have otherwise never even travelled out of their own state. This is what gets my goat about foreigners. It's obvious they disapprove of us here. They don't understand our ways and start to try to change things. We all chuckle along because the Singaporeans don't give a fig for what a westerner thinks. Your contract is up and you are gone back to the United States, or to Europe, where everybody can bleat about their rights.

You have rights if you can win them.

You have to push and shove and barge and bite for your rights.

Then you deserve them.

There is no point trying to make everybody equal. Darwinism is the only biological imperative that makes sense. Before I had Philip and Bernard I lectured in Eastern Cultural Affairs at the university. I enjoyed it tremendously and there are times when I yearn for the uncomplicated life of an academic. There might be some vicious political manoeuvring in the background, but the research aspect always soothed me. Coming to my senses in a darkened library after hours of reading and thinking was oddly comforting.

But back to the 'odd thing'. Little Ping had been so full of excitement last week about the fortune teller that I was surprised that she now seemed so reticent to speak to me. She kept changing the subject and Joyce was particularly wittery. In the end I had to bang my glass down and insist, as politely as possible, that they share with me, their oldest friend, what was going on. Joyce looked at Little Ping and Little Ping looked at me. Little Ping reached over and grasped my hand and squeezed it.

'I don't want you to worry, I'm sure it's nothing. Stupid fortune tellers! What do they know?' Joyce nodded enthusiastically.

'For goodness' sake!' I said. 'Why would the fortune teller say things about me? You went for help with your *infertility*.' I lingered over the last word just to make sure Little Ping knew exactly where she was in our pecking order. Little Ping shrunk back a bit, as I knew she would, and withdrew her hand.

'He talked about you, Eunice,' Joyce muttered. I stared hard at Joyce until she looked away and then glanced at Little Ping. Both women looked genuinely frightened. The situation was becoming uncomfortable and, as ever, my discomfort translated into anger. I rang the tiny bronze bell that was on the table beside me, and the maid approached unseen from the shadows.

'Brandy,' I snapped.

'Yes, Madam,' the girl replied. 'Do you want glass, Madam?'

I just stared at her. I know it's unfair but I can't help it. I want to lash out and I'm too concerned for etiquette and gossip to do it to my friends. Lisa faded away and I returned to the present.

I took a deep breath and looked sweetly at Little Ping. 'Tell me,' I asked, with a touch of a smile playing about my lips.

As the wretched story unravelled I began to feel the first twinges of doubt. Apparently, Little Ping had indeed queued for two hours in some odious HBD to have an audience with Lim Chew, who is famed for his predictions, but the man refused to talk about her at all. Instead, he insisted that a woman called Eunice was under a curse. Demons had been summoned and she was the target. Her life was in jeopardy as was her husband's career, and their place in society was under threat.

This charlatan 'knew' that my husband was a politician and little details about our lives that he couldn't possibly have known without 'spirit guidance'. Even though my first instinct was to laugh it off and make fun of Joyce and Little Ping for believing such fairy tales, a chill descended to the bottom of my spine and squatted there. And though Joyce and Little Ping agreed to laugh it off too, I could see disquiet skitter across their faces, which seemed suddenly etched by centuries of belief and fear about demons and evil spirits. I called them peasants and responded sharply that sophisticated Chinese women do not become affected by legends and gossipy old fakers. After that we drank brandy and coffee and all became more intoxicated than we should have, but there was a tension in the air now. Something had been spoken about, and it is well known that once something is acknowledged it can become real.

Later, after Joyce and Little Ping had teetered to their cars and their drivers, who sat waiting impassively, I felt the chill again and wrapped a shawl tightly around my shoulders. I sat outside in the cooling dusk and tried to relax, reassuring myself it was a degree or two of body heat lost due to the alcohol. The over-indulged Labrador from three doors away began its nightly performance, and oddly I took comfort in that dull bark. I thought to myself, all is right with the world, Eunice. You have nothing to fear. It's an infertile woman's fancy. But still, even as I repeated the mantra, it occurred to me that I was clinging to it in a state of sudden desperation, that the clammy shiver at the base of my spine was a dark foreboding. My thinking began to spiral. Had I burned enough offerings for our ancestors at the Hungry Ghost festival? Was I too harsh on Little Ping in the company of other women? Too harsh with my children and not obedient enough with my husband?

I began a rigorous inventory of my actions over the last month, pulling my words and deeds to pieces. And as I racked my memory I began to rock as I would a child and found a brief comfort in it. As I rocked and muttered, I became aware of Lisa standing just inside my field of vision and I turned sharply.

'What?' I snapped at her as if she were a Karanji stray.

'I clean car now, Madam?'

I dismissed her with a nod but before she disappeared, like the long shadows on a mountain at dawn, I could have sworn I saw the twist of a smile tug at her lips. I can't be sure but I'm almost certain that the little miss was enjoying my discomfort.

LUCILLA

19 Sabre Green

Tonight I go out with a friend of my Ma'am's. His name is Connor and he is Rory's nanny in Scotland. He is a good-hearted man and makes me laugh. I was sure he was gay, lah! But no, he just sounds it. He has big green eyes that are hidden behind glasses and big whiskers that come down the side of his face. He is also from the mountains and he keeps asking me to marry him.

It was Halloween last night and all the children from the neighbourhood dress up and go round doing trick or treat and collecting candy. I took Rory round with his little pumpkin basket and my Ma'am and Connor dress up like vampires and scare the children until they squeal like bats. They are very comfortable together, almost like they are related. Ma'am says Connor is part of her heart family.

Yesterday, I tell Ma'am I want to work for her always and Ma'am sighs and says she wants so much more for me and that I am too good for this job. And I say, even when I get married, please I work for you? And my Ma'am hugs me and says, you can stay with me forever if you like. You are my heart sister. And we both have tears in our eyes.

My Ma'am doesn't mind me using the family's cutlery and bowls. Not like a Chinese employer once, who gave me a bowl identical to the dog's and expected that to be that.

I can hear Rory hovering at the top of the stairs, too scared to come down in the pre-dawn shadows.

'Morning, Lucilla,' I hear a little voice pipe.

'Morning, Rory,' I reply. His little figure come slowly down the stairs. He is clutching his favourite soft toy, Sheepy, and sucking on his binky. 'Wait, Rory, I put light on for you.' And he waits until I can light those tricky stairs for him. Wooden and knife hard, they would be unforgiving to a falling child. Once he is settled in front of the television to watch a programme and wake up, I stumble towards the kitchen again and make his favourite 'chocomilk'. This is the only way Ma'am and I can get him to drink milk. The milk in Asia is very different to milk in Scotland, my Ma'am says wistfully. The cows range on green land up mountains and by rivers. The herds are huge and very expensive and their milk and beef win prizes and are full of Scottish goodness.

This milk is from Thai cows. Skinny, fawn-coloured, rib-showing, sorry excuses for cows that graze on stubby grass gnawed right down to the earth. They do their best, poor beasts. They are treated with contempt by the farmers who only know about survival and feeding their families. I wonder to myself what conversations these animals would have with each other if they ever met. Their lives are so different and yet maybe they would have some experiences that were the same.

I have been having bad feelings lately. Feelings when my mouth goes dry and my fingers become shaky. My dreams of my village have been very frightening. In these dreams it is very dark and a black storm is making itself known. The villagers are inside their shacks, trembling and cold. All the lights are out and as I walk through the village my neighbours hiss: *Get in, get in! She comes, she comes.* And I know who comes because I can see her in the jungle shadow. There is a smell of rotted things and evil. Even in dreamland I can feel death spreading out from this thing. All Filipino children are told of the Aswang. In some stories she is a witch or a vampire. In others the figure is more flimsy, less solid, but the fact that she is demonic in some form is never questioned. The Aswang comes out at night and she feed off innocent people. If you dream that a person you know is attacked by the Aswang then that person is in great danger and their life could be threatened. Now in my dream mist swirls around my ankles like in a western thriller and as I walk to my parents' house the air grows colder and I begin to shiver. My skin is clammy, and although I want to turn and run and hide my face in my grandmother's skirts it is impossible. I am stilled with fear, until the spirit pushes me towards the house. It is dark but I hear a faint sucking sound like a dog lapping at cold mountain water. My father lies on the floor a few feet away, his head broken and the blood, oh! the blood. Everywhere. He is pale and lifeless. I push the heel of my hand into my mouth to stop the scream that lies in wait. Edging further into the room I see my mother, in the arms of the Aswang, who holds her like a lover. My mother wears the faded green shirt that she bakes in and a skirt of yellow flowers. Her legs drum gently against the dirt floor. Mama, I whisper, too scared to run at the demon and tear her away from my mother's neck. The Aswang turns to face me, and smiles, showing sharp bloody teeth. Teeth stained with my mother's blood. The witch rolls her eyes at me and laughs. Then I wake up sweating, shaking and with a terrible ache in my head. I lie on my bed with my face in the pillows that Ma'am brought me. I feel sick. My stomach churns with dread. I crawl to the kitchen, still early enough to be bathed in darkness, and fill a glass with water.

MA'AM LESLEY

35 Sabre Green

I replace the card that Ralph has scrawled to Jocelyn and heave myself
off the bed. I don't feel particularly upset and that surprises me. The
overriding sensation is relief. Sex has been such a complicated affair
for so long. I've never felt pangs of desire when reading risqué books
or felt a stirring in my loins if something X-rated appears on television. The idea of pornography is bemusing. I have never used sexual
oddities to stimulate me, but I can relate to why people would.

It all boils down to the simple fact that all I really want is an uncomplicated life. In a novel I would be the granite-faced housekeeper. Not
the one from Mandalay – too much passion; but the solid, uncom-
plaining and dark-skirted figure whose presence is unnoticed for the
most part. I would move silently through a dark house, gently guiding
the other servants towards what was for the greater good and attend-
ing some austere house of God on the Sabbath. I would watch grim,
slate-coloured clouds gathering over the house and grounds and cross
myself with relish. I would be respected but avoided, with the taint of
the religious novice about me.

I would eat my meals away from the other servants not because I
was being snobbish, but because I cherish my privacy above anything
else. And the others would recognise that and not think ill of me. I
wasn't born to be lady of the manor. I've been beaten and bullied into
this role like an overstuffed matron squeezing into a corset from her
youth.

Most people long to just be.

I long to *do*.

Although each day seems to meld and flow almost invisibly into
another, I am aware that I've received no post for a long time. No letters or cards, packets, or even property adverts which, in Singapore,

45

are relentless. As I've mentioned, the house phone too is silent. Perhaps Ralph doesn't bother with the house phone any more. I stopped asking Ralph 'difficult' questions some time past. And any questions at all a few months ago.

His violence towards me has become habitual. I don't think he means to hurt me but my ongoing incompetence is too great a disappointment for my husband, and each sight of me solidifies this disappointment further. A stone of abject failure cracked and hardened by ebb and relentless flow. I only wish he would refrain from striking me in front of Jocelyn. She enjoys my humiliation and there is nothing of sisterhood in her. Rather she is a single battleship, primed and ready to defend. She has spirit, woman, Ralph would snarl at me when I ventured to suggest Jocelyn was rude even when extended the utmost courtesy. And so I have left the subject of Jocelyn alone and she has risen and contorted and threaded herself through my life like beautiful but merciless bindweed. The balance in the house is changing and I need to be careful or I might lose my footprints in the shifting sands.

'What are you doing?' Her little-girl voice breaks over me like a black sea. 'You get out, this my place, get out, GET OUT!'

And get out I do, although I am thoroughly pulled, pushed, slapped and cursed as Jocelyn shoves me out and onto the kitchen floor. Red faced, she screams and screams and I am mesmerised. Swollen with fury and panting with the effort of dislodging a great lump from her bedroom, her tirade lasts some minutes. Finally, she slows and a sly cast shadows her face.

'You clean kitchen floor to say sorry or I tell Mr Ralph.'

And that is that. The seminal moment between us and how it might go for the next hundred years. I have a choice. I can stand up and brush myself off and tell her to pack her things. She is leaving. I will phone the agency, in front of her, and tell them I am very dissatisfied and I want her out of my house immediately. I can ring a friend and discuss the horror of the situation over gin and tonics.

But what friend?

I do none of those things. Instead, I stare up at her and simply reply, 'Yes.'

'Yes, what?'

I hesitate, feeling myself on the brink of something extreme, like diving off a cliff hoping the wind will catch and spiral me down to the ground like a hopeful seed. But I am tired, so very tired of this pretence. Perhaps it is time to take a step back and just see where it takes me.

'Yes, Ma'am.'

Our eyes meet again and she nods once. 'You cook tonight. Or I tell Mr Ralph.'

I am surprised to feel a smile on my face.

I know and understand this place. It is where I have longed to be. And as I clean the kitchen floor, methodically and beautifully, I think about dinner and what I might cook. Some women have a talent for clean and tidy. I am one of them. I can put a household in order with the artistry of a blacksmith. A blueprint appears in my mind of where best to put things and where to store the leftovers and it all fits together like a dynamic puzzle. I write a list. Beef Wellington, with a ruby port *jus*, followed by chocolate mousse, and I dredge my memory for a suitable sombre red that Ralph will approve of. I trudge up the stairs to my bedroom. I am fat and unfit and sweating like a racehorse.

My entire wardrobe seems to be draped across my bed and Jocelyn is twirling in front of the mirror. I see her feet tucked into a pair of my Louboutins, which swamp her tiny feet and make her look, for a fleeting moment, like a sweet small girl trying to impress her mother. She catches sight of me in the mirror. I'm not sure what I had been expecting, perhaps some residue of embarrassment or a blush at being caught out, but I had underestimated this cuckoo.

'Your feet are too big? Why so fat?'

'Those are my clothes,' I venture.

Jocelyn shrugs. 'You too fat to wear, why waste?' And the challenge at the end of the sentence is laid bare. She holds the threat of Ralph's violence in between us like an angry sky.

I shake my head and try to think of a single thing to say, but I just want some peace. I certainly do not want Ralph's anger directed at me any more. I am almost certain that he will accept this switch between the women of his household with relief and I might even receive some kindness for being so accommodating. I feel myself being swept away by lethargy, a disassociation that happens when I feel threatened or something is too difficult to deal with.

'I'm going to go and do the shopping.'

I wait for an acknowledgement but receive none so I go back downstairs, find my purse and a shawl-type piece of clothing and open the front door.

The idea of a taxi is appealing, but I decide I will get some exercise and enjoy a stroll. As I emerge from the house into the midday sun it is clear that I have made a mistake. It is blisteringly hot. The heat assaults me in thick waves and almost immediately I am sweating. I pull a straw monstrosity over my hair and step out onto the steaming road. The humidity hangs visibly in between the fronds and palms, emboldened by the lack of wind. It is very quiet out except for the odd car, or a maid wandering back from the shops with heavy bags stuffed with groceries or walking the vast shaggy dogs that Singaporeans are so fond of and that are so inappropriate in the tropics.

I smile at a few of the maids and they cautiously smile back. Any westerner is treated with reserve until it's known if they are friend or foe. If you slip up and say something negative about your employer and that gets reported back, well, you could lose your job and your family their livelihood. I hope eventually I can get them to trust me. The cheeky young woman I met earlier is nowhere to be seen and I trudge on down the road with a lift in my heart and a feeling of expectation, of promise.

The sun is high in the sky and something has changed, shifted, but I have no idea what it is. I am ready to be patient and let the play unfold.

SHAMMI

112 Sabre Green

I don't feel so well today. My head aches and my stomach feels like fishing knives are gutting me. There is no point saying anything to Madam. She doesn't believe in illness. I have to work regardless. My head is very hot and even though I drink and drink my throat is dry and rough.

It is not a good day to be ill. Last night my Madam told me that the family was going on holiday and I was to go to work at her friend's house. She said I had to work extra hard as her friend was very fussy and she didn't want any complaints because it would reflect badly on her. A taxi would take me. I was to be there for fourteen days and during that time I would be expected to perform all the duties that I do for Madam as well as look after the three children and the grandmother. This seems a lot of work for me but I keep silent. My head is throbbing and if Madam strikes me again I think I will sink to the floor and stay there.

I enjoy the taxi ride. It is the first time I have been out of the house in, perhaps, months. I ask Uncle if I can let the window down in the back just so I can feel the wind on my face. It makes me feel a little free for one moment and then the sadness hits solid, like Madam's hand, and I have to pant to stop the tears from falling. I am full of despair and as I look out of the window, as we fly down the AYE towards Tampines where Madam's friend lives, I think of all the other maids in the city that are sad. Huddled behind chain-link fences, dry lipped and dry mouthed. Hollowed-out eyes and lank hair. Grieving for their children, their marriages and their lost youth.

I feel ancient, like a crone from the village. I am dust beneath the plastic sole of a Little India slipper. And I'm hungry – so very hungry.

Hungry for love, ravenous for touch, greedy for freedom, famished for comfort.

And there is none for me here in this city of flowers and tears.

We draw up to a large blue house. It is an odd colour blue for a house. The type of blue that rich boy-babies wear. It has four pillars in the front and I can see three floors. It will mean a lot of work for me. The taxi stops and Uncle gestures to the house.

'Yes,' I say, 'I think.' I give him fifteen dollars.

He looks at me. 'You wan receipt?'

'Yes, Uncle.' He clicks his teeth in annoyance and I think, why did you ask then?

His hair is greasy and swept back from his face in a hairstyle that is twenty years too young for him. His lined face betrays the unnatural total sooty blackness of his hair that sits densely like charcoal in a box. Eyes squint at me, then he sighs and he says, 'Work hard, lah? Be good girl.'

'Yes, Uncle,' I say, even though I am past twenty-eight years.

I could have three children by now and a husband to keep me warm at night. I could have. I could have! And what do I have? I look down at the small, battered case at my feet and I see my frayed trousers and bleached-out shirt and I am so ashamed. And Madam cut my long hair last week. She said it keep falling in the food. She used big pinking shears with a crinkle edge to hack it off. Oh! My beautiful, silky hair. I felt the last bits of my hope, my heart and myself fall in a pile on the dusty floor among the stripes of black silk. Now it is short to my ears and looks odd. I don't think it is cut straight, but to complain would be too dangerous.

My English is not good and so I don't know how to question things in this country. My Madam say that if I displease her she can send me back to Indonesia or, worse, to jail. She say badly behaved maids in Singapore are flogged. Lucilla, from next door, who works for Ebony Ma'am, tries to talk to me but I point at the newly installed security cameras. Madam says she look at the film at night to see that I am not slacking off like bloody Banglas.

How can I be lazy? I work from before the blushing dawn to hours after dusk. I want to ask about my wages. I know I must pay back

money to the agency but months have passed now and still I have
nothing to show for my labours. To work this hard, to be this sorrowful, for nothing.

'Are you the girl?'

A tiny, birdlike woman is darting forward on impossible foolish
heels. She wears layers of red silk with ruffles in electric blue. Her face
has thick make-up. Her eyeshadow is peacock-feather sharp. It makes
my head ache to look at her.

'Yes, Madam.'

'You can start straight away,' she snaps. I gesture to my bag.

'Where should I put this, please, Madam?'

Then she sighs, clicks her teeth and steps close to me so I can smell
her sour breath. 'I don't want a troublemaker, lah. You will put it
where I tell you to put it. You will speak when I let you speak. You
will eat when I say you eat. Now come.' This is not new to me, this
hateful way.

I follow her to the kitchen trying to acquaint myself with how it
all works. New kitchens are hazardous if you don't have a patient
employer. I'm expected to find where everything is quickly and without fuss.

I ask again where I might put my bag. If I have a room.

Madam Peacock lifts a heavily plucked eyebrow. So thin it might
be a pencil drawing. She gestures with her head to the outside door.
Outside I see a mattress, stained pillow and dirty cover.

'Maid's room all full.' I nod slowly. I need to sit down. 'You lucky,
tonight we go out. All family. No eating from our food. No drinking
from our cups. You have your own cup. Plate. There are ready noodles in that cupboard. You can have one tonight.'

'Thank you,' I say.

She ignores me as one might a black speck amongst one million
black specks and disappears.

A gentle breeze blows through this part of the house and I feel it
soft on my skin, nudging me to a smile. At least here I could imagine
I am free. I don't care about sleeping outside; it will be cool and private. I can pretend I am back in the village. Perhaps Madam will let
me bake her *rotis*. Or perhaps not.

There is a cracked old mirror fastened to the wall and I catch a glimpse of someone so strange I think the woman is behind me. But the woman is me.

My skin is marked and I have the ends of an egg-yolk yellow bruise around my eye and my lip is swollen where it split last week. My hair is chopped without reason or style. My eyes are large and fearful. The light of hope has faded and I feel meaningless. How do I hope to endure when I am so wounded? If suicide were not a mortal sin I would have thrown myself off the roof months ago. How desperate do you have to be before killing yourself becomes unimportant? I have ashes in my mouth and ringing in my ears. Temptation is everywhere. Knives and burning, pills and high places.

It hurts. Oh! It hurts. I look like Koti, who thought she was a soothsayer and marked her face with twigs and threatened to eat all the children.

I am poison.

I am nothing.

I am a dark blemish on your radiance. You cannot love me.

And so, I cannot love myself.

MADAM EUNICE

134 Sabre Green

I woke up today with an inglorious hangover and felt foolish, pretending to my husband that I had a touch of the flu but he wasn't to worry.

Chinese men don't care about suffering very much, especially the older ones. Suffering is a badge of honour. If it hurts do it harder. Our people have experienced mass suffering for hundreds of years. The sleeping bear has experienced famines that have eradicated millions of peasants and country folk. And still the Chinese plough on breathing and living and making and denying themselves. Privately, I wonder if that denial is caused by our imperial guilt. In the same way the British people tend to go overboard with the Singaporean Indians here. As if they could make up for their ancestral swaggering by smiling too wide and inviting them to a few dinners. But the Chinese have many smiles. Compensatory smiles, bitter smiles, vengeful smiles. Unlike the Thais whose every smile is the same whether they are about to kiss your neck or slit it. We are a complicated people and should not be underestimated.

A few days after the disastrous Mahjong affair I realised that I had received no contact at all from Joyce or Little Ping. This was particularly odd as usually one or both would ring me to gossip and arrange the next meeting. We would circulate hosting duties every week. It was Joyce's turn and nothing had been arranged. I had left a message on both their phones but still nothing. I felt suspicious and excluded. A very odd feeling for me. I am used to being what the westerners call the alpha female. My husband has the best job and the highest salary. I have sons. That fact, in itself, usually sorts the pecking order. Little Ping languishes at the bottom but irritatingly not only does she not seem to mind – she doesn't even notice. Joyce is much more submissive and behaves accordingly. But it is Little Ping's deference that I need. I want her fear to translate to obedience. Being frightened of me is one thing. But ignoring my position is quite another.

I have a manicure appointment later. The maid will do the weekly shop. She has her list, which I reviewed earlier, and enough cash to cover it. I will of course examine the bill minutely later and check the change. I think the girl would be too scared of the consequences to steal, but you never know, and I have had bad experiences before with dishonest maids.

I think I will drive by Little Ping's house and see what is really happening. I don't have to go in; I can just park and observe from the car or do a slow drive by. I am feeling very annoyed with myself, and increasingly furious with my friends.

And the suspicion that I am being shunned grows, and I feel quite rabid with indignation. Here are two women whom I have had the benevolence to befriend when, let me be honest here, they are well below my social rank. But I accepted them into my home and my heart because they seemed lonely and unsure of themselves. I shan't jump to conclusions. Both of them know me well enough by now to understand offending this particular Tiger would be very unwise indeed. I have quite a reputation for legal revenge. I have ostracised women for disagreeing with the type of flowers I have chosen for a fundraiser. I have made unfortunates less popular than lepers for interrupting me during conversation. I allow myself a little smile. I enjoy being feared. It gives me a bit of a kick, actually. Most Chinese people of good character are the same. To be strong you must be feared and prepared to do that which others do not have the mettle for.

From my window I watch that fat, western woman paying for a taxi to take her maid shopping. Makes me crazy. These Filipina women have attitude enough. Don't go filling her head with taxis and an easy life, makes it harder for her in the end. I watch this young woman with her hair swinging down her back like the fronds of a passion flower, laughing and getting into the taxi as if she owned the place. Her employer even waves her off and mouths a thank you. How naive. But then, this woman is struggling, you can see it. She wears native costume – huge sarongs wrapped around her body. And there are shocking rumours about her husband and the maid. And she is so fat! No control, lah! Disgusting.

It will all come to a bad end. You have to have boundaries with these people. Village girls need to be guided and protected, not allowed to have ideas above their station. It will make it harder for them when they have to return to poverty. The best lesson these girls can learn (and the most valuable one I can teach them) is hard work. It might sound harsh but most of them have families relying on their wages. The harder they work, the less likely they are to get into trouble.

There is talk at the moment in our circles and in the *Straits Times* that the government is very close to putting through a mandatory day off for all maids. This is very foolish of them. Freedom is not a prize. It must be earned. If I want to give my maid time off then I will. The government should stay out of it. Already there has been a barrage of letters to the papers condemning this proposal. Many employers feel quite rightly that their lives will be seriously curtailed by such a development. Who will look after the children at the weekends? And the elderly parents? The weekend is the only time we can have time without the children. It would be a serious inconvenience.

The other concern is what the maids would do on their day off. If it does come to pass, I want to have some control over what mine does. If she gets pregnant and sent back to the fields, I will have the double inconvenience of having to hire a new maid and teach her the ropes. This is a long and arduous process. I have little patience in general and these girls drive me mad. Their English is poor and they seem to have trouble understanding my accent. *My* accent! It is flawless! I won several prizes for my diction at school.

Already there are online spats between Chinese employers and the westerners. One stupid female implied that we were monsters and modern-day slave traders because we didn't believe in a day off. These idiots live in the clouds. How dare they cast aspersions on us? We are only thinking of our maids and how best to protect them. They are there to work for us. We give them a roof, a bed and food. Our own hours are long and we expect employees to sacrifice in the same way.

It is not selfish, just a different perspective. It is becoming a hot topic in the very worst of ways.

I drive to my manicure. The girls are very good here. Gentle with no distracting chatter. If it is empty enough, sometimes I nap, and I think I might snore as sometimes I wake to stifled laughter, but I can't say I let it bother me. I wait in the car for a bit, admiring my long, lacquered nails. They gleam like a crimson glaze on a freshly fired pot.

Little Ping lives off Orchard Road in one of those huge serviced apartments. Clearly they have more money to spend because she is barren. I drive past slowly. My mouth feels inexplicably dry and my nails tap like pecking chickens. I see cars in the driveway that I recognise as Joyce's and those of two other passing acquaintances. I slow the car down and I open the window. A faint clacking sound and shrieks of laughter confirm my suspicions.

The Mahjong afternoon has gone ahead without me.

My hands grip the steering wheel so tightly that my nails score marks in the leather. I am gripped by rage, and my reflection in the rear-view mirror is of a pale woman with eyes glittering with fury. My smile is terrible as I press hard on the accelerator and roar away.

LUCILLA

19 Sabre Green

When I first came to Singapore it was 2006. I was full of hope and excitement. Everybody knew someone who was a maid or nanny. We had shared those stories by the fire. We would giggle about the girls that had married the *ang moh* and discuss how big the *ang moh* were. The more brazen worldly girls would say, big everywhere! And we would stare wide-eyed at the fire and chew on our meat and wash it down with Coke.

There were horror stories but mostly they were ignored like a troublesome cough. There was so little choice for us village girls. The road well travelled seemed to us the safest. So for most of us it would be service of one kind or another. Some fathers were not as loving as mine. They believed that daughters were there to serve the family. And as it is much easier for a daughter to work in Asia than it is for a son the matter was settled very early on. Some fathers in Thailand and Cambodia were not anxious if their daughters became prostitutes. They were not Catholic like us and had no worry about sin the way we had. So we dismissed the stories because we had little choice and we pretended that we would have a wonderful time and the fairy story would come true. The lies start early.

In the Philippines what happens is we go to an agency, and they represent us in Singapore or in Arabia. I wouldn't go to Arabia. Already I have heard that two maids have lost their heads and many others are beaten for small things like not bowing low enough. There is no comeback if you get into trouble and no help either. Most of the girls who go to Arab countries are Muslim. They have to wear the veil and be totally obedient. Worse even than Singapore – the Arab employer is even worse than the Chinese employer. Here at least there are some employment laws that protect parts of us. The bric-a-brac parts, odds and ends that don't really add up to anything for anybody except the government, my Ma'am says. Many maids do not read well and cannot check if what their employer tells them is right. My Ma'am never makes me sign anything without reading it first to me. She goes through it slow so I understand her words. It is not always what it says that I don't understand, just that she talks very fast sometimes and we laugh about it. At the agency in Manila the contract I sign says what I am entitled to. Cellphone, day off, breaks from work and a good wage. This contract I am signing seems good. It gives me some freedom and guarantee I can contact my mother and father.

This is what happens when I arrive in Singapore. We go through customs and immigration with our representative. She doesn't talk much but does answer our questions. When we are led outside we are met by the agency owner who gestures to a filthy van. Inside it smells of sweat and smoke and something else. I can identify it as evaporated fear. We huddle in the back like frightened mice trying to make conversation to help us feel comfort.

'Where are you from?' I ask the young girl who is trying to be bright and brave beside me.

'My name is Clarita, from Manila. I live with my parents and we need the money.' She shrugs as if all this is to be expected. 'I am going to work hard and marry a nice western man. I'm still young and pretty. They like us like that.'

I smile encouragingly. 'I hope it works out for you, just remember to read everything before you sign it.'

Another shrug. 'I don't read well. But I have other talents,' the girl says, thrusting her tiny breasts out towards the setting sun. Her laugh is like a wind chime. I notice that the two men watch her carefully, as if memorising her for later. She is so young with the innocence of youth that can believe, *I am invincible. The world is mine.*

I know the world is not hers. I know this world will crush her within a few weeks.

The agency owner who looks like the devil with black hair that sticks up and red, red lips like bloodstains shouts often, banging her hand on the steering wheel for effect.

'You will not talk!' she shouts. 'You keep quiet and speak when we tell you!'

We exchange looks because we are unsure what to do. This is what I expect but her attitude still shakes me. Even Clarita looks nervous. Her brashness disappears for one moment. Away from our families, most of us for first time. We are paralysed with anxiety. One girl who I learn is called Ana has left her babies behind and milk leaks onto her blouse. She probably paid 600 pesos for the cheap, flimsy thing to impress in the big city. She cries silently rocking her head from side to side. I reach out quietly and take her hand and squeeze. She squeezes my hand back tightly but her weeping continues.

We drive for what seems like a long time. The adrenaline is wearing off and I can feel myself shivering. I have such foreboding about this place. I cross myself quickly and say a prayer to St Jude. The sky is streaked with purple clouds as dusk settles on Singapore. It is a wondrous sight so I try to point it out to the other young women to raise their spirits. Grey faces and swollen eyes turn to the skyline and try hard for a smile. It is clear we are facing a harsh time. I do not know if we will be taken to a brothel and forced to work. We are at the mercy of the woman driving and the granite-faced men she has watching us.

The city flashes with artificial light. Buildings tower above us and there is a scattering of people on the streets. I see Chinese women who look like dolls tottering towards bars and Bangla men in groups whooping and chatting like noisy cubs. I see a handsome western man, even in the dark his blonde hair shines like the *gumamela* flower. He is tall and confident and is much older than his girlfriend. I am amazed to see that he is holding hands with this tiny Chinese girl. She looks self-satisfied and haughty. As we pass them she looks into my eyes and draws her index finger across her neck. I rear back in shock at this violent gesture from such an innocent-looking girl.

After that I keep facing forward and pray silently for protection and peace. The van changes direction and from the position of dying sun I think it must be north. The roads are smooth but the driving is haphazard and we are flung backwards and forwards against each other and the seats, which prompts sharp cries. One of the granite men cuffs the girl nearest to him across the head as easily as yawning. After that we practise silence.

The van pulls up by a large house in a very tidy neighbourhood. Even in the darkness I can see how clean everything is. Not a blossom or a banana leaf out of place. I wonder who is responsible for this cleanliness because it still has not occurred to me that there are thousands of maids who rise early and continue to work constantly to keep this Singaporean fantasy alive and that I am about to join them. Struck by the strict and regimented look of this street I think to myself that I much prefer the wild and bedraggled beauty of the jungle around my village and the mountain streams that cascade down slab rock and the vines that weave into pools of pure cold.

We are pushed out of the van and made to stand in line in silence. I see a flicker of movement from the corner of my eye and turn my head to see a slight girl, Indonesian probably, cleaning a car. Her movements are practised and silent. She catches me looking and nods at me. Somehow the gesture gives me a little hope and I turn up one corner of my mouth in reply.

The wrought iron gates swing open with a gentle thud and we are herded through them and up a driveway towards a wooden door at the side of the building. We are pushed into a small area which I realise is the laundry room. Ten of us squeezed together, nervous and fretful, realising that our situation is very hazardous. A few straw mats litter the floor and large containers of water are dotted about. It smells of women and fear. We are lined up roughly against the longest side of the room.

'Passports and phones,' Devil Woman barks.

Silently we hand over our documents and phones, our links with our families.

'Please, Ma'am, when can I have my phone back, to contact my babies, please?'

Devil Woman's response is to reward her with cobra stare.

'This your phone?'

'Yes, Ma'am.'

The silence threatens to drown us as it stretches out. At last, Ana whimpers and Devil Woman responds by dropping her phone on the floor and pounding it with her foot until it shatters. Plastic and rubber skitters across the floor.

'Now you won't miss it, lah. I do you big favour.'

I see that Ana is frozen with anguish and panic. This throwaway cruelty is to become very familiar.

'You sleep here. Too late to eat now. Too much food make you lazy. My name Madam Joo. You call me Madam. You work here every day until we get you jobs. You work very hard or I send you back to Philippines. I keep your passport and phone. Safer that way. Also the law.'

Of course it is not a Singaporean law at all but it is Madam Joo's law. She is our lifeline and our deity and our keeper. She is very convincing and I have no doubt any one of us who defy her will be dealt with harshly. We settle down for the night and sleep a little, especially the village girls who are used to mats and earth floors. When we need to relieve ourselves we knock on the door tentatively and when nobody comes we squat over the sink in shame. The heat builds up in the tiny room very quickly and the stink of our waste makes the humidity even more cloying. The fragrant frangipani from outside have no place here. Cockroaches run up and down the walls but the drone of mosquitoes sends me into a reluctant sleep.

The next morning most of us are awake by the time the banging on the door starts. Up, up! she shouts. Banging the surfaces all the time. We are pushed out of the door and down a corridor. Another tiny tiled room opens to the left. All of us are shunted into this room.

'Take your clothes off. Shower now. Dirty dirty. If you use toilet only flush after four girl use. No flush after every girl. No waste water. Go to jail!'

If we take too long she bangs at the door and tell us to hurry.

Always *Bang! Bang! Hurry! Hurry!* Many years later when I watch a film about a prisoner of war camp I am rendered dumb by the similarity. The same shouting and the same daily humiliations.

When I first tell my Ma'am the beginning of my story she cover her mouth with her palm and cry as if she is in pain. My Ma'am feels things very deeply. She explains to me about the Holocaust. About the terrible suffering of the Jewish people and other 'undesirables' during the reign of the Nazis. She tells me that the guards used to harass the inmates like that in the death camps. Camps, she tells me, where men, women and children were worked or starved to death. Or were selected for the gas chamber and burning. I listen to Ma'am in silence and then we both weep for different things and the same things.

Sometimes now I still fall asleep with in my ear the shouts of Madam Joo and in my head the memory of those men with their sour breath and their roughness and the blood trickling down my thighs onto the cracked tiles and my innocence lost in a careless brutal moment.

MA'AM LESLEY

35 Sabre Green

I haven't ventured out of the house for a long time. Jocelyn has always done the shopping and everything has quite miraculously appeared where it should. I can't remember when I stopped caring about what I looked like or indeed what Ralph did or didn't do but for the first time I have a sense of purpose.

It is desperately hot. One of those Singapore afternoons when the sky burns with blue and the humidity sticks to your lungs making breathing difficult. Large as I am, it is even more of a struggle for me, and I find I have to rest several times in the shade of a banyan tree. Sometimes, I wish we lived in Fiji where fat women are idolised. I suppose I could lose weight but I just haven't the energy. I know that sounds odd but it's nothing to do with being lazy. I feel so low sometimes that I just want to lie in a darkened room, go to sleep and wake up years later. I imagine waking in a room covered in thick cobwebs. I stagger to the mirror, collapsing several times because my muscles have wasted, but when I study my reflection I am beautiful, slender, with taut facial skin that radiates with vitality. When I realise that Ralph has abandoned me I experience an intense, almost orgasmic surge of euphoria. I am free. Then a door will bang somewhere and I am jerked into the present with all the finesse of an unstable blancmange.

I have brought a bottle of water with me and gulp at it. When I set off on this adventure I had planned for the shops being a twenty-minute walk away. That would be twenty minutes for a person who isn't carrying an extra four stone, but I am determined. I want to prove to myself that I can still do normal things. And even though I must cut a comical figure struggling down the concrete pavements being passed by grandmothers and the tiny birdlike women, I keep going.

Entering the shopping mall is a harder task. I panic at the thought of so many people at once, but caution myself that if I focus on the task in hand I can achieve this. If you are not used to social interaction, if your world has become so reduced in size so that peering through the curtains is how you stay in touch with people, then shopping malls are terrifying things. The noise for a start seems deafening. We live in a very quiet area. One of those throwbacks to 1950s Singapore. A gentle, green enclave in the middle of an urban catastrophe. Even taxi drivers have trouble finding it and you have to shout, Jalan Lempeng, Jalan Lempeng, at them. For some reason the Chinese don't become offended by shouting. They seem to relish it, even approve of it.

Even though there is much I don't understand about Chinese culture there are parts of it that I really do enjoy. So much of it is jolly and proud. No one worries about making too much noise and red is prominent. Berry, crimson, terracotta, blood-orange, cherry, brick, scarlet, auburn, fire. I love them all. My favourite lipstick that I have but never wear is shockingly, wonderfully, unapologetically red. A sinful red. I don't wear it because Ralph told me I looked like a leaking Marseille whore. After my marriage Ralph took exception to make-up, boxed up my Chanel lipsticks and Laura Mercier foundation, my fragrant, comforting Sunday Riley cleansers and a huge palette of Mac eyeshadows, and dumped them next to our bins.

The sliding doors open and I catch the most magnificent wave of air conditioning which offers enough relief from the heat for me to push through the doors to the icy mecca beyond. I heave a sigh of pleasure as my skin starts to pucker with a sharp chill and it is delicious. I walk through the mall to the end past the little pop-up stalls that sell everything from painting-by-numbers sets to dumplings to impossibly small underwear. The Asian children are adorable and I love watching them running about like turbo butterflies. I can only do it for so long before a lump in my throat warns me that I shouldn't dwell.

Wandering through Cold Storage I notice a surprisingly large amount of western foods and become unfashionably joyful at finding a Waitrose cheddar stocked amongst the Australian cheeses. I reach into the chill cabinets for flaky pastry, a large cut of beef, some foie grass, two bars of very dark chocolate, some cream (Australian) and free range eggs. I slip an extra big bar of Dairy Milk in for me. I speculate I will need some fuel for the long slog home. But chocolate never tastes as good here. I think it's the heat or the excess sugar. It melts so quickly you don't get that rich sensory experience in your mouth.

Singaporean malls are not lush, fluid experiences but sharp and harsh. Electricity rages through the floors, powering the AC units and the pulsating lights, and hiding is impossible. The pop-up stalls are filled with traders shouting and gesticulating. I have a fierce hunger for gentle, cheerful hours spent around the Fishponds Farmers' Market in Bristol, which hums with a silent language that I understand perfectly. But I pay for the shopping and congratulate myself that for once I am part of the greater world. The cashiers are cheerful and polite as they pack all the grocery bags and lift them into a trolley which I wheel out into the purging heat. I head for one of the sky-blue Comfort cabs that wait passively outside. I gesture, the driver nods in agreement and pops the boot, waiting stoically as I heave the bags into the stifling space. Only a very few cab drivers will actually help you with the shopping; most are content to watch.

The journey back is uneventful; I direct him through the roads until we hit Sabre Green. I notice with some surprise that Ralph's car is already in the driveway and feel wrong-footed at this sudden change in routine.

As I push my way into the house I hear giggling from upstairs and then Ralph's meaty guffaw. I feel my jaw clench painfully but I resume unpacking, stopping from time to time to swig gulps of icy water from a bottle in the fridge, and I realise that I am excited. For the possibilities of tonight. Perhaps, at last, I can show Ralph that I'm not just an obese and totally inept past-it wife. That there still might be some use in me after all. I lean on the kitchen counter and smile to myself.

The click of heels on the stairs and the laughter that follows are ominous and I stiffen with worry. My husband and Jocelyn appear together in front of me. She is wearing one of my Alice Temperley dresses, an empire-waisted one that dazzles with sparkling stones, and she is weighed down with my jewellery. I don't mind this so much except that the pearl earrings in her lobes were my grandmother's.

Without thinking I hold my hand out and demand them back. Jocelyn looks outraged, but Ralph is incandescent. He walks away and returns a few seconds later with his father's old walking stick. And he sets about me with a routine I am familiar with. Long, swishing thuds on my back, avoiding the kidneys and short, sharp lashes on my face and shins. The pain is an excruciating almost tender thing like when you've a terrible toothache that has gone on too long and you can begin to identify the different types of pain through throbs to hot lances of agony, then the sudden retreat before it starts again.

'Please,' I murmur. 'Ralph, please, not my grandmother's earrings.'

Jocelyn's giggling is the last thing I remember.

I don't know how much later, but these are the next things that I know: that I am on a morphine drip and I have concussion. That my jaw, miraculously, was left alone – I don't think it would have survived another beating. Ralph comes to see me in hospital only once to explain the rules. As he towers over me, the nurses mistaking his attention for love, he makes it quite clear what he expects. I will not speak about this to the medical staff. I can say I fell down a short flight of stairs at home after one too many. After that, I am very much alone, and instead of using the time to get stronger and seek help I feel my resolve draining away with the saline drips. I am asked about my injuries but in a brusque way, and the nursing staff are polite but not comforting, and there are moments when I wish I had died.

After ten lonely, painful days I sign my discharge papers and sit on the hospital bed, a Gucci suitcase that I don't remember buying at my feet, wondering what to do.

The truth of it is I have nowhere else to go except for 'home'.

Clutching a bag of opiate medicines I return to my house of pain.

SHAMMI

12 Pasir Ris Terrace, Tampines

I wish I could wake without this ache in my heart. Something feels broken, bent, disconnected. I've become uninterested in my welfare. Day after day I feel myself becoming more numb; even the slaps from the children do not hurt as they once did. The humiliation burns less bright now.

This Madam is very fussy and she expects high standards. Before, she had two maids to do all the cooking, cleaning, washing, looking after the aged grandmother who also has a memory disease. Care for the children, put them to bed and feed them. For these two weeks it is just me.

Grandmother is incontinent and if her pads slip in the night it is extra washing for me. Madam expects all sheets and pillows to be handwashed. I have to use a cracked, plastic bowl and a separate tub to rinse. It would be so much easier by the river. In my village as we wash we sing songs and tease each other about flirtations with men, pretend and real. We help each other with the heavy sodden sheets and lift them over the rocks to dry quickly in the sun. There is a cadence to our scrubbing, a connection to the women before us, as we pound and laugh our way through the boredom.

However hard I try to recreate that happy scene it makes my head hurt and I have to stop. I feel feverish still, and flushed. If I look in the mirror there are spots of scarlet on my grey cheeks. I wonder if I am dying, and oddly, I do not feel threatened or anxious about death. My parents would be able to mourn me properly knowing that I tried to serve them until my last breath. This afternoon I go to the doctor's. I haven't had my periods for three months now. I suspect it is lack of proper food but my Madam won't hear of it. She seems to think that the loss of my menses is a positive thing. You lucky. No mess for months. No cramping, no pain. No baby. I always smile inside at her insistence on this possible future pregnancy. It would be an immaculate conception considering I have no freedom at all. The doctor's 'appointment' is a forced health check all maids are expected to have, by law, twice yearly. We are tested for all manner of diseases including HIV and have to have a pregnancy test. If we refuse then our passes are cancelled and we are sent back home. So we bite our lips and squeeze our fingernails into our palms and suffer the indignities with silence.

Today, the youngest boy pulled my hair so hard some came out in his hand. When I cried, he slapped my face. I looked up in shock to see my Madam standing in the doorway nodding her approval. You never reprimand my children. If you are stupid and lazy they are allowed to reprimand *you*. You disrespectful to my children I call police... You go to jail... I send you home. Always the same threats hang in the air. To be sent home is the worst outcome because in many instances we would not be allowed back to Singapore. Then our choices become even more limited and dangerous. You understand that many of us are village girls. Taught to be submissive and respectful as is the Asian way. Female purity is honoured in our culture. A fantasy that puts women on a pedestal will never have a good outcome. She will fall from grace quickly and painfully by the very men that put her there.

I know my English is not good but I try. If only Madam would slow down a bit I could catch up even more. But she speaks fast, like a hail of nuts, and if I don't get it first time then I have to just nod because the alternative would be painful. I think about asking Madam for some headache pills but she only believes in Chinese medicine. Maybe this is why she is so bitter. The muddy draughts that smell like rot and sweat make me retch.

If I were back at Sabre Green I would try to whisper to Lucilla and she might sneak some tablets to me. On my birthday, Ebony Ma'am pushed a box full of lovely things over the fence for me. There was chocolate, a bracelet, two pretty dresses, some underwear, money and a tiny cake. I pray over the bracelet – it is pearl and silver. I like to think it shines with protection by the angels. Ebony Ma'am gave me a lovely smile. I carry that smile with me in my heart like cool *lassi* on a steamy day. I wonder about that lady and her good heart. I think about how she met her husband. Was it by a pearlescent seashore or did he rescue her from a Bengal tiger that had escaped from a rajah's zoo?

She wears different-coloured gemstone dots on her forehead. Sometimes ruby, sapphire or emerald. Her eyes sparkle with goodness and love and when she cooks I press my forehead against the wooden fence that divides us and inhale the sharp spices that remind me bittersweetly of home. The fragrant air shimmers in the space between us. Chinese food uses large amount of oil and fish sauce. It never smells fragrant to me and sometimes I gag over the wok I use to cook for my employer. My lips twist into a tiny smile as I think about spitting into the food. And then I pinch myself. What is happening to me? I never used to think like this. I feel poisoned by my life here, poisoned by the double standards and my fear that something terrible is going to happen.

Tonight, Madam went out after the children were put to bed. She always kisses them on forehead and fusses with their blankets as if she has spent two hours bathing and cleaning them, not I. Shammi, you go on downstairs and clean up kitchen. Walk dogs after. Then clean car. Plants need watering.

I stumble downstairs and start on the washing up and clearing away. After a few minutes I hear the front door slam as Madam leaves. I have no idea where she has gone. I start to hum as I wash the dishes, allowing some hot water into the bowl, a luxury usually not allowed. When I'm on my own like this I sometimes imagine that I'm back in the village and if I turn round my Ebu will be sitting on the mat shucking vegetables for the stew. And she will gaze at my face and beckon and I will lie with my head in her lap and she will stroke the hair back from my face and I will feel at peace.

A pair of heavy hands are placed on my shoulders. The smell of him. Oily, overweight, cheap cologne mixed with sweat. My face tenses and I hold my breath. I feel his breath against my ear.

Meihua, Meihua.

His breathing gets harder as hands begin to knead my shoulders and my upper arms. It is painful because I am frail. Why does he do this? He cannot find me attractive. I'm skin and bone, my teeth are terrible, my skin is flaky, my hair hacked and lustreless. Every night he forces himself a bit further on me.

Tonight his hands slide over my hardly there breasts. He moans and I can feel a hardness pressing into my lower back. What I should do is take one of the knives and stick it in his neck but I just keep humming and washing, like an idiot. Then sounds from upstairs force him away from me and just like that he is gone and I have never seen his face.

It occurs to me that this need he has is not about sex but more about ownership. Like a cracked rowing boat that he has rented – this Sir owns me for fourteen days and will do with me as he wishes. The sense of power is what makes me so alluring. It is the worst type of cliché and a complicated game that I cannot hope to win.

MADAM EUNICE

134 Sabre Green

My revenge on Little Ping has been slow but beautifully crafted. Being respectful of hierarchy is important in Chinese culture and Little Ping has cut ribbons through ours. And she has paid.

First, I began to make subtle mentions of her unfaithfulness and always mentioned Joyce as the source. As I spun and wove Little Ping into tighter and tighter circles of deceit I gained strength from her dismay. She began to call me and beg my intervention to find who was spreading these terrible lies about her. I sympathised, in character, and assured her I would do anything I could to help. Her husband had heard the rumours and had become very angry. When she told me that he had hit her for the first time in their marriage I stifled an attack of the giggles. It was too funny. Watching her gulp her tears down, her face unbecomingly flushed and hot.

I felt powerful and I have always enjoyed that feeling.

The culmination of her calamitous downward journey is to take place at a charity event for the Chinese Women's Association. This brittle yet sparkling occasion has long been seen as the event of the year, and it is a perfect stage to set Little Ping up for her big fall.

I have, as usual, bought a table which cost my husband around 8,000 dollars. This is quite usual and I am happy to tell anybody who asks. Chinese culture encourages one to demonstrate one's prosperity and talking about money is completely acceptable. Discussing salaries, school fees and prices of houses and holidays is customary, and they are considered appropriate subjects for polite conversation. The westerners wince at this, which is very amusing. It is seen as the height of bad taste to 'boast' about one's financial or fiscal position. People who do it may be tolerated if they have enough money, but are excluded if they don't. It's also a class matter for westerners. The older the money, the less it is discussed. The aristocrat and the artisan alike despise the nouveau riche. The aristocrats and the artisans chug along with each other and disregard the rest. Our class structure is more fixed. You would have thought that the reaping ideals of the Mao Tse Chung would have smashed it to death. Using the clumsy yet effective anvils of paranoia and fear to bludgeon China into a cohesive, single unit. But the system is tougher than it looked and is thousands of years old. A land and a people do not lose their cultural faith and mores even if they are forbidden. Look how the Restoration bounced back in England after Puritan rule. Overnight London was injected with colour and vibrancy, Charles II was resplendent and the country rejoiced. Ah, the British! They have always been sweaty, drunken barbarians with a sense of entitlement and pale snobbery that has allowed them to rampage through some countries and contaminate the shores of others. Although that served them better a hundred years ago or so. A great country bought down by champagne socialists. I think that is the term.

One thing that is very important in our culture is skin colour. The darker your skin, the more likely you are to be a farmer or a labourer, someone unrefined. An elongated fingernail on a little finger indicates wealth and a profession that does not require manual labour. My skin is the colour of lilies. Pure, creamy white and without blemish. I have the whitest skin of my peers, a fact I am very proud of. I have never exposed it to the sun in my life. I have the skin of an empress and the attitude to match.

This evening, Little Ping and her husband, and Joyce and hers, are guests of mine at the table. Or Joyce is. Little Ping thinks she has been invited, but in fact there is no room at the table for her. She will arrive in all her glory, slightly muted from the stress of being gossiped about, and approach me. I will step smartly out of the way while she looks at the place cards and when she fails to find her name beautifully calligraphed onto creamy parchment she will look at me, a confused smile attached to her mouth, and I will glance at her and hold her treasonous eyes for a full five seconds watching intently as she begins to understand. It will be delicious.

I am wearing a jade-green Vera Wang gown with matching satin shoes. My hair is ebony-sleek and in a high bun. My skin glistens under the dimmed lights. I feel astonishing. And I watch my husband with interest as he works the room, and he actually does just that. He researches who is on the guest list, and then, if there is a dignitary who doesn't happen to know an author or politician or land developer, he will step in and broker the deals. A business card first and then a complex series of mini meetings. He has quite a name for himself, my husband, and tonight he looks rather dashing in his black tie. Our eyes meet and I nod discreetly at him. What we lack in passion we make up for in ambition. I think that is why our marriage has worked.

Oh! I know full well he takes mistresses sometimes for a short while – sometimes longer. The Polish girl, ruddy cheeked, huge bottomed and built like a farmhand, lasted almost two years. The little Chinese language student over three, and she had her own apartment that he paid for. We don't discuss these things; it would be indelicate. But I'm very aware of these women and they are not in the least bit threatening. It is quite usual for a Chinese man to have mistresses. They have just taken the place of concubines in the second bedroom.

My great grandfather, Li Gang, had several concubines that my great grandmother, Ai Lan, accepted wholly. They would share his bed, prepare food, clean the house. Menial duties. It was not the most beautiful or the most sexually accomplished concubine that was the danger. It was the simplest, purest girl. Usually from a farm, sold by her family to stave off the ubiquitous starvation that followed the plague of famines in the Breadbasket and other areas of China: the Great Leap Forward became the Great Hunger. This girl would be a virgin. As my great grandfather Li Gang grew older, he became captivated by one of his youngest concubines. Her name was Mei and she was fourteen years old. The only one allowed to rub his feet, she rose in stature almost to equal his own wife, but in the end she died suddenly, painfully, wracked with terrible pains and vomiting blood. Li Gang alleged poison and suspicion fell firmly on the other concubines who railed and cried and denied everything. Eventually, no evidence could be found to corroborate his suspicions and harmony was once again restored. My great grandmother Ai Lan never admitted to being involved but it was most likely a conspiracy of women.

Women can be vipers and turn on each other like maelstroms. Sisterhood is a pretty idea but women are naturally competitive and the older we get the more cut-throat we become. But the tendency for older men to look for younger, more fertile mates is part of natural selection; they are driven by a biological imperative and there is no point getting sad about it. Better to make the most of the good times and be respected and revered in later life. No Chinese man wants a wife who scolds and, although we are represented in most professions, it is still expected of us to maintain a beautiful, serene home and be the traditional wife and mother. Blood-on-the-sand imprints on the Chinese psyche. Our historical culture is too deep rooted for us to change it now. If the shock and awe of Mao failed to frustrate our natural inclinations then I think they are set in stone.

I check my immaculate hair in the mirror and relish what I see. I glitter like a jade dragon. Shimmering with vengeance and possibilities.

Then something catches my eye in the far left corner of the glass. I see a tall, robed figure standing immobile in a way that is unnatural. Something feels odd and disconnected about it. The head is bowed and a cowled hood conceals the face. I squint to try and see more. Then a chattering group of guests distracts me for an instant and when I glance up again the figure has vanished. I spin round and search the room discreetly but I can see nothing out of place at all. The Singapore butterflies are out in great numbers, the fine wine is flowing and the business chat is animated.

Ah! Little Ping and Joyce have arrived. Joyce is too pudgy and ten years too old for her Alexander McQueen creation, and Little Ping looks fragile and nervous but nevertheless rather beautiful in a crimson Marchesa.

I make my silken move towards my husband and wait with anticipation for the sweet inevitable.

LUCILLA

19 Sabre Green

Hurry! Hurry! Your time is my money! This is one of Joo's favourite phrases and she smirks as she says it. It is probably the only honest thing she shares with us in these harsh, hateful weeks. As well as our passports and phones we have been ordered to hand over our bags. Phone cards and money are contraband and illegal in Joo's house. We sleep in the sealed, shuttered laundry room side by side. Our prison cell, no more, no less. I watch the nightly battles between tiny geckos and large cockroaches and the lizards watch back with their unblinking basilisk stares like tiny collaborators.

We are allowed three moderate bowls of noodles per day and unlimited water from the containers. The tap is out of bounds and Joo checks the water meter daily and if it moves too fast then we all forfeit a bowl of noodles. The realisation that we are purely a commodity to her arrives quickly but I am surprised to feel so apathetic towards my fate. At 5pm on our first evening we are given our first bowl of noodles and harangued the whole way through it. The shouts and pushes become knitted into our daily routine, but I begin to suffer from heartburn because of it. We are split into groups of three and the maid trainer begins her work. The maid trainer is bought in by the agency boss to show novice maids how to clean and wash efficiently and effectively. We are taught the difference between an HBD flat and a house, the right way to ask questions and the best deferential manner. These are long, arduous and monotonous days. I haven't been able to contact my parents and I fear for their anxiety. I lift the shutter that covers the window a few inches and peer out to a scene that reflects a very different world. The sun shines, the blossoms fall and I wonder if God is even aware of me. Two different worlds exist – there, and here. I am not very sure which one is reality.

One day we are taken to the agency proper. This time we travel by MRT and I find it clean and quick. All of us relish this supervised freedom and I see Ana glancing at the exits more than once. Don't do it. It's just not worth it, I whisper urgently. I don't think I can bear it, she replies. I miss my babies and my breasts hurt. I've got lumps and red spots and I feel sick.

It's true that Ana does not look well. Her eyes are too bright and her skin too pale. We have all lost weight over the past few days and most of our already tiny frames can ill afford it. Show me later, I say. And when she does her tiny breasts are swollen, ripe to bursting and red splotches cover both. I can see lumps dotted about and recognise that she is suffering from mastitis. My sister had the same thing when she was breastfeeding. Ana's predicament is made worse by the fact that she has no way to express the milk that is now blocking the ducts. She needs medicine. I approach Madam Joo and explain the situation. You make trouble for me? she says. You want to cause problem? Troublemaker goes back to village in shame. I am prepared for this and quickly tell her that Ana is a hard worker but if she becomes ill she will lose more income for Joo. The old harridan understands this logic. Ana gets her medicine and recovers quickly but Joo never stops watching me after that. Her ghoulish face caught between curious and distrustful and her eyes inscrutable.

I find out later that the two thugs that Joo employs are her sons. Brutish, stupid and in sexual overdrive they leer and grope, pinch and whisper. They are the ones that stand guard at night outside the laundry room door. The window is barred anyway, the metal frames bolted tight against the wood. They never try to enter when we are sleeping because they are terrified of their tiny monster of a mother and though they push against the limits they are much too cowed to try actual assault. But to endure the day-long barrage of sexual comments and the endless mauling is so hard for us. There are so many invisible unknown rules. To answer back or to scold these boys is not sensible so we try to stay in pairs for safety.

At the agency we have to wait on benches around the office. There are thousands of these tiny little offices dotted about Singapore serving every catchment area. I notice Blossom Wide Resources, Sincere Maid Station and Sunnyvale. Pretty names for ugly business.

At about ten in the morning Chinese women who are prospective employers begin to wander in and they glance at us with less interest than they would a duck on offer at the wet-market. And so the process starts. We all hope for a western employer but none comes through the doors. It's not that we expect the *ang moh* to be the good fairy. They also can be snappish and cold and forget your birthday and sigh and jealously guard their husbands but you are much more likely to get a weekly day off and a slightly better salary. These snags of information are handed down from maid to maid through what is a well-constructed oral grapevine. Every aspect of your employer is discussed. It is always the main topic of conversation or at least the initial one. It makes you more popular however if you sigh and complain like the other girls.

You will keep any happiness that you might find to yourself because it is a rare thing within our community and to discuss it is to make others sad and jealous. Other maids who are living in much less forgiving circumstances with fussy aggressive employers don't want to hear about your happiness. The fact that your skin begins to plump and your hair begins to shine again is bad enough. Everything is compared. From food rations to hours, Ma'ams to Sirs, charges to off days. It is quite normal for the other maids to disbelieve that such happiness exists and will disregard such 'fabrications' as boastfulness or crazy talk. Friendships have been spat out and tossed aside and enemies made and never forgiven over employer talk.

A flat-faced pig-nosed woman comes over to me. I stand up quickly with my head slightly bowed and wait for the inevitable questions. You have children? Boyfriend? You work hard? Healthy? Strong? I don't want lazy maid. Last maid was a terror. Whine and complain like little dog. How old? Muslim?

And then after a long appraising look and a nod at Joo she walks out. Joo calls me into her tiny, rabid office. 'Sit down. Madam Y want to hire you. Here is the contract. Do you want me to read it to you?'

I shake my head. As I read through the contract Joo's long yellow nails beat an irritated staccato onto the desk.

She sighs heavily several times. 'I don't have all day. Problem? No? Then hurry, hurry.'

But there is a problem because this contract is unrecognisable from the papers I have signed in Manila. There is no provision for a day off and until I pay back my 'debt' to the agency I will receive no wages. My hours are 5am to 10pm. I am not afraid of working hard. I will work the full day and night if I get money to my parents.

'This is a different contract,' I say.

'So?' Joo shouts, her annoyance bulging out her eyes and blooding her cheeks.

'There is no day off here or public holidays,' I say as quietly as I can.

'You work first, pay off debt, and then see. Why you expect so much, huh? Are you lazy? Are you going to be a problem? Your mother sick? She needs your wages. Are you selfish daughter or obedient daughter?'

The futility of saying to her that I wouldn't be paid wages for eight or nine months anyway is beyond me. The apathy I am feeling is more like I am thinking this is not really real. When you have no power at all and there is no room for a discussion minds often retreat to a more peaceful place.

I pick up the pen and I think perhaps now I am signing away my life.

MA'AM LESLEY

35 Sabre Green

I'm not sure what I am expecting when I return to the house. I am still in a moderate amount of pain and wince as I retrieve my bag from the back of taxi. The driver has looked at me oddly a few times. My face isn't looking particularly pretty: a riot of mud-coloured bruises decorate my face. I stand at the gates for some time staring at the house. I suspect it would look quite innocuous in gentle, dappled sunlight but the afternoon glare of a relentless sun is unforgiving and the house stands stark and combative. For some reason I glance up at the top floors I become aware that Ralph is observing me. There is no wave or greeting, just an ominous stare. I think it is now that I realise that he probably wants me dead or to quietly disappear, and I feel chilled. I have no safe harbour, no friends and certainly no champions. I am as adrift as a Victorian governess, reliant on my husband for whatever scant provision he might make for me.

If I were sensible I would keep my head down and my mouth shut. Find a way to squirrel some money together and then leave. But if I were to leave where would I go? This is my burning question. My family have ceased contact and the friendships that grew when I first arrived have vanished with my own withdrawal. The police? They don't like to get involved with expatriate problems and are more likely to support Ralph.

There really is nothing for it except to pick up my bag and begin the torturous steps to the front door. As I walk I become aware of the soft wind, the almost sickly fragrance of frangipani and my own mortality. Fear bites into my marrow and my breath quickens as the adrenaline spikes my blood. I swallow, once, twice. Trying to encourage some saliva onto my lips.

The house has not changed at all and this leaves me surprised. I had thought that perhaps all traces of my existence would have been removed like a shabby secondhand suite that had been re-upholstered long ago to make do. It is clean and the sun streams in through the top windows, arcing across the marble floor, dividing it like a chessboard. For several moments I just stand, my plastic bag still in my hand, swaying slightly trying to get centred. I have an urge to giggle violently but stop myself when I realise that Ralph is standing on the little oak landing just above me.

'So.'

I wait for more but nothing is immediately forthcoming.

Ralph moves down the stairs to the yew bar cabinet that is an heirloom and very pricey. My husband loathes it, thinks it has terrible lines and is as dumpy as a maiden aunt. I think it is quite beautiful but have never had the courage to voice that particular thought, having learnt the painful way that Ralph's rules on speaking about certain subjects are as mercurial as a Scottish summer. He pours himself a large single malt – large for three o'clock in the afternoon – and leans against the wall, watching me speculatively.

'So. Things have changed whilst you've been away. Jocelyn has become pregnant. I know this might be a shock to you, and I've not behaved in the most gentlemanly fashion about it, but as you know, an heir, a son, is… well, it's everything. Not your fault, of course, Biology, genetics. Whatever it was. But I'm delighted. Absolutely delighted.'

I miss the end bits. I think he is talking about having to change arrangements. That Jocelyn is going to need care and attention. Of course, she would have to move out of the maid's room. For all the scenarios that I have contemplated this has never been one of them. I have understood they are having an affair and have remained as dignified as possible about it although, until now, I have received no absolute admission. And I am a coward. I am terrified of Ralph's systematic violence.

Ralph has paused somewhere during this uncharacteristic outpouring and is clearly waiting for me to reply.

But I am dumbfounded. 'Congratulations,' I manage.

A nanosecond of relief lightens his face before the conceit returns.

'In the circumstances I'm afraid divorce is the only way forward. I have to make the child legitimate before the birth. I'm sure you see that. You are a good girl, Lesley. I'm sure you don't want to make any trouble for me. Obstacles and such. Not a good idea. I think that would probably end badly for you.'

Another conscious pause to make sure I understand absolutely the consequences of anything less than obedience. So Jocelyn is commanding Ralph, as Anne Boleyn did hundreds of years ago, and she had better give him a son otherwise her currency will become useless for all the same reasons. If noble birth and powerful family members could not save Anne Boleyn from the axe then what hope does Jocelyn have? I feel quite protective of her suddenly. Maybe there is something I can do to help this petulant, arrogant little girl who has no idea what she is taking on. Hubris does not protect youth from the evils of this world. It may delay them for a while and even lessen their impact but eventually the wheel of fate must turn.

I pick up my bag and start to move up the stairs. Jocelyn will be more comfortable upstairs for the time being. 'In the spare bedroom?' I ask.

Not the spare bedroom, no.

I am still standing with my back to Ralph, hovering with one foot on the step that leads to the second floor.

'So where?' I ask.

The silence that follows communicates more than his words ever could. It takes me a few seconds to catch up. To comprehend that I am destined for the maid's room and am mistress of this house no longer. As if I ever had been!

'You have a choice, Lesley. You can leave but no court will compel me to give you alimony as you cannot bear me a child. I can cite mental stress, terrible mood swings and, of course, I have a witness to this. Or you can stay on and look after the house and Jocelyn for a bit while the dust settles.'

And I realise just how mad Ralph actually is. Not in a sectionable way, but mad with greed and lust in the way colonial men of a certain background are prone to be. He honestly believes he will win, believes it with the absolute certainty that is born of those years of education at a public school with a history that started in the four-teenth century, a history that my grammar school might have envied but was better off without.

At this moment the little fight I may once have had deserts me, and I feel my body become tired and old. Self-pity floods my already list-ing and fragile psyche. I move off the stairs and through the kitchen and push open the door to the former maid's room. She has been very thorough; I'll give her that. All her clothes are gone. A few shoeboxes lie scattered about giving the impression of post-coital lethargy.

It occurs to me that they might have had sex in this room, but I bat the idea away quickly. What does it matter in the great scheme of things? And I am too tired, much too tired, to contemplate any other indignities. There is so much I need to think about and I need time to do it. Some relief is required. I hope that perhaps now, as I won't be disappointing Ralph as much every single day, he might turn his attention elsewhere. Maybe not to Jocelyn while she is pregnant – well, probably not, but I don't want to think about that too deeply. It is the most disturbing part of my marriage that, although I have tried never to underestimate my husband, I've done just that, and done it when it matters the most. I used to think that if I could keep as quiet and invisible as possible, the violent episodes would minimise and I would find a safer place in this wheezing, tubercular existence. But I had misjudged my husband's affection for brutality and his talent for it – sadism is a talent. It takes a particular type of person to create mon-strous mazes within a relationship that are governed by decrees and statutes that disappear and reappear like invisible ink. As volatile as a mistral and as deadly as a rabid dog. The submissive person spends his or her life navigating choppy waters, setting off traps and flares, blun-dering though tests and exhibiting failure like a wartime art gallery.

I lie fully clothed on the bed, the sweat from my body chilling my bones as my body temperature fluctuates wildly. Pain medication, shock, fear and chronic fatigue are competing for my wipe-out. I give in. The narcotics in my body can gently remove me from worry for a few short hours.

And I am barely aware of the cockroach that I think runs over the bed in the night or of the vocal Labrador two doors down. Or the mostly hushed but sometimes shrill conversation that is taking place in the bedroom above me. Can I hear her plink-plink heels on the stairs? Is that the door opening? Can I sense her standing over me with her fists clenched or her leaving shortly afterwards? I drift in and out of restless sleep and pray to have answers in the morning. But nothing comes easy for me any more.

SHAMMI

12 Pasir Ris Terrace, Tampines

It will happen soon. It is inevitable as the sunset and the fresh sprigs on the banyan tree. As sea salt encrusts barnacles and a broken string disrupts play. Sir is playing a waiting game and he has the patience and the desire born of the master's right. I am conscious only that I will not fight. I will accept it and turn my face away from the drool that will spool onto my cheek from his mouth and then I will send myself to a river and dive and swim until I am transformed into a glittering fish that jumps and twirls and is forever free. The mossy stones will be no obstacle. Evolution will direct me to the source and peace will await me there.

But that will be then and this is now and I have to find a way to accept the now, in my present, to accept the inevitable assault on my body. The rape that will not be rape. That will be consensual in his eyes because I do not react when he pushes himself against me. My silence and immobility is understood as willingness. This is the justification that he will allow himself.

As I peel the potatoes, whittling down the white flesh until it is almost nothing, I can see myself in each piece of starch so small that it is pretty much useless. I think of my life here as a treadmill of predictability. I will die, or I will be deported, eventually. Both scare me although one offers more relief than the other. I am no good at home. No use to my parents in the village. I can't grow food from my bare hands or perform miracles. Money will not pop out from behind my little nephew's ear. I have to stay. I'm already too broken for Orchard Towers although the men who trawl the brothels of Geylang may not be so fussy. It is as if I am wishing death on myself. I don't want to feel this pain any more. I think God has abandoned me. I say this out loud and I've never voiced it before. It makes the idea more real and

I'm feverish with anxiety. My thoughts are becoming staccato and jolting. Things are not connecting. Sometimes I come to, and I find myself standing completely still and I have no idea how much time has passed.

I need to make a decision about myself and I fall to my knees and pray for what might be the last time for guidance and comfort. For a sign that I am still in the Father's grace and that he loves me. I only have four more days here and if I can just hold on and take whatever comes with fortitude and courage I will survive. And then I realise I can't remember what either of those things feels like.

When I feed the children and get slaps for my trouble, I bear it stoically. They delight in these stinging blows, not maliciously, but with the consummate glee of a child who is without boundaries. It is a game for them. How many slaps does it take to make the Indonesian maid cry? Not many is the answer. Lack of body fat and iron makes for a bruised landscape. If I were a painting I would be quite beautiful. Their mother either ignores it or smiles encouragingly. Can you imagine smiling as your children beat another human being? So much sadness behind the shuttered doors of Singapore.

I start to prepare the vegetables for dinner. All of this must be done by hand and they must be cut into impossibly small slivers for stir-frying. My bones ache in my hands after several minutes and I shake them out. A squirrel runs lithely across the border fence, beady eyes alert and aware. I envy the creature its freedom and its brain too small to contemplate the more complex details of life. How I wish I could stop thinking sometimes. To float in an unconscious shell, ferried as if by coastal tides, buoyant in ignorance and bliss. I think about the sea often because it is a great leveller of humankind. All are equally vulnerable beneath the surface; ruler, peasant, eastern or western, man or woman. The swell and roughness of the waves have no desires or premeditating motive. They exist and act on the caprice of the moon. There is a freedom in these thoughts that comforts me, but I allow myself the luxury of them only sparsely. Too much dream comfort makes the reality of my life unbearable.

Madam has returned from her outing. When I hear the car swing its way through the gates I am slightly late for the 'standing outside' ritual that she insists upon. I get a slap across my legs for that, but not outside. She waits until we are in the darkened hallway. I wince but hardly flinch. Is it a positive or a negative thing that the hurt hardly bothers me any more? She is angry, I can see it etched into her face and the pinched state of her mouth. Something trivial will have happened and it has irritated her. She runs through a list of chores that she has expected me to have finished. An impossibly long list that I could have had no hope of completing, and Madam knows this. I have accomplished all the washing, the food preparation, the weed pulling and before she went out I cleaned the car, but I haven't managed to iron all the sheets and pillowcases.

Not good enough. Lazy. Lazy. You stay awake until you finish all the chores. I know you stand dreaming. I don't pay you to dream. Her litany about idle village girls is her favourite, and drones on for some time. It is hard not to be affected by the constant barrage of criticism. However rusty your soul has become and your body a negative frame, the insults still make contact. Pummelling away at your self-esteem like a drunk boxer. I mutter my apologies knowing that nothing I say will make any difference. She is bored, frustrated and spiteful. A hateful combination. And yet seeing her with her children you would challenge my version. She is full of mother love and tenderness. Her children are her entire world to the exclusion of all others in the family. She reads stories and encourages their learning, holds them when they fall and soothes them in illness. She is patient, tender and awed by the beauty of her offspring.

Meanwhile, the dismissive attitude towards us, the maids, until we have the status of the lowest beasts, is so deep in this culture that employers drop insults and jibes like litter. They have no recollection even of doing so. It is as natural to them as breathing. But our lack of education which they see as ignorance doesn't make us stupid. In our world, education is a luxury, not a necessity. What good does education do if you can't afford to stay on past eleven years or take exams that might earn you jobs? What good does it do your family when they need paper dollars to survive? Pencil shavings will not buy rice or flour. You can't barter text books for medicine. Everything must be paid for in blood, sex or tears.

The monsoon season is upon us and the sky has become a dark grey bruise. Rain will come soon and the heat will break for a little. The humidity hangs low and the air is thick. Even the birds are quiet in the tembusu trees, delaying their feast until the weather has settled. It is oddly quiet when the birds stop their chatter. I find them friendly company in my isolated state. Even their stares seem softer, less pre-historic.

As the sky darkens the yellows and greens of the trees and plants seem to hum with a natural vibrancy. The vermilion stems of the sealing wax palm flicker in the shadows and bend in the prevailing wind. The rain starts with tiny drops, then splats, and finally a tor-rential downpour that makes the soil dance with its intensity, and a comforting, earthy odour accompanies it. Soon the gullies and drains are riotous with water and small lakes and rivers pool in the parks and sally down the drainage ditches.

The Javan minah birds gather in gossipy groups picking off the worms as they head up towards the pattering rain. It will probably pour down for about two hours or more, hard and defiant. It will wipe clean the surface of Singapore and drown a few cockroaches and other street vermin and then stop as suddenly as a snapped finger. You get so used to it that the beginning and the end of the storm become a continuous process.

I only have four more days to bear. Then I will be back amongst the devils I know.

MADAM EUNICE

134 Sabre Green

Oh! Little Ping's fall from grace was perfect. Her trembling mouth, her look of incomprehension, the slow dawning realisation that I had planned and schemed this for weeks. I think it is important for your enemies to know when you have outwitted them. Discord and unease chip away at their marble hearts until the victor decides to accept them back into the fold – at a reduced rate, of course – or to dismiss them entirely from the circle. I haven't yet decided what is to be Little Ping's fate. I am actually quite fond of her and she is one of the few people who can amuse me. Joyce is much more tedious. In fact, I can't remember why I am her friend at all. I suspect it is something to do with our husbands' work, although they are not on the same pay grade.

Joyce is lacking in accomplishment. There is nothing she can do well. I suppose her peasant stock is more prominent in that respect. I can sing reasonably well, arrange flowers, play traditional instruments and cook an enthralling Beef Hor Fun. Joyce works three days a week at a hospice for the terminally ill. I suppose it's good of her. Not my cup of tea at all. I just don't have the patience. I do my bit. Well, more than my bit. Look at the CWA dinner. I helped arrange that and earned thousands of dollars for charity. I prefer to 'do' than to talk. I find it difficult to just sit. If I do, I feel myself pinging with energy. My body starts to twitch subtly and I have to move.

Little Ping and Joyce have been silent again. I thought I might receive some sort of apology for their behaviour over the Mahjong party but clearly they are still under the misapprehension that I have lost some power.

You should never underestimate a tiger unless you are suicidal.

I've had other things to worry about. I have seen the elusive ghost again in another reflective surface. This time I was washing my hands and peering out of the window into the dark garden when exactly the same figure materialised behind me. I still couldn't see its face but this time it looked as if it would remove its hood, and then the maid knocked at the door and asked if she could go to bed now. I *tsked* at her, and told her to water the plants, then she could go to bed. And it was the minute the maid knocked that the figure evaporated, and I was alone. I was left with a feeling of uncertainty but more than a decent gobbet of relief. I felt sure that bad things would happen if I ever cast my eyes over its face. I know this all sounds absolutely insane and, believe me, I am not normally a superstitious woman. Not overtly, and not when you compare me to other women of my generation. Certainly, I respect traditions like Hungry Ghost. It is paramount to appease one's ancestors with a ritual burning of paper money and papier mâché versions of elaborate and fine gifts. We even make extra food and put it in front of an empty chair for each of the ancestors that we want to worship. Food and incense are burnt all through the day and night for a month. I once heard of a very new expatriate woman living on the East Coast who smelled the burning late at night and called the fire brigade saying that an elderly couple with possible dementia were burning what looked like money and valuables. How could the firemen keep straight faces? I'm sure the street laughed at her for months afterwards. I know we did in our salons and on our cellphones: *Did you hear about that Caucasian?* Gossip was shared and clucked over for some time.

Ghosts and demons are not strangers to me. Culture and religion are steeped in myths and frightening tales that may or may not have some truth to them. What I mean is, to see a ghost behind me wasn't the most frightening thing that could happen. There are many references to ghosts in Chinese culture and they have been worshipped in one form or another for thousands of years. Even Confucius mentions them from time to time, although he counsels keeping a distance between us.

What I am more worried about is discussing it with anybody. I had what is termed, I suppose, a breakdown when I was in my forties. I think my husband's affair with his Polish mistress was over and he sought comfort from me. I don't know if it was the onset of the menopause or the shock of him coming to my bed, but I began to cry at the smallest things. I lost weight, couldn't sleep and would power-walk around town trying to out-distance the pain that would engulf me if I stopped. It was a raw and tender time and I suppose I had some sort of conviction that life was not feasible for me any more.

I don't want to labour this point but suffice to say I was prevented from throwing myself off the sky deck at the Marina Bay Sands. I'm still incredibly angry with myself for choosing such a public place. The papers got involved and I don't know how much my husband had to pay to keep our names out of the story but he managed it. I was settled in a nursing home, a strange choice for recovery, surrounded by elderly Alzheimer's patients and the odd depressive. It was the most peaceful I had ever felt. I had no competitiveness and no fight left in me. And so, for the first time in my life, I just let myself be. All the patients were just existing in the twilight world between sanity and dementia, life and death. But it was a very tranquil place, considering. There was a small but fragrant garden ringed by bougainvillea and a creamy yellow and pink frangipani whose flowers were as aromatic as orange blossom. I could time my recovery by my sentience of the garden.

When I was very ill my life occupied only as far as my peripheral vision, blurred and sepia tinted. The fragrances from the blooms were nuances, nothing more, but, as I recovered, more colour seeped into my consciousness. It was as if I was awakening inside myself, like a snail that, having retreated into its shell when threatened, then emerges when danger has passed. While I was in the grip of the depression I took very little notice of my fellow patients. Chronic depression has the effect of quarantining the sufferer. Feeling isolated from the flow of life and unable to access a single joyful thought in any minute in any day is apparently an exhausting and debili-tating state. For me, it was bliss. I gathered myself and my emo-tional strength ready for life outside this sanctuary where nothing was expected of me bar taking my medication on time and the odd talk with a doctor.

The bad part was when my husband visited. He was desperately uncomfortable, wearing a business suit on a Sunday because his grandmother had always told him to look smart around doctors. Everybody else was drooling and in elasticated trousers and he was wearing a Hugo Boss suit. I would turn my face away to the wall when he came. I didn't have the energy to deal with his discomfort. When the nurses left he would pinch my arm and try to shake me out of my gloom. Once, he slapped my face in frustration. But never in front of the nurses.

I asked him not to come until I was ready to leave. But he ignored me, I suppose for the sake of appearances. And then as my sanity returned I began to smell the woman on him. He reeked of her and it made me nauseous. It was during these dark hours that I reconsidered my marriage and moulded it into what it is today. I had never loved my husband, but I think I fell out of like with him then, too.

LUCILLA

19 Sabre Green

With my first employer I had had only a mattress on the floor beside the children. The first Sunday I came to work for my present Ma'am she showed me to my room as if I was royalty. It wasn't huge but there was a pretty quilt and matching pillow, a basket of toiletries and not cheap ones either. A mirror, some flowers and a bedside table. I tried to get things I thought you would like. To make you feel at home, Ma'am said. To tell the truth I felt at home from the day that I met her.

I am sitting on the hard benches at the agency. I am wanting to transfer to another employer, an *ang moh*. I want a day off to be able to attend church and time off in the evenings and enough sleep that my head isn't full of bees every day. And I see this smiley woman come through the doors holding the hand of the most beautiful golden-haired child. As she stands waiting for Joo to see her she smiles at all of us. There are eight of us lined up on the wooden benches, and I see her take the time to acknowledge everybody.

Her little one makes a sudden break for the glass door. Without thinking I dash to his side and guide him gently back to Ma'am. The smile she gives me speaks words. *Salamat po!* she says and squeezes my hand tight.

Joo appears at the door scowling. Always scowling but she changes it slightly into what I suppose she thinks is a smile. Ma'am grins at her and goes in. Two minutes later Joo beckons me in. I stand in the doorway but Ma'am gestures for me to sit in the chair beside her. Joo is talking to me in Singlish as if I don't speak a proper language and then she turns to Ma'am and speaks very western. My Ma'am looks confused. Why is she talking to you in that ridiculous accent? she whispers while Joo's back is turned. I cover my mouth to stifle a giggle. We share a conspiratorial look and then Ma'am winks at me. I come away with one day a week off, and all evenings. All public holidays and my birthday. My wage is set at 850 dollars, which is very high wage for a foreign domestic worker. I feel the sweet rush of happiness and want to call my mother and tell her that her prayers have been answered.

Ma'am says, 'I hope you will be very happy with us, Lulu. May I call you that? You are so pretty. You look like a Lulubell.'

I tell her she can call me whatever she likes because I am so joyful.

This I hope will be a turning point for me. The beautiful child who is named Rory looks at me and beams. I feel my heart wrench. This child I could love.

As I have said I have a boyfriend. I don't speak about him very much because I am a private person but also because he is my secret, except from my Ma'am. Having a 'boyfriend' is a very good thing to have in Singapore. Firstly, maids get terribly lonely. Many of us have left love behind in our native countries and comfort becomes a precious thing. Secondly, it often stops an amorous Sir or at least gives him pause to think. Sir has no idea what your 'boyfriend' looks like. He could be a huge Malay with warrior ancestors or a passionate beefy Scot or a possessive emotional American. It is our security if you like.

My boyfriend works long hours as a driver carting the wealthy Chinese, Malays and Indians around the casinos, bars and hotels in the town. He also gets the airport run. I never get to see him on Sunday until past 4pm but then we make up for lost time. We eat out in simple hawker centres, chicken rice and noodles. Sometimes we go to a cheap seafood restaurant and share chilli crab or prawn stir-fries. Mostly we just get on with each other acting as large debris in the aftermath of a tsunami.

We can pretend we are a normal couple in a society that doesn't condone us. There is usually a party at the weekend, often a dinner party with everybody bringing something to eat and drink. A Filipino tart or some satay and chicken. And twice a month a group of us will drive over the causeway into Malaysia and go clubbing in Johor Bahru. It is no problem getting in with a passport and everything is cheaper there. Malaysia is huge compared to Singapore. Vast tranches of tropical rain forest and idyllic coastlines and a bubbling metropolis. It reminds me of the Philippines and I think that is why I have such great affection for the country. The Malays have much more evolved cultural identity and are more tolerant towards workers. Although corruption in Asian politics is rife and the nepotism in the top jobs and the courts is shameless. I have never been to Penang or Kuala Lumpur but I plan to soon.

It is a sad and shocking story in the paper that catches my eye in Mr Mong's corner shop. Another maid has died falling from an HBD flat cleaning the windows. Some employers still expect you to climb out on the windowsills to clean the outer panes. I think a law was talked about being passed but nothing yet. I pray for her family and if she had children. I cast my mind forward to her body being collected at the airport and the funeral that follows.

Was she a mother, daughter, sister? Did she feel relief and relax as she fell, giving herself up to God, or scrabble for a handhold as she began to panic? Were her last thoughts meditative or was her mind blank with terror? When this happens it sends ripples of muted outrage and fear through our little communities. What if I am next? We think and share and shake our heads in unison. Feeling momentarily guilty that we are still alive to share a picnic in the Botanical Gardens and mock the gangs of Banglas that jostle for superiority. And do any of us feel envy that her life is now uncomplicated? She has no guilt or shame or fear. No anxious sending of cash to Western Union addresses in Manila or Leyte or Candy or Rangoon. Queueing for hours sometimes on a Sunday as every foreign domestic worker waits patiently to send money home. Imagining the recipients gratefully relaxing as the bills will be paid this month.

I always send half my wages to my parents. They put some of it aside for medical bills but my Ma'am contributes. She says, they are like my family now, Lulubell. I have never had a pet name before and I try it out again and again on my tongue and around my mouth savouring its warmth and character. Ma'am has asked me to call her by her Christian name but I can't. There needs to be some boundaries between employer and maid otherwise things can go very wrong. I say to her that even when I marry I will still call her Ma'am. It is a symbol of my respect but also of my love. When I say my Ma'am that is how it feels. She is mine, this *ang moh* who has shown me more love than I thought possible.

Ma'am sometimes invites me to lunch at the Marriot on a Sunday. I meet her and sometimes Rory up there. We eat sandwiches and fries and maybe have a glass of wine. The servers are mostly Filipinas and they love that Ma'am takes me out. We have become celebrities. I sit looking out at the river of people passing by, Chinese to temple, Filipinas to Lucky Plaza, Banglas watching the girls go by. Sometimes, you see western men at a table with three or four pretty girls. Ma'am thinks this is very funny since I told her last time that one of them was a man. Now we always look for the Adam's apple. It's hard to tell because the lady boys are so accomplished at being beautiful. Their hands are sometimes a little too big and their jaws a little too wide but their poise would be envied by anyone. Do you think he knows, Ma'am asks, and what does he need *three* for? I raise my eyebrows at her and she squeezes her eyes together and bites her lip in amusement.

One time in the Marriot a Chinese woman was staring at me. I was used to it. I recognised her from the neighbourhood, always scowling and head up in the air. She didn't like me sitting at the table as an equal. I shrugged it off but Ma'am became crosser and crosser.

'What the hell does that old bat think she is doing?' And then Ma'am turned her chair and stared right back at the stone-faced woman. And they just stared at each other and Ma'am's face got red and her breathing got rapid and she gripped the arms of her chair and began to rise. 'Right, I've had enough of this.'

I placed my hand on her arm and pleaded that it didn't matter and she was not worth it.

'But it does matter, Lulubell. You matter.' And she came round to my chair and hugged me tighter and then tighter still as if by keeping me close she could dispel all the poison in the world. And in that instant I saw the faces of the Chinese woman, the *ang moh* man, the Filipina servers and the Bangla boys and wondered how it would all end.

MA'AM LESLEY

35 Sabre Green

I've been having vivid rolling dreams, which seem to have gone on all night but in truth it's probably been just the last few seconds. I wake slowly, my face full of sleep and opiates and I'm hot, sweating through the sheets hot. I lean up on my elbows and then it comes charging back into my consciousness like a limp rerun of a soap episode. If I wasn't so dazed by these painkillers I would probably weep with despair, but I find myself curious instead.

Curious as to how my new life will reveal itself. I swing my legs gingerly off the bed and feel for the floor with my feet. A blast of nausea blindsides me and I clutch the duvet to steady myself. Easy, girl, I caution. Slowly, slowly I stand and then overwhelmed with a desperate need to pee I hobble to the loo that adjoins Jocelyn's – now *my* – room. It's not too bad. Quite cosy really. There is a shower, which is fine as I've never been a bath person. I like to feel I'm rinsing the dirt off not absorbing the roads of Singapore through my skin.

Later, I stand outside on terracotta tiles warmed by the sun and watch huge snails trail slowly through the garden. We have a big garden by the republic's standards and when we first arrived I spent hours at the nursery in Clementi Road with the idea of creating a fragrant, tranquil space where Ralph and I would sit in the evenings and our future children would gurgle and crawl and trip around on chubby wrists and legs. Now it represents the loss of all those things. But the bougainvillea always thrive and their wooded stocks grow and their blooms shimmy in the breeze from the South China Sea.

The colour of things here makes me tremble. Nature is intense and at times intimidating. The flat browns and greens of Hampshire in the winter and even the brick-red clay cliffs in Devon pale in comparison to this garden state in flower. But Britain in the summer could rival it.

I think of the rape and linseed fields in the Wiltshire of my youth; its pear-drop yellow and dusty blue squares have burnt themselves into my memory.

My grandmother loved horticulture. She had a taste for gaudy, overly sweet roses. Blue Moon, Peace and Black Magic. Polar Star, Iceberg. As a nine-year-old I would pore over the garden catalogues committing the colours and names to memory. I have vivid memories of watching her defy the hosepipe ban to water her flowers and the inevitable, ugly rockery and I remember thinking how mundane her activities were and how much effort it all required. It has taken me years to understand why she loved it so much and even now, standing amongst the plants that I have cared for and helped to achieve their present beauty, I feel a closeness to my grandmother and to the natural world.

A connection born of millions of years of an arrogant notion that we live in harmony with nature, when the truth is that we are barely tolerated by the elements, and when this tolerance ends the earth lashes out like an older sibling keeping its charge in line.

I have an urge to run naked into the garden with my arms open wide shouting at the sky with pure joy and acceptance. But I am aware that it is the strong pain medication that can make exhibitionism seem like a really good idea. I bite my lip, quelling my impulses. imagining Ralph's outrage as he witnessed my sky-clad romp. His disbelief would make it worth it, but the battering that would follow would not.

I find myself in a strange state of suspension. Part of me is terrified of Ralph and his nonchalant aggression and I have no doubt at all that he will eventually kill me, death by misadventure. But there is another Lesley that is pushing its way to the front of my personality – a stronger, less meek woman. I can't work out if this is disassociation from the abuse and Jocelyn's alleged pregnancy, or if I am beginning not to care about my present circumstances. I suppose I am like a novice standing at the gates of the convent full of radiance and total belief in her actions before turning to wave a final goodbye to her family. Her lip begins to tremble and she has to turn away, to face the gates, to will herself to concentrate on the small but compelling sculpture of the Holy Mother, and, taking a deep breath, to corral her courage as a child does before returning to school after the holidays.

An unusual, chill wind blows through the gap in the houses to the back of our garden. It catches me by surprise and I shiver involuntarily. I can hear a trilling of a small bell inside the house. It becomes more and more insistent. I wander back in, tying my sarong around me tightly because I have actually lost some weight. Not much, but it's a start, and I feel lighter and less out of breath. I go back through my room and into the kitchen feeling the floor strong and hard beneath my feet. The bell is coming from upstairs, and so I duly begin to climb, summoned by an invisible dual force of curiosity and bemusement.

The door to the master bedroom is ajar and I push it gently. Jocelyn is lying on my bed, eating chocolates and watching television. Nothing has really changed except she has moved upstairs. She regards me coolly, weighing up my attitude and what she might need to do to crush it. I cock my head to one side and return her stare. Jocelyn takes a deep breath and I brace myself for a list of incredibly arduous and complicated demands.

'When I ring the bell you come. You come quickly. You will make three meals a day and anything else I ask for. You will treat me as important person. I have Mr Ralph's baby here. I am very important now. You will respect that or I tell Mr Ralph.'

It is almost comical. She is such a petulant, bolshie little thing like a toddler who isn't getting her way. I feel another wave of sorrow for her, not understanding where it is coming from.

'Of course, I will help you as much as I can.'

'No! You will help all you can. Or Mr Ralph... ' and she mimes hitting me across the face. I sigh and nod.

'Should you be eating those?' Pointing to the Charbonnel et Walker champagne truffles she is stuffing her face with.

'Shut up! Not your damn business.' Jocelyn's pixie face screws up red and hot. She thumps her fists down on the bed either side of her hips and starts to bawl. Tears leap out of her eyes and down her face, a turbulent salty stream. These are tears of bitterness, grief, frustration, and something else. Is it fear?

'Would you like some herbal tea and fruit?'

'I want champagne and cigarettes and dancing!' she screams.

I understand now that the trap, if that's what it is, that Jocelyn has set for Ralph has not been thought through. The difference between the fantasy of having a baby and the reality of it is kicking in. Jocelyn is a very rare Filipina in that she does not have a natural maternal bone in her body. She is an endless teenager, hormonal, self-absorbed and skittish.

And she is terrified.

The pregnancy hormones are making her feel vulnerable and ill and for the first time she is acutely aware of her situation. But I feel very little towards her. The momentary empathy has drained away to a few drips and her plight doesn't really affect me.

But the baby's fate does. And in that tiny moment of greed and need I make a decision to save that child from its parents. I have no plan and no supernatural message has written itself on the screen doors outside.

It is just my instinct, my gut reaction that I need to stay here and suffer whatever presents itself because I have a greater purpose. A raison d'être.

A baby.

SHAMMI

12 Pasir Ris Terrace, Tampines

One more night to bear. One more night to grit my teeth and fall asleep with my clothes on – jumping at even the minutest sound of a gecko gently flexing its tail on the stucco walls. A single night to pass with my heartbeat jumpy and profound, my blood pressure bulging out my veins and arteries in readiness for fight or flight. I have wedged a cracked but solid garden chair against the door that opens into the house. My mouth feels desiccated as if every single drop of liquid in my body has been spent on keeping me alert through the night. I gulp water from my big bottle and despite the cloying heat shiver through my thin clothes and musty blanket.

More than once I've jerked upright mistaking a noise from the neighbours or a natural creak from the house as the doorknob turning. This is not a healthy way to pass a night but what choice do I have? I'm protecting my virtue, which is my dowry. If I am violated tonight it will be the end of my marriage hopes. Prospective in-laws are not interested in the hows or whys of your loss of virginity; they are only interested in the physicality of it. Being raped or coerced against your will is something that a woman is supposed to prevent at all costs. Even to die trying is thought honourable, and preferable to the concept of damaged goods. They don't want a daughter-in-law who didn't try hard enough to stop her own violation. Or a wife for their son who can't have children because of the damaged caused. It is not a two-way street in this world. For women like me there is no grey area. No territory open for negotiation. It's right or wrong, white or black, positive or negative. The world is so much more complicated than this. The real world has a million consequences for each choice. And the women? Well, we are left to sweep up our own leftovers. Place a pad between our legs to stem the bleeding and pray to God that the rapist's seed lacks the courage to go the distance.

Dawn is breaking over the grey outline of the building blocks nearby. The sun's colours are playful at this stage of its cycle. Cocktail bold. I feel a tingle of hope. That I might have just managed to survive this last night intact and will leave this house as I came in.

I hear the sounds of the children waking and quietly open the door. The kitchen is clear bar a baby cockroach that scuttles towards the cooker and the safety of darkness. I will it away before Madam sees it and scolds me for the rest of the day. I am leaving at 9am and the kitchen clock tells a story of early morning. I wait at the bottom of the stairs for a little, straining my ears against the damp silence. What action will be the safest? Should I start sweeping outside now – at least I will be afforded the protection of being visible to the outside world.

Even the most conservative of Singaporeans would revolt at a sexual assault being perpetrated in daylight. And so I put the kettle on and walk towards the front door, grabbing the broom from the small hall-way cupboard. The deadbolts slide back easily and the third lock is a 90-degree twist. Morning greets me with the smell of victory and freedom. I suddenly long to be able to return to what, despite every-thing, feels like my own mattress again, and to sleep in that familiar hallway, content and drowsy from the baby's breathing.

Madam comes through the door and regards me sourly because I disappoint her. Even as I sleep. Even as I breathe. I slow my sweeping but keep my head down.

'You make breakfast and tidy bedrooms before you go. Also, the plants need to be watered. Did you finish the washing? No? What you expect? That I do it after you gone? You are such a lazy girl. I will tell your Madam just how lazy you are.'

And she will tell her and my Madam will delight in punishing me for it. But even when I am forced to hit my own face with her shoe, trying to avoid my eyes and nose, but aiming for my mouth because it bleeds easily and Madam stops suddenly when she sees the blood, even when that is happening, that is still my home in Singapore. It is the only one I've got and it is where I belong.

My Sir is too old to try anything. He might want his shoulders massaged or his legs petted from time to time but it is not a sexual need. It is not threatening and he usually grunts and then falls asleep very quickly. He has never shouted at me. If anything he is unaware of me. We are taught during our maid training to put our backs against the wall when a member of the family comes down the stairs if we are sweeping them. And to bow our heads if we carry some washing through the living room while the family is watching television. My Madam dislikes me eating in front of her so I have to squirrel it away in the kitchen behind the huge, silver refrigerator before she catches sight of me.

But that is better than waiting for my own rape.

After the sweeping is finished I move back through the front door and towards the kitchen, checking the marble floor as I go. It looks pristine, but an oily smudge or a fingerprint can start my Madam off for hours.

I see his shadow before I see him. A long crooked shadow that stretches out from the kitchen doorway towards the oak dining table. He is represented as shade. His shadow hands clawed and long, his back bent and deformed. I brace myself but can hear Madam starting down the stairs with the children, so surely I must be safe. I turn into the kitchen and I am grabbed, quickly, violently. He forces me back against the wall between the kitchen bins, his right hand around my throat and his big-lipped mouth against my ear.

'A little present.'

And he thrusts his hand up between my legs, tearing aside my cotton underwear and pushing his fingers up inside me. Brutal, sharp, agonising. And then it is over and he is gone. I lean back against the wall, holding onto the bins for balance. My mind is blank, my eyes stinging. I turn my head slightly to the doorway. Madam stands there staring at the floor. There is an ocean between us. A field of landmines, a mountain range, chasms of space. There is everything and nothing between us. She has a choice then; I can see it in her eyes. Deciding which way she will go. I'm almost sure I see a flicker of sympathy in her eyes. I wait to see what will happen because I can't move my legs yet.

She makes her choice and leaves me to it.

I make it to the mattress on legs as weak and shaky as a newborn foal's and collapse. I have so few things to pack up. I take my time. My sense of victory has vanished and I'm left with a feeling of impotence. He was always going to win and I was foolish to think that I could outwit him. He had all the time in the world to bide and a feudal attitude towards possessions in his house.

The tiny spark of happiness that the dawn had brought with it has been whipped away on a gust of sadness that threatens to end me here and now. By the time I manage to get outside to wait for the taxi I am emotionally numb. Conscious only of the throb between my legs, the trickle of blood gradually soaking my underwear and my overwhelming shame pinned to my lapels like Akar Saga seeds.

MADAM EUNICE

134 Sabre Green

I loved my grandparents. They were able to show love without conditions or buttoned-down emotions. They never showed that they cared one yen if I was a disappointment because I was a girl; instead they revelled in my star-crossed gender. For during my youth I was acutely aware that I should have been born a boy, and this ultra-feminine silhouette you see before you is a fairly modern take on Eunice.

For years during early childhood I tried to become boyish enough for my father to take notice. I had much more to me than either of my brothers. I was more intelligent, more resourceful and more ambitious. From the age of four I was bringing home certificates and commendations for my language skills, my maths, my reading, and for deportment. The aim was to transform my father's attitude so that he took me seriously. I would cut the lawn and watch sports on television, attempt to understand the maze of Chinese politics while at the same time being feminine and obedient.

I often wonder whether I would have tried so hard if I had realised that my father knew exactly how remarkable I was but was so constrained by his concrete beliefs and creeds that he was buried in them. Incapable of movement either forwards or backwards, he remained static and unconvinced. Life was a disappointment to him. Brainwashed by the cult of Mao, his whole life had been mapped out by a party that despised and condemned individual thought. My mother always argued that he was good man, but the physical hardships created by the famines, and the paranoia that was created to deprive party members of any committed relationships save for complete devotion to the party, meant that men like my father paid an emotional and a physical price. In his later years he was physically frail and always had a look of displacement about him as if he wasn't quite sure where he belonged. And he was incapable of trusting even his own family. Even as a younger man he would remain apart, detached from and uninterested in family life. I have no idea how he produced children. Perhaps we were conceived before his mind broke. But I am sure that even had I understood the extent of the damage in my father's heart and mind, I would never have stopped trying to impress him or buy his love with achievement. One of the many useless roads insecure children travel for their whole lifetime. And I don't need a psychiatrist to tell me that my choice of husband was directly influenced by my father. We are attracted to those we understand and share a connection with. A shared passion can be as strong a connection as deep love or friendship. And my marriage is centred around our joint ambition.

But lately I have been distracted by glimpses of my hooded figure. I've been ribbing myself about these sightings attempting to keep it lighthearted but the truth is I'm on edge.

The apparition is appearing with more frequency and there seems to be an urgency about it. I jump like a scalded cat every time I see something flicker or move. Constantly seeing black shapes weaving in and out of the edges of my vision does not make for good sleeping and I've developed an unsightly eye twitch.

Seeing the doctor is out of the question. Our family physician is my husband's golfing partner and would inform him immediately of my visit and the reason behind it as he has every other time over the past twelve years. My husband's generation is unimpressed by the ethics of confidentiality, believing that secrecy breeds secrets and even medical secrets set a dangerous precedent. Much better to have everything out in the open, making blackmail obsolete. Also typical of his generation, Dr Fong has kept his own transgressions out of the public eye, notably two sexually transmitted diseases picked up from one of his playmates in Thailand. The good doctor's professional hypocrisy rages long and hard in keeping with the norms of the old boys' network. These trips to Thailand and Indonesia for golf and other leisure activities are an annoyance that I suffer. I know what happens – I'm not blind or deaf – but I have no interest in my husband physically so I am content to let him dally providing he is responsible and does nothing that could harm the children.

After a disturbing incident three years ago, my husband has used a pseudonym in certain situations to protect his shreds of dignity. A young woman he had a brief liaison with took umbrage when the affair was cut short. She became enraged and used his business card, which she had kept, to wage a war of emails and texts at me. It is the most surreal experience to receive an email from another woman who calls herself Candy writing that she is distraught for hurting me but do I know that my lying, cheating husband has being doing X and Y with her for months. I might have taken that email and her subsequent tirades more seriously had they been from a woman called Victoria or Pauline.

This incident was never discussed directly between us, but I left printed copies of the emails on his study desk – underneath the children's reports file. The messages stopped abruptly and a rather splendid diamond choker made its way onto my dressing table. Tiffany-blue for betrayal. I have so much jewellery that most of it lies neglected without skin to dazzle on: a safety deposit box in a bank in Central Singapore plays host to a collection of jewels given in guilt and shame. A thousand pieces for a thousand adulterous acts. I store them, in keeping with the tradition of other deceived wives, as insurance, for the day, should it come, that my life becomes unbearable and I need to take the children and run. This plan of mine is at odds with my external ideology and most forbidden, but I don't believe in playing the odds and have a feeling that when the rainy day comes it will be a tsunami.

But I do need to discuss these feelings of disquiet with someone, and I'm running out of options. Little Ping and Joyce have disgraced themselves and I have heard nothing from them since my victorious coup at the charity dinner. There are very few women I trust in my circle because, truthfully, I am not enamoured of them. They tend to be gossipy, flighty, incredibly bored individuals whose ambitions have been eroded to the point of insignificance. Values and personal beliefs have faded into a void so large and so vacuous that they may never resurface. These are my social peers and, privately, I am disgusted by them. Publicly I never lose face, welcoming each and every one into a holding pen in my mind that I have created specifically for them. Once here, they are allowed to see exactly what I am willing to share of myself, and I present a pretty fierce public face.

Boredom creates a careless viciousness in some people. An intended slip of the tongue airing another's trusted secret, the destruction of character behind closed doors, and the mob mentality that women can display when given enough freedom and few boundaries. The *tricoteurs* of the French Revolution proved this as they knitted their way through countless beheadings, crowing from the front row and erupting with laughter at the sight of twitching limbs and the rusty sawdust clumped with blood mocking the stained and fallen wigs. I have no illusions about women and their capabilities both good and bad. I've seen and read enough conflicting stories and examples of each side of the female spectrum. The mother rage that kicks in in all animals when their young are threatened. The adrenaline that flicks the fear off and gives rise to incandescent fury leaving the imprint of a goddess. All-powerful, and possessing a terrible beauty that will haunt a man for the rest of his days. I often wonder if the myth of female deities stems from this powerful state a woman can ascend to. Eyewitnesses as far back as the Roman Empire have written about women moving pillars to free their trapped children underneath. And millennia before that, was not the mother goddess in charge?

And then the flip side. The spurned woman, the scorned woman. When love turns to hate and the imbalance created sets off a chaos in a woman's mind. Inventing pregnancies and sending anonymous texts to other wives and leaving hateful messages on an answerphone. Threats, bluffs, shadowy figures with deep pockets and the chilling possibility of long knives and sharp-edged tools.

Tomorrow I am taking the children to China to visit their grandparents. Old they may be but still almost perfect replicas of the parents whom I remember from my youth. The boys need to know them. They will be worshipped and spoiled and shown off and it will take a month to talk them off their twinned pedestals. But it will be worth it just to see the glimmer of pride my father has in them and, I fervently hope, in me. The little girl never falls from the black lotus and my need for approval is still as raw and salty as a sea urchin.

There is a secondary motive. I am hopeful that if I leave the city the figure will stay behind, rooted by its own history and ghostly labour. If it doesn't, then I will need to visit a specialist in this subject when I return, to lay this demon to rest.

LUCILLA

19 Sabre Green

Today my Ma'am and Sir fly back home for the summer. It is always a sad time for me because the house seems so empty and forlorn like a bird without song. They stay for two months and then return in August missing the coolness, but happy.

Good to be back, Lulubell, Ma'am will whisper into my ear as we hug, long and hard. Ma'am never packs early, usually the day before travel, always throwing too many clothes and shoes in because she forgets what she has at the other house in Scotland. She explains that it is little more than a flat and very small. It was their first home before they had Rory and Ma'am can't bear to part with it. She says the memories are etched into the walls and the woodwork, erratic but timeless like atoms and house martins.

The Scottish street where they live was named after the market that used to take place up the road, and Ma'am says her neighbourhood borders a very troubled one that has crime and high unemployment. I have visions of gangs of feral children with knives coming through the windows at night and poking until you give them your money, and then they flee cackling like miniature monsters against a sky of plum and tar.

Ma'am has showed me photographs of her wedding. Ach! It was beautiful; like a fairytale, like every wedding in every film I have ever seen. And the love that shines between them is evident in every picture – eyes never leaving each other for a second, each aware of the other's physical presence at all times, and this radiance that spans the room and beyond. This is the wedding that I want. To a loving *ang moh* who will give me my fairy tale and not expect too much in return. Singapore reeks of sex from its gutters and from behind closed doors and from the desperate men roaming for it. The more that Singapore tries to lock the sex up in a tidy and secure place the more it agitates and seeps into the republic's consciousness, oily and slick. Coating the streets and tongues of men with desire and shame.

When I was younger I would attend the tea dances in the Towers. It is very different on the tenth floor, and the tea dances start in mid-afternoon and carry on until the evening. Although there are unspoken rules that the women who attend are all maids on their day off and not ladies of the night, most who are single would like a western man and so the place jumps with hopes and giggles, sweat and pheromones. And now when I walk past if I am heading for Lucky Plaza I watch the men who cast a hopeful eye on Orchard Towers. Some are disdainful with guilt, others are bright eyed, innocent and sheepish, others still are fatigued with the depravity of craving something more realistic than the life they have spent years creating. Letting hedonism drip endlessly onto a now mundane and exhausting existence. These are the older men you see propping up Harry's Bar in the week and in groups outside at the weekend. Sometimes older Chinese women will be hanging around them laughing a little too hard and drinking a little too quick as if aware that their currency is almost redundant.

And I cringe at the hypocrisy of these men who get fatter and older and there is no consequence for them, only a constant supply of nymphs to worship them, and the women have to hold on to their figures and faces of twenty years ago with a feverish intensity, calling themselves Ginger or Bette when their native names are so much more beautiful. But this part of Singapore, this restless, ugly swirl of humanity, recognises and rewards artifice and deception. The natural order has no place here.

My friends scold me because they say happiness is a luxury and gives you too much time to think. *If you were sad you wouldn't think so much about this shit, lah. Too much time. You should swop employers with me. I want to be happy and think too much!* Always my friends ask me if my Ma'am needs another maid or nanny. I think they suspect that I'm lying about my employer because nothing can be that good. In a time where false hope and expectations harm you far more than acceptance and stoicism I can understand their annoyance and envy. And my position is unique. Almost unheard of – one of those myths and legends that continue to convince girls and women that they should come to Singapore and be slaves.

I've seen the sad-eyed lady boys in the bars, dressed to kill and impossibly beautiful, being dismissed and derided by men who are definitely not their equals, and every time they are dismissed a little piece of them falls onto the floor like a discarded handkerchief and they visibly have to pull themselves together like corset ties, tighter and tighter, to stop their courage and self-esteem from leaking out. And every time a piece falls to the floor it is ground into the dirt and detritus and becomes absorbed by it, staining the soul in minute incre-ments like skin as it ages.

I wonder why they do it. Why hold yourself up for ridicule and rudeness every night from fat pigs with no dignity themselves? And they would reply that they love it! The drama, the mystery, the friendships and the quixotic search for love. And while some of this is true the sadness weeps from their pores and expressions and the lac-quered hair and kohled eyes scream for some peace, some comfort. The endless giving of themselves takes its toll on their looks and their futures. Most of these men have already isolated themselves from their families by being gay. To take that further, to subject the family to ridicule and God's fury is indefensible to most Muslim fathers. In Leyte, we are more accepting.

Maybe our Catholicism has given us a history rich in sin and blood. I know that if my brothers were gay my parents would love them no less. They would pray for them more but could never cast them aside because of such a tiny thing as the wrong love. Divorce *is* forbidden, so falling out of love is difficult. Filipinos stay married but might move on from each other. And the maternity wards in Manila are so full that there are often two or three mothers with babies to a single bed. The care is good but the great lack of basics in the wards is a testament to the loyalty we have to our God and his laws even if this modern world does not understand or make room for them. My Ma'am says she is a Catholic in her heart. She says she was never born to be a Protes-tant with its muted colours and simplistic texts and insipid teachings. Catholicism is a real religion, she sighs, dramatic and decorous, always fighting its own history and sin. Much more suited to the trials and tribulations of humans, Lulubell. And I nod and smile because sometimes I just like to listen to Ma'am talking.

She is passionate like a Filipina and full of colour and taste. Like her cakes. Sometimes she will bake Blue Sky cupcakes for Rory. She just adds a little indigo colouring to the icing and Rory says they taste beautiful like *blue* would. And he nibbles away at the fondant on the top and leaves the golden cakes naked and bold and Ma'am chuckles and says it's because he is so sweet, that he only likes the icing. Sir like all parts of the cake and grabs several to take into work. He says it reminds him of home when he is away sad with the short loss of his family. At work Sir misses his wife and child even after a few hours. That is a man of love and honour and I am proud for him to be my Sir.

MA'AM LESLEY

35 Sabre Green

Ralph has gone away on an extended business trip to South Korea. I know this because his itinerary was bunched up in the pocket of his blue linen suit. I have no idea what he is doing there but it's clear he had meant to destroy this bit of paper and for some reason had forgotten it.

Jocelyn became quite hysterical when he told her. Perhaps her inability to keep the real Jocelyn from beating her way into their lives, now, is taking its toll on Ralph. I see his hooded eyes often resting on the horizon as he waits for answers. Now she has given in to him and they've had sex, Jocelyn's image is forever tarnished in Ralph's eyes. Had she stayed quiet, submissive and demure her future would have been assured, but like another of Henry's star-crossed wives, the naive and earthy Katharine Howard, she is so egocentric that it is impossible for her to play the political games needed to keep her out of danger.

For some reason, now she is pregnant, Jocelyn can only be herself. And the very worst of it. Petulant, angry, wheedling, hysterical, hypersexual; in different degrees her hormones have unbalanced her. Ralph has begun to stay out later and often he doesn't return home. His once supple Aspinal briefcase is stained and dog-eared as if the owner has stopped caring about it. Sometimes, when I wake at six to get started on my new duties, he is asleep on the sofa, sweating and snoring, dishevelled by some pain that he keeps close and will not discuss.

The monsoon season is bashing the island to bits. The rain is spiteful and seems to relish breaking up the barbeques and parties by the many swimming pools. Weather can be malicious and I am reminded of the mistral that drives men insane as it screams its way down the Rhône valley banging on the shuttered houses incessantly, crying to be let in. It nips the heads of the sunflowers and suffocates the laven-der, birds are boxed to death by gusts of wind so strong they are slammed to the ground in groups, feathered corpses littering the mud beneath the native trees. This squall feels similar, as if it brings death and pestilence. Riotous fungi will grow quickly on the rain tree's fis-sured bark and lime-green moss will start to grow and creep along the footways like zesty trimmings.

There is a stench in the air that is unavoidable. I think it is olfactory misery.

I do what I can for Jocelyn but I'm not at all sure what is going to happen to the three of us. Subtle changes in the dynamic have left me dry mouthed and sometimes breathless. I'm more curious than fright-ened because I am still Ralph's wife in legal terms. The subject of our divorce has not been mentioned since the night I arrived back from the clinic and Ralph is probably treading water in panic trying to work out what to do. There is something else that is uncertain about him. He is losing his patina, his gloss. The slicked-haired, Beau Brum-mel that I married and moved to Singapore with has almost entirely disappeared. Perhaps the demise of his lotus fantasy has taken its toll.

The reality of a pregnant Jocelyn – a seething, uncontrollable Joce-lyn – has shattered any romantic notions that he might once have had. This reality is messy and unattractive, fibrous and bitter. It is unfair to expect any person to be able to live up to the illusory courtly love that a hard-lacquered romantic might bestow upon them. Women tend to fall flat on their faces when they have been assigned the role of a Pre-Raphaelite heroine. The well-dressed fallen woman rising with fragility, but radiant with a new-found purity, just doesn't exist now and it was probably never a feasible option. Men and woman are gloriously messy and our encounters together even more so. Love is a kitchen after a family has finished their breakfast. Littered, gob-bled, spent. But whatever the details, we can be drawn together in such a primal way that it is impossible for us to avoid it. Infatuations along with hope are the most dangerous notions to have. The power of lust can define a country, decimate reputations and lay waste to those promised lavish obituaries. The hysteria that accompanies lust and its greedy explosion is condensed by its prologue – a torpedo trail of wretchedness.

Today, in this present moment, I am thankful for the soft sound of my sweeping, the cool and restful marble beneath my feet and the calm that has begun to enter my heart. I'm not sure when I stopped being quite so frightened. The fear just started to drift away the less Ralph noticed me. This reversal of roles has benefited me greatly. I have time to reflect and make considered choices and I love to keep a house in order. I shop and make plans and make wholesome meals and fresh fruit drinks for Jocelyn. I hand-make chocolate truffles without the alcohol and Jocelyn continues to listlessly pass them from her hand to her mouth – an efficient conveyor belt. I hear her talking on her mobile phone – sometimes panicky and loud, often whispered and tense.

Her family situation is a mystery to me – even at the beginning, before she became openly hostile, we never talked about friends or what she did on her day off. Jocelyn kept herself at arm's length from the first day of her employment. I think I was to blame in many ways. Having staff was anathema to me. It felt odd and wrong and bamboozled my socialist sensibilities. I was never comfortable with having her live in and in the beginning would almost fight her for the washing up. At first, after considering me for a few seconds, she would point her finger to her temple and move it in a circular motion before retiring to the park for the rest of the afternoon. And I would finish the washing up, smugly thinking I had won the battle without understanding that Jocelyn's plan did not include me and I was irrelevant from the off. Ralph was hooked very early on, particularly after witnessing her scrubbing the hall floor on her hands and knees in obscenely small denim cut-offs. Poor Ralph. He really didn't stand a chance and Jocelyn knew that he was obsessed with having an heir and worked that angle with as much accomplishment and guile as a souk trader. And began her project of pushing me further and further out of the kitchen and further and further from the heart of my own home.

And now some of the cards have fallen and I watch where they lie, trying to interpret how the fates will intercede or intervene or

just let the blood flow for kicks. As Ralph loses his substance and
Jocelyn is panicked into silence I continue to sweep, revelling in the
smooth, long strokes, a ritual practised and ancient; whether on the
dirt floor of a slum in Mumbai or a floor of limestone slabs in Hampshire, women have moved and removed dirt from their living quarters for centuries. It is the most domestic of duties and doesn't involve
expensive electricity or patented vacuums. Just women brushing and
clearing spaces for their families to grow and sleep, eat and weep. A
continuum of the feminine calling.

My thoughts do touch on my future. I have not worked for years
now, and would be useless in an interview, and my experience would
be rubbed out by the arrival of new qualifications and youth. Even
though I don't fear Ralph so much any more, there is still a residue
of general fear that clings to the inside of my skull and cleaves to my
heart. I was never confident around people and my marriage to Ralph
has perfected my insecurity. Do certain things ever come back once
they have been beaten out of you? A broken jaw is easier to mend
than a broken mind or heart. The knots and scars of a damaged psyche
are impossible to see with the naked eye, which is so odd considering
how deeply they are felt.

It suited Ralph for me to be isolated, and he worked on that stu-
diously, like a trail of ants determined to bring a large crumb back to
the colony. I wonder what people think has become of me. Perhaps he
has told them I've gone back home or we are divorced already. Perhaps I am dead from a terrible illness or freak snakebite in the Bukit
Timah Reserve. The last time a friend called was over a year ago, I
should think.

And it has been a relief. I never connected with any of the women
here. They are too confident and pristine. Most are very slender.
Entirely thin, resembling anaemic sticks of celery. Or less often they
are huge, gargantuan and rolling with flesh. Shopping, like I did,
with acute embarrassment for larger ladies' clothes in BHS and Marks,
pretending that they were content with being chubby and that their
husbands loved it. Heaving shapeless sacks and grossly misshapen
blouses out of suitcases hoping wildly that something might look a
little fashionable. And as they hang there, desolate and saddened by

their cheapness, rubbing up against something smaller from long ago when we had figures that were effortless and careless, the truth of a fat woman's self-deception weighs heavy.

I was never happy being fat but it was a useful way to shut people out. A truly physical barrier against a hurtful society and a life that had taken a spectacular wrong turn. I think back to that first dinner party and, even with the wonder of it all, of being courted and seduced, it was not long before the cracks began to show and Ralph presented the malevolent and syphilitic Dorian Gray replica that has haunted me most of my married life.

SHAMMI

112 Sabre Green

Today I had to go to the doctor's because something isn't right down
there. There is blood and it still hurts. I have cramps that double
me over with pain and leave tears hanging from my lids like acid.
The Chinese doctor is brusque and rough. Pushing and pulling and
prodding. He doesn't prepare me for the physical examination and as
he pushes the speculum in, my thighs clamp automatically round his
hands. He slaps my thighs apart with a stream of furious Mandarin and
I bite my lip until scarlet beads pop up desecrating the pinkness like
sin.

He pushes his fingers inside me and I experience a flashback so
intense I think that I will die from fear. I can hear the keening sound
around me and my body rocks and rocks itself – the doctor is staring
at me without empathy, more perhaps curiosity mixed with irritation.

'You lost virginity. Understand? No hymen. No virgin any more.
I will write your Ma'am. Take bloods for pregnancy test. You wait
here. Stop crying. No good crying. Should have thought before acting.'

He bangs the door as he leaves and I pull my trousers up and sit
underneath the examination table, my knees pulled up tight to my
chest and my eyes protected by my forearm. I can't hold a thought in
my head; it is too messy. Although the casual way that I have been
spoken to has inadvertently helped in some strange way because I feel
too numb to keen any more. But I am frozen stiff with shame and loss.
I hear the door open and squeeze myself tighter, hoping that I won't
be humiliated by the doctor again, pulling me out by my arm and
shouting instructions that I can't follow. It is in fact a young woman.

Her English isn't very good but neither is mine and we make do with just holding hands for a while. In the end she kisses my forehead and gazes at me unhappily.

'Sorry, lah.'

I bite my lip and nod and the woman leaves as quickly as she arrived. I stay for a while on the white-tiled floor underneath the safety of the examination table. What am I supposed to do? I start to chew the raw skin around my nails, frozen by indecision. I am teetering on the edge of a chasm. Shall I fall and embrace a hellish death or trudge on hoping that I will somehow be saved?

I begin listing escape hatches in my head. One is to go home. Just to leave, plead illness of a close relative or my own terminal disease. I think I once heard about transferring to another employer, but it was in a language I didn't understand. Even my own contract was gibberish to me. I signed it because there was nothing else to do. *Sign or you sent home. Think of your parents, the shame you will bring with you.*

I could escape on a junk and sail the South China Sea until I reach our village on the coast. I would cook for the crew, fresh fish and seaweed rice, and I would learn how to be useful. I imagine being captured by pirates in the Sulu Sea and being held prisoner but the captain, a bronze-skinned schemer who is attracted to baubles and gold, becomes infatuated with me with one glimpse and we sail the endless water, pursued by the authorities. Never resting or staying still. Our only constant being the moon and our promises of devotion to each other.

I think it must be a hopeful sign if I am still able to harbour fanciful notions in my head. There must be a certain amount of living left in me if I can still imagine a future, however absurd. And I cling to this tiny piece of life that honours my beating heart. A life raft in a sink hole, a sturdy vine in quicksand. I feel like a child misplaced in a frantic crowd. So for now I will place my secret shame in a small corner of my mind. There is so much else I have to keep inside me, and a time will come when I have to make a journey into that painful place to look at what is hidden there. Yes, a time will come and I will try to be ready for it.

Eventually the door pushes open and the doctor appears again. He is less brusque. He says I should rest. The bleeding will stop. He seems anxious for me to leave.

I take the MRT the long way round, not really caring that Madam will be angry. It takes so little to make her furious I think she must enjoy the feeling.

Ebu always said there were two types of women in the village. The ones who fed off anger, who felt empowered by it and drew strength from its fire, and those who were made numb by it, chilled by its fury, who turned the other way whenever it approached them. I am the latter. Confrontation has always bothered me. I don't enjoy seeing another's rage. It is unpredictable and sometimes dangerous, like a drunk whose internal hate becomes a war with the world. Angry people seethe like maggots on a corpse. Their eyes bulge and their skin changes colour. You feel a distinct change in the atmosphere, like lightning recharging or the smell of madness. When they move, odourless vapours follow them; they trail wrath like hot coals. True anger changes the face of a person and that is too otherworldly for me. I trust the constant and the usual. Even my employer, who is so hard on me and finds new ways to punish me every week, is consistent and unbroken in her enmity. It is oddly comforting. I can't pretend to understand the rituals of her inhumanity, but I don't fear them any more.

Sitting on the MRT I feel the nearest to the human race that I've felt in a long while; it is crowded with schoolchildren returning home and teachers from the western schools looking flushed and grumpy. I can buy anonymity along with my ticket. Nobody knows anything about me on the train. They may guess, if they have a bored moment or two, but I am not worthy of consideration. A young Indian mother sits passively as chubby children pull on her braids and nose rings. She winces through the pain adoringly. These woman are too beautiful with their saris in bright caterpillar colours and their kohl-rimmed eyes. Endless glinting bracelets stack along the lovely burnt-butter skin of their arms, and when they move or shift a harmonious tinkling accompanies them. I often look for Ebony Ma'am who lives next door to me.

But she is rich and has a driver that takes her smoothly through the city to a destination unknown. Sometimes, I think about bumping into her and she is shocked to see my thin body and sadness and furnishes my room with sweetmeats and deep soft covers and buttered crumpets like the Little Princess. Except I have no room of my own, just a mattress outside the children's room. And I'm not even sure what crumpets are but I often wonder how my mother came into possession of that very western book she read to us both every night. On the inside of the cover there was a stamp in English.

The Strand Hotel
Rangoon 1941

When I held the book close and felt its fragile pages with my fingertips I wondered who else had heard this story, who else had found such peace with the saving of Sara Crewe. Ebu used to call me a dreamer but when she was unwell she would lie with her head on my lap while I smoothed her long hair from her face, my fingers drawing shapes on her rough, familiar skin, and wove stories of animal changers and princesses who are abducted as babies and then found again.

And so I breathed the magic of hope into my Ebu, wishing her strength and love through my stories. Hoping the describing how it would be to fly, like an eagle, to have that freedom as a natural, daily choice, would free her from the bondage of her ill health and her worries about her children. She wanted better for us all, but how could we achieve it? To push us to improve ourselves was a lost cause. Village children do not become successful and wealthy. Our lot is to serve and die and seek happiness only if it is within reach. It is a simple and effective way of staying as safe as possible. If you don't reach for too much then you are less likely to lose what you do have.

I wonder when I will be able to see my parents again. A savage burst of homesickness on this modern train circling and backtracking its way through the day. I watch older couples sitting together, maybe a hand clasped or a smile between them, and feel naked with grief.

Sometimes, it hits me like that. A pain so fierce and clinical I fear my voice has been lost for ever. I grieve for my parents who are still alive. For the children I haven't had yet, now for my purity that has been punctured, for my husband who remains a figment. I feel weak from pain and grasp the sleek, metal pole to stop myself from falling. My eyes feel wet with tears but I'm too tired to brush them away and they fall unchecked onto my dusty cheeks and dripping onto my shirt.

A Caucasian man, young and ruddy, is standing in front of me and is gesturing to his seat. *Please, please.* He takes my hand and helps me to the seat. This act of kindness renders me more vulnerable than the generalised bullying of my daily life. It threatens to give me hope, comfort. I bow my head and can't even thank him. He just pushes a soft paper tissue into my hand and looks out of the window above my head until the train stops at Outram Park where he steps off.

I stare at the floor, memorising the specks and inconsistencies on the vinyl, willing the pain to fade away. The tissue is sky-blue and as yielding as a baby's skin. I hold onto it tightly and possessively as the train speeds onwards oblivious of the humanity inside.

MADAM EUNICE

Zhouzhang, Jiangsu province, China

It was a terrible mistake to come here and whatever comfort I thought that I might receive is invisible to me. The children are being spoiled and have become tetchy and demanding and I feel as if I am an outsider in my own family. It's easy to forget the differences between us. The shabbiness of my mother's local pyjamas. The frayed cuffs of my father's ugly shirt. The mouldering environment within which they make their home.

But I have spent hours walking along the clifftops and shores of my birthplace. The countryside is astonishingly beautiful, unspoilt and uncomplicated. This is a fertile province that has produced fish and rice for centuries. Zhouzang, where my parents have lived all their lives, is crisscrossed by canals and I worry about how they will steer the heavy barges when they become too infirm to hoist the poles. But I have misjudged the strength and tenacity of my mother before, with bloody results.

My mother was a believer in firm discipline. Like many Chinese, she viewed the cane as an essential part of child rearing and not in the least unkind. In a vast country with no social services and where infanticide is still practised particularly in rural areas, children learnt quickly to respect their parents and obey without question. My father was too detached ever to become involved in our punishments, but my mother performed them with gusto. The livid stripes and the crusted blood on the backs of thin, pale legs were displayed with pride by schoolchildren, us included. We showed off our wounds and tried to outdo each other with stories about our bravery and the length of the beatings. We always had this common ground; our quiet friendships blossomed from our weals and we took a strange comfort from the ever-present tart, metallic odour of drying blood. Our teachers would remain unconcerned about our injuries, preferring instead to preach about the party and its greatness, impressing on us heavily the need for obedience and thoughtful endeavour.

We were stoical about our lives, and even growing up during the complicated 1970s we never felt we were hard done by or lacking something. This was our existence, and the total sanction on foreign media meant we had nothing to compare it with. All the books, text books and novels were approved by the party. Our school clothes were uniform smocks and trousers and our haircuts were pudding-bowl, hatchet jobs. It was as if the government wanted us to resemble each other like mannequins.

In the same way as some mothers dress twins identically to protect their sameness, the party insisted on this for all its children. If I hadn't been able to escape to Singapore when I did, embracing capitalism and establishing myself as an ornament to wealth, I would have stayed much like my mother. My cuffs fraying and my hair greying as the years sped by towards death.

Returning was always difficult. I had carried a lacquered casket of guilt for years, admonishing myself for not removing my parents from the poverty they seemed to revel in but simultaneously aware that they would never leave their beloved China even for a visit. The longer I was away the less they trusted and the more they venerated me. I was paraded past gaggles of their friends with my mother beckoning each and every one to feel the softness of this or the cost of that. And I would be pushed and jostled and on one occasion actually scratched down my arm, while disbelieving and disapproving elderly Chinese inspected me and found me wanting. The fact that I had left the province for the temptations of Singapore marked me as maverick and, because my parents were not now living in a golden palace with servants, this indicated my lack of filial piety.

So why did I come this time, despite knowing deep down it would be a failure and an acute disappointment? Every time I returned I harboured a secret belief that they would see me as deserving of their love and pride. It is a waste of my energy and continually frustrating but I can't let it go. An unseen force propels me towards their displeasure over and over. A Hainan gunship churning the waters of my familial ties.

The coastline yawns upwards towards Shanghai and the weather is slightly more temperate than Singapore, whose humidity is legendary. I have brought walking shoes with me – brand new and agonising as my feet break them in with the resulting bloody froth of blisters. But I stride on regardless through the scrub and marsh flowers, watching the common rose and red lacewings weave their way through, and trying to discover calm from the natural beauty of my surroundings.

As I stand on the path using my hand as a sun guard, I notice somebody standing in the distance. I think perhaps a fisherman or walker, although the Chinese mainlanders are not known for their admiration of nature. I begin to slow and the wind drops suddenly and completely. I try, strain, to hear the world about me, but silence clings like a sticky malevolence. It is as if the world is concentrated around me and time has stopped. The figure is still blurry in the distance – half rubbed out on the horizon – but I can see it turn towards me. My mouth is as dry as a cuttlefish and I shiver in the noonday sun. The figure flickers like a faulty bulb and then begins to drift across the stubby grass and salty rocks in my direction. Rooted to the spot, I can only watch and wait as it makes its diabolical way towards me.

As it comes closer I can see a face of melted wax, eyeless with only black crosses covering the empty sockets, and its mouth – a scarlet slash of a mouth with what seems like icicles hanging from it. The fear is so overwhelming that afterwards, huddled like a child who has been whipped unfairly, I realise my trousers are damp and I have wet myself.

Sobbing and humiliated, I run for home not caring about the curious gazes of fisherman and villagers. When I appear in the doorway my mother draws in a harsh breath and the children stop their playing. Mama? Bernard asks. I can only stare at him, incapable of words. But it is my father's reaction that scares me most. A man incapable of engaging with the world on any level, he raises himself slowly from his chair and points at me. His face ashen and his eyes bulging with terror. *Mogui! Mogui!* Demon! Demon! he screams.

The children begin to sob and my mother pulls me through the door and pushes me into the back room.

'Wash yourself! Wash yourself and then you go. There is something travelling with you, daughter. Take it away.'

I find myself with the children in a taxi that has seen much better days, shuffling to the nearest airport in Zhejiang. The children are sniffly and I hug them fiercely. As they burrow into me I inhale the fragrance of their hair and skin not bothering to try to make sense of what has happened. I just try to concentrate on the present and on expanding this tiny moment of peace. I spend the rest of the short journey staring out of the window noting every mountain and wave and ship that I can see.

Flashbacks of my father collapsed, pale and shaken, refusing to meet my eyes and turning his head from me. Was my mother right? Did evil travel with me? Something malign and otherworldly intent on my downfall? I should be in a strange way both comforted by my father's terror and ability to see the 'ghost', because it suggests that unless we are sharing a unique episode of madness, I am not being threatened by another breakdown, and also terrified, because out there is something much more unsettling.

I will have to contact Little Ping and confide in her. I am hoping that she, ever the manipulator, will be swayed by my need and fallen circumstances and will fall over herself to help me. While gossiping wildly behind my back, naturally. I am beyond caring to what lengths Little Ping might go in order to revel in my precarious position; I will take care of that later. Reducing her once again to a supplicant who heeds my every word and seeks approval at every opportunity. I need to see the fortune teller that Little Ping visited to find out more about what he told her. I don't relish the idea of four hours in a run-down HBD but this is my only avenue to the truth. Something is happening around me and I need clarification.

My father saw something and I have to conclude that this time the spectre seemed intent on doing me harm. Its initial reluctance to show itself and the distance it has kept from me has gone, and the subsequent violence with which it has launched itself into my path indicates a much more troubling time ahead. I need advice and some protection and I will happily endure the sexist, insane ramblings of the man who is at the centre of this conspiracy against me.

I will use the rest of the journey back to Singapore to mentally prepare for whatever it is that is pursuing me. I concentrate on my breathing and relax my muscles, one by one, listening to the sweet breaths of my children as they settle into sleep.

LUCILLA

19 Sabre Green

It is an odd day, lah! My Ma'am and Sir have returned from Scotland and I am happy. But there is a strange vibration in the air while we await the stinging winds from Indonesia. Ma'am says that the governments are burning palm-oil fields and the winds have changed direction and are heading for Singapore and that it is going to be bad. And Ma'am's face darkens and her fingers grip and clench the sides of her sarong so tightly that creases leap quickly into the fabric. They mirror the worry in my Ma'am's face.

When Sir arrives home he pours himself a large whisky drink. Just a touch of water, Lulubell, as he often reminds me, and he returns again and again to the window searching the sky for something. For a sign maybe of the 'perhaps' terror to come. Sir huffs and sighs and concern attaches to his face like shadow to the parched grass back home. And the more he drinks the ruddier his face becomes and yet his movements become more deliberate and controlled.

Alcohol is too expensive for us to drink much of it in the Philippines. It is a sodden luxury peculiar to the west and my Muslim girlfriend says it makes whores of its women and monsters of its men. I ask her why she thinks this is so peculiar to the west and not to humans generally. Her Malay prejudice kicks in and a sneer speaks her disgust quite beautifully as she launches into a diatribe about the perilous west and the gentle, misunderstood east. I find her views quite hopeless and frustrating. And yet, when she hurls these hateful ideas at me it is in the gentle, hushed tones of a supplicant at prayer outside the mosque just before Fajr. Her skin is dark honey and her veils bright and spirited like ship's pennants blustered by the wind.

My Ma'am takes me aside and presses a box of masks into my hands. I protest but secretly am glad that she loves me enough to think of this. So far it is easy to breathe and there is nothing spiteful in the air but we know it is coming and the beginnings of panic creep to the very edges of the country and its blot begins to spread through the reservoirs and into the trees, past the airport and towards the Johor Strait where Malaysia sits smugly thinking that it is not to be troubled.

Rory arrives home in the school bus and there is a sense of urgency even there. Auntie, usually so talkative and quick with laughter and a pinch of cheek, hands Rory over and shuts the bus door robustly with only the twitch of a smile that recedes quickly like the tide before a huge wave is due. The birds are silent and I stare up at the big rain tree opposite the house and search for signs of my demon. And ask for a blessing from God and all manner of things from all manner of things.

The tree stays quiet, remarkable only for its wooden history and its stillness. Not one leaf is turning. And there is a smell in the air. Like madness or violence. Or the smell of a desperate scream from a frightened mouth and I begin to feel my stomach clench and coil with worry. The very realness of this day, of this time.

Ma'am asks me to run to Mr Lim's shop. Quickly, Lulubell, before it hits. Just a few supplies.

And Sir says loudly that he will go but Ma'am gently dismisses him and asks me to take Rory. It is clear she wants to speak to Sir in private. So Rory and I leave for Mr Lim's. Only four minutes away. Mr Lim of the rich friends that like Filipina girls. Of the bulging eyes and greasy, sweat-stained widow's peak that flops like an opium addict. And why should a man who resembles a bothersome tree frog make me feel these things? It is all about his power and my lack of it. I find myself simpering and half-smiling from behind my hands like a good little Filipina girl. Tactics to keep him happy and to keep him from noticing me too much.

Rory swings my hand and picks up flowers off the ground to give to Ma'am. I don't think a child has ever loved his mother more. Sometimes it is difficult to know where he begins and she stops. I squeeze his hand tighter and smooth his moon-darkened, ripe-wheat hair away from his smooth forehead.

Mr Lim looks different. For a start he is not sitting behind his counter surrounded by the pink invoice books where he totals every item that each family buys on tick. Every time you bring something to the counter he looks you up and down before announcing the house number and your role there. I am number 19, maid. Rory number 19, first son.

Nor is he tending the rows of tiny cages each containing a single sunbird that hops from perch to floor and back again in a monotonous round, only its bright, black, basalt eye showing intelligence of its surroundings. Even the birds' plumage is dull. A dirty green and a flash of stained yellow around the eye. The western Ma'ams all get very worked up over Mr Lim's birds. But the fact is they will not fly away. If he cleans the cage they step out and wait, shivering, feathers clutched tightly around them, until he shoos them back in. Maybe they have nowhere else to go. Or perhaps the world seems much more frightening when they are away from their cages. Once you stop thinking about your circumstances and become secure with confinement then nothing else is possible.

For some reason this thought frightens me and I squint up at the sun, noticing for the first time a faint, dark corona settling around it. I pull Rory close.

'Quickly, darling. Quickly!'

We step through the door of the shop and into the darkened room with its dusty aisles. I can see three other women standing like out-of-place wooden dolls. One is a twitching Chinese employer I recognise from around the green, another the sad-looking western Ma'am I have tried to speak to sometimes, draped in a sarong. The third is the Indonesian maid from next door. She is so very thin and the small light has vanished from her face and from inside. I can see the demons are making casual calls toward her soul and can see but not completely identify the battle that rages inside her. She has awkward hair and a broken tooth. I try to smile but her gaze never rests for long on a person, only on things. The floor, a speck of dust, her feet with such sad toes.

Mr Lim appears from nowhere heading straight for the entrance and jamming all the locks with whipping sticks.

'Now we are safe. Now the haze cannot touch us,' he shouts authoritatively.

We all stand united in a brief moment brought about by Mr Lim and his odd behaviour. The girl, Shammi, I think her name is, reacts first and with surprising vigour.

'You must let me out, sir. You must. Please. My Madam will be so angry.' And as she tugs repeatedly on his sleeve her little face is pouring. From her eyes and nose and mouth. Salt and froth, snot and saliva.

The western Ma'am tries to comfort her. 'I'm Lesley,' she starts. 'Don't be frightened.' But she is shrugged off.

And then the sound of cans and boxes falling and the Chinese Madam falls to her knees, arms outstretched, gulping huge breaths and beating at her head and scratching her face with nails scarlet both from polish and blood and the little Indonesian is the first to react and she tries to stop the woman scratching at her eyes, imploring us to help.

Rory lets out a long, tremulous wail and his tears and fear join the already well-stoked fires of pain and fright starting all around us. I glance at the shop front that is haunted by Mr Lim's shadow and I think nothing good will come of this.

MA'AM LESLEY

33 Sabre Green

There is something wrong with the air today. It is like breathing scorched earth. A bitter myrrh in the atmosphere but it's not until after I've served Jocelyn her lunch that I catch the news story on the cheap television in her old room that is now mine. The haze is coming, the news reporter exclaims and we watch the news footage of irate Singaporean politicians shaking their fists in the general direction of Indonesia and then other clips of Indonesian politicians doing exactly the same thing to Singapore.

I know about the haze, of course. It has far less legend attached to it than the mistral or a volcano, but it can make life very uncomfortable if the winds betray us. Fickle things, winds. Like hormones and cats. I have experienced it in other years before now but something stalks the air today in a way that it hasn't previously, and a nigglesome sense of alarm hangs about like a spite and sin. Singapore, for all its darkness and faults, is safe. You can rely on it to be safe. The dual threats of flogging and death are generally presumed to be working deterrents. But once again man's rape of the natural world is roaring back.

I am anxious about any potential threats to the baby. Woodsmoke in concentration is hazardous and the pregnant and elderly are most susceptible. What to do with Jocelyn? Should we all move to Malaysia for a few months?

The air is definitely heavier as I run up the stairs to the sound of Jocelyn coughing. And sudden pain, somewhere in her abdomen, makes her start, and the colour leaches from her face as quickly as the sun's final dip beneath the horizon.

I manage to get her breathing under control but she is clearly terrified, tears coursing down her face. You learn a lot about people living at such close quarters with them and Jocelyn's emotions are as free and abundant as a high waterfall in late summer. But in that moment I also realise that my protective reflex is bound up with the child in her belly. My child. And I will do everything I can, beyond reason, to make that possession possible. It is an extraordinary moment. I realise that I *can* love again. That I have the chance to give and receive a sacrament far greater than faith. An intangible belief, just out of focus but there all the same.

I check Jocelyn for bleeding and find none. 'I need to go to Mr Lim's and see if he has some masks. The index has risen and I don't want to take any chances with you.' I speak quietly, not wanting to agitate her.

'With this you mean.' Jocelyn points at her bump and pouts. 'What you care about me?'

'I care about both of you. You and the baby,' I counter.

Jocelyn looks unconvinced but I'm not interested in placating her. I am on a fairly urgent mission and it is important to be outside for as short a time as possible.

'I won't be long,' I yell up the stairs.

The air has thickened and become angry. Now I can actually taste the woodsmoke and my eyes sting, my breath shortens and not a soul can be seen. It is as if the world is ending. Even the status-enabled cars stand idly in the carports and underneath shelters. The birds are silent, censored by an atmosphere squeezed tight with portent. For the first time I begin to feel a very real panic. Nature is so unpredictable.

I pull my scarf tightly around my head and mouth, uncaring of the spectacle I must create, and make my careful but hurried way towards Lim's shop.

Lim is an odd sort. He survives mostly because of the Singaporeans and expats who live in the Sabre Hills area. But his dislike of us is barely veiled. I have felt his flat, onyx stare and it makes me uncomfortable because it is designed to do just that. I have never asked for his credentials or cultural references or he mine. I am interested but to achieve that purpose would mean engaging in conversation with him and the thought of this makes me even more uncomfortable, so I have avoided it and make up disturbing fantasies in my head instead.

I noticed that he was selling masks yesterday when I took a city cab back from Cold Storage with the shopping. I suspect they will be horribly marked up but for all I know we are living in black market conditions. Walking into his shop it occurs to me that I've not been here too often, but my overriding impression is of a shabby bomb shelter. It looks dirty and unkempt as if the owner can't really be bothered but knew an opportunity when he saw one. Rows of depressed packets, jars and tins line morose Formica shelves. Only the overworked fridges, heaving and sighing their chilly way towards unremarkable deaths, give the impression of life. Today there are only a few customers and I panic briefly, thinking that all the masks have been sold by now, but looking around I see plenty in a couple of fabric bins next to the deplorable 'beating sticks' that many Singaporeans still use on their children.

I notice a very fragile-looking Indo girl with an odd haircut. Much too thin with a grey shadow that moves about her face. There is something inexplicably sad about her, and the nervousness of someone not used to being out in the open. Her eyes twitch and blink like a cornered animal and her breathing is shallow and laboured. The Filipina girl, Lucilla, smiles brightly at me and the contrast between the two women is harsh and too bright to consider for long: her hair is glossy, each strand bouncing with theatrical vigour and even though her body is slight it is well fed, nurtured and happy, and she has that beautiful little boy with her who always smiles at everybody.

The last customer is Chinese and seems hazy and insubstantial. Her face is fully made up, but horribly smudged, which makes her look more sinister than tragic. She has the odour of madness. I step towards the counter just as Lim blocks the entrance and locks the shop firmly. His eyes are flush with the fervour of self-justification and my heart begins to flutter as the little boy starts to wail.

SHAMMI

112 Sabre Green

I sit in the kitchen, squatting with my bony bottom barely scraping the kitchen floor and my knees bent. I am quiet and watchful like the feeling inside the house. I am alone. I managed to operate the radio earlier and I know that my employers have left to escape the poison that the wood devils have sent to Singapore. They have left me to its mercy.

But this is something I am accustomed to. The house seems less vindictive in the family's absence. Less inclined to betray me because even though I am locked in Madam forgot about the tiny window in the store cupboard by the kitchen. A space small enough only for a child to escape through. And through lack of food I am now small enough. I thank the spirits in the house silently for not betraying this mistake.

I move very, very quietly like a refugee from the war hiding in the ruins of a building. Like my family did when the bad city man returned to bully my parents into growing the drug plants. We hid in a secret hole cut into the earth floor of our hut. My grandfather had dug it decades earlier and we used to store sacks of grain and dry fruit. I bite my lip so hard it stops the beginnings of a sob as I remember the sea-coloured batik covers on the walls and the wood animals that my Bapa would carve for us stacked neatly in one of the dirt corners. They seem so far away from my heart. My brain does not work so well and my world is covered with gauze.

My employers are away for the next three nights. How can I be so exact? Because they have left me one brown apple and nine packs of noodles in a pot. I have the money that Ebony Ma'am has given me so if I can gather my courage I can buy other food and some fruit at the store and maybe a mask. I have never been there before and the thought makes me nervous but my eyes sting like Andaliman pepper juice has flicked up from the spice table and splashed in my eyes. The wood devils have sent fog so thick and poisonous that my throat feels dry and raw and my breathing is heavy and hard. Staying still is good, it doesn't hurt so much, but I must make the effort and get to the shop.

I ask Jesus for courage and pray for salvation. Lying flat on the brown-tiled kitchen floor that cools my cheek and soothes my mind I watch a trail of black armoured ants make their way from the locked food cupboard to the outside, flowing silently under the store door. They are heroic. Tiny, tiny things, barely living but surviving. I envy them their togetherness. A little army marching for a common good and hope. My Madam could learn a lot from them.

I wake with a start. I realise I must have drifted off to sleep for a bit. The shadows in the garden have lengthened and the firecracker flowers have crept back into themselves preparing for the evening. What time does Mr Lim close his shop? Will he serve me or accuse me of stealing the money?

Oh, when did every action start to require so much thought? I'm weary, God, so weary. I cry for my mother and for my poor, sad heart.

There is a cicada on the windowsill. I find this strange because they are naturally shy creatures. Its tobacco-brown body is shiny and strong in the gathering dusk. Its legs create a music that is long past bringing memories back to me of the village and the gentle nights by Ebu's fire. It rests on the cheap, steel window edge and I think that it must be brave to be in this strange, troubled place and play its music for me. And that I must be worth something to this world. If the little creature can be brave then so can I.

The window is tight even for my tiny frame and I catch a fragment of my blue shirt on a jutting, rusted nail. Better that than my skin. I wiggle myself through and land lightly on the concrete outside. I feel awkward and unsure like an elephant calf born early but I remind myself that I am committing no crime. I keep that mantra in my head. I know that I can I am small and light enough to climb the security gate that guards the side entrance. I know that the streets will be empty as the air thickens and lungs begin to burn. No one will be bothering about me while I try to pretend that I belong in this outside world.

The first thing I notice is the largeness of everything. I don't remember the last time I was outside, free to hunt the honey and sail into the wind. A dusty black cat emerges from the little park across the road, swaying oddly with its docked tail. They do that here. Hack off the kittens' tails or drown them in the big drains at the back of the houses. These people are so careless with life and haughty with death. The cat and I exchange furtive glances before it totters off to raid the bins of a nearby house.

I can see Mr Lim's shop in the distance. I suppose this makes it sound kilometres away but of course it is only a few hundred metres. The tarmacked road and wide pavements are identical in this area but the flowers and plants explode with a revolutionary beauty. It makes me laugh, but only a little because the air is too choked with the devil fog to see the efforts that go into curbing the gardens and their wild ways. To think you can control the grass, the soil, the roots, the sap!

It is a curious feeling, this fire in my belly. A rush of protest between my ears and down my arms. My fists clench automatically and my lips purse with displeasure. I am sitting in judgement of something and I relish every moment of it. To experience even a tiny chunk of power is quite wonderful and I stamp down on any thoughts of fear or worry. This feeling is golden. Like my mother's voice and the milk from our Jamnapari goats. It is delicious.

Something near to confidence brims inside me and the shop is smaller than I had thought. I had always imagined it would be so big. So unattainable and angry. But it is shabby and old. Bare and slipper-less. The tiny birds in their cages are agitated by the heavy air but are too weak to sing or chirp and I have no time to comfort them.

Mr Lim is not to be seen and I keep my head down shuffling down the rows of food. I make my way to the back carefully and select some fresh fruit. The mangoes are blushing and smell of rain and leaves and the apples lie rounded and chubby like a serene Indian god. I take one of each and move up towards the counter clutching my ripe fruit. The masks are in cloth bins by the entrance. I can see them but a queue has formed and I don't want to draw attention to myself. A fearsome-looking Chinese Madam stands in front of me and I automatically take a step backwards to distance myself. She is behaving oddly. Pulling at her clothes and muttering. I glimpsed her face only once in profile and it is a devil mask. A ruined mess of black and red and I look away quickly.

The Filipina girl who works for Ebony Ma'am is holding the hand of the lovely little western boy she looks after. There are times when she still tries to talk to me but I have to gesture silently to the camera that follows my every movement and records my daily work and she nods in understanding and a sad look comes over her face. Her face is not so friendly now – lines of worry crisscross her perfect tawny forehead. The other shopper, an older western Madam in a sarong and slippers, there is a sadness on her face too. I feel a kinship and a mounting desperation that nobody is safe from the pain in this dark place.

Hidden by bars or hidden by make-up. It is all the same. We are all the same.

The shopkeeper has appeared again and he is hopping about like a ragged flea. His face is flushed and I can smell no good on him. My heart pounds as he shouts and gestures at us. What is he saying? There is a rush and the sound of water thunders in my ears as I watch him bolt the door and my mind nearly breaks in two. And I run to him screaming, imploring him to let me out because someone from my Madam's family will be checking on me later and the consequences, if I am not in the house, will be terrible for me.

And then I hear the child start to sob and I know we are at the mercy of Mr Lim and his mercy is not to be tested.

And then night seems to arrive early and the floor and its mismatched vinyl tiles rise to greet me like a lonely dog too long without its master.

MADAM EUNICE

112 Sabre Green

Today I am fevered. I can feel a sickness invading my blood. It is as if evil has come to stay. The children have been sent home from school because of the hazardous pollution index and their off-tonal screeches of delight reverberate through my head like the sound of the piano tuner.

It is unusual to have my sons home without the iron-banded presence of my husband and I usually enjoy this time enormously. But, today, I am hiding in my white bedroom, a haven of pales and mutes, and still their boisterous play interrupts my thinking. The walls of the room start to pulse and my nerves begin to bounce in time. This makes me anxious because usually this room is the safest space for me. I do not share it with my husband and even the children are discouraged from entering unless absolutely necessary. The maid should never be in here except to clean or bring me refreshment.

But today even this room feels like an enemy presence so I crawl towards the ivory bathroom with its cool and creamy Italian marble, step into the shower stall and push my forehead against the wall. With one hand I fumble for the tap and turn it to its highest setting, barely conscious of the scalding water battering my skin. The water pounds my head and body and suddenly I can hear and see nothing except the water. I sink onto the floor of the shower, the tiles exerting a momentary chill against my skin, and sit hunched against the wall allowing myself to be carried away with the steam and heat.

I think about the haze. Rationally, I know that it is an environmental problem. The palm-oil fields being raped by companies who care little for the place or the people who live there. No point bleating about it unless you want to be seen as lambs ripe for slaughter. Yes, the realist in me has no doubt that this haze, this dense, uncomfortable smoke-laden atmosphere, is unavoidable. As I have often thought, when we have done with this world, it will come to its end and it isn't for us to argue with that.

But the Eunice who huddles in the shower, whose hands – ugly claws marked by blue veins and chipped varnish – are outstretched before me, this Eunice feels differently. I am not rational as I sit gibbering, my hair plastered against my bony face, my lips chapped and painful. The air outside has been sent to haunt me. To punish me for something I can't fathom. I rack my brains for histories of a family curse. Of something I have done to anger the gods and make my life so. Surely not, I am only living my life as any good Chinese woman would. Adhering to the Asian principles of face and a fierce pride that are celebrated as an integral part of my culture as well as being imprinted into my personality like a wax stamp.

I do not feel like the Tiger woman that I have shouted about so often. I am little more than a field mouse who has lost her way back to the wheat barn. The rough furrows of soil are confusing and every screech is from a hungry owl tracking my progress. I am weak and naked. Unkempt and unarmed in the face of this backlash. The air is toxic and leaks its poison into my mouth and throat, scraping its grey fingernails hard across shell-pink skin and then pushing into the dark places of the lungs. I feel that if I don't move I might die here. And so I do move, levering myself upright and stumbling, staggering, falling into each step. I forget that I am soaked and that my make-up is dissolving onto my cheeks. My clothes leak as I haul myself down the stairs, so weak that I have to sit for the last part and slide over each step, shaking and jittery.

The maid is polishing the windows with a scarf tied around her mouth; the air conditioning is woefully inadequate and when she sees me, she pulls her scarf down and her mouth opens in a slack peasant shape and I retain a spark of old 'Eunice' and want to slap her face. But even thinking such a thing saps my energy and I am left with just enough to walk the hall, gingerly like a novice model on a Milan catwalk, and make it through my front door.

Outside is deserted and in my highly sensitised state I can feel the silence and see the poisonous trails. The air is red with them. The road and park are empty but I see the lights on in Lim's shop. You can always rely on greedy Lim to be open in times of trouble. He is probably charging double and rubbing his trotters together as he does. And so what? He is just operating from a sense of survival. He has always treated me with an obsequiousness that I have accepted but felt disgusted by. Lim is too oily, too smiling, too deferential. I fear that like my maid he laughs behind my back. But his lights are on and I need something to shine on me today. I need some illumination and a way to find my path.

The status BMWs and Lexuses are parked as usual; few are moving. But then someone drives slowly past me, or it seems they are. My fear is that time is slowing again, that ghastly precursor of the arrival of the thing that stalks me. The woman driving, beetle-black hair and an anus mouth, scowls at me. And the reflection I see in the car window is an exact representation of how I feel inside. Orange-tinged lips snarling with apprehension. Torn, my colours run, my edges double-blurred. Hissing at the back of the retreating car and the woman's obvious disgust makes me feel stronger for a second and I carry on limping down the road.

I am trying to remember what brought me here. I wipe the back of my hand over my mouth and then start thinking that I'm bleeding, but it is just the waxy stain of lip pigment radiating across my hand like infection. I sigh deeply. This cannot end well, I think as I enter Lim's shop.

I sense other people and I do see them, their details leaping out at me with a sickening precision. Two are maids, I presume. One a sick-looking Indo farm girl and the other a Filipina, far too smug for her own good. Glistening with health and happiness as she clutches the hand of a small western boy with a delightful smile. A western woman that I think must be his mother stands apart from them. She is dressed horribly in a sarong, her rather unkempt hair scraped back and her insipid watery blue eyes flickering back and forth from the boy to the door.

Lim appears from somewhere gabbling about saving us from the toxic air and that no one must leave until the authorities tell us. The idiot must be having a panic attack – his eyes are unfocused, his glasses slightly off key. In a moment of clarity I start towards him to read him the riot act but am beaten to it by the Indo girl who has become quite hysterical, pulling on his arm and slobbering over his cheap, blue shirt.

And then just as I am feeling rather more part of this world an evil palsy is cast over it rendering me frozen. The hooded figure appears behind Lim and a little girl is beside it, her dreadful mouth agape, her eyes crying blackness. The figure lifts a free hand to its hood and pulls it slowly back to show its face for the first time.

And I am scratching at my face and eyes. I would rather be blind than have to revisit such horror again. I barely see the Indo slut sink to the floor and the only sound left in the air is the little boy's wailing siren.

MR LIM

Sabre Green Corner Shop

I am master of all I survey.

That being a dismal little whore of a shop pandering to fucking westerners and *sabi* maids. I serve them every day with a grimace on my face and a very dark heart. It shouldn't be this way. I was born to much greater things.

My great uncle was a famous Singaporean politician. He was tortured by the Japanese during their cursed occupation of my home. And the Japanese know about torture. Just watch a sushi bastard at work. The clinical filleting, the slash–slash of ink sacs and the acidic balm of citrus. I have no Japanese patrons and I am glad. We Chinese loathe the Japanese. It is a historical hatred. They are betrayers by nature. Wasteful, egotistic and demanding. For such a small nation their arrogance is embarrassing. Little tin starred soldiers acting as if sacrifice was such an extraordinary thing. To be celebrated. Pah! We Chinese men know the true meaning of sacrifice as part of our moral code. We nail it to our hearts with our kin's blood and savour the pain with smiles of the penitent.

I can even smell them. Insipid and wan like the noodles they consume. My sacrifice is this dank little shop serving those who are not fit to collect my piss and my damaged reputation because of one small slip. I had no idea she was so young. Why would I? So I got a bit rough – I thought she liked it. Pah! And the little bitch ruins my reputation and forces my family to turn their backs. So I know about sacrifice, Nippon bastards.

I learnt a long time ago there is no one to trust in this world. Except for my sunbirds. My beautiful song-fire birds. You know how much they are worth. Thousands of dollars. Their olive plumage and twist of yellow around their eyes make them exceptionally rare. A small fortune hopping and tweeting about me during the day and safe in the shop at night.

And those stupid western cows sidling up and looking shocked. Pretending to ask interested questions about my birds when really all they want to do is complain that they are in cages. This obsession with freedom? We are all in cages from the moment we are pulled from our mother's womb. I've learnt to ignore their eyes and their bleating. If a new cow asks a question I generally ignore it and smile in a meaningless way.

My birds love me. When I clean their cages they are nervous and hop around me urging me to finish my task soon. If they are so unhappy why do they never fly away? They have plenty chance but they don't because they love me, Lim, and my love is like a gentle father.

This haze is worrying me though. I have the television tuned to Media Corps and the pollution is a hot topic. The index seems to leap up every twelve hours. How will this affect my birds? They are my children and without them I think my life will shrink and become unmanageable. I have already brought them in and their cages stand scattered around the back of the shop until I can work out the best way to protect them. And still I watch the news, the lipsticked statue mouthing five depressing stories for every positive one. Her lacquered hair shiny in the studio lamps, thickly black like sweating asphalt in the midday sun, distracts me from the printed ribbon at the bottom giving the hazard index of 401.

This is very dangerous for us. The masks I sell are flimsy and unadventurous. Why would I buy anything more industrial? The politicians promised us it would never happen again. That our collective health would never be threatened in this way. I'm sure their collective health is just fine as they lie on batik sun loungers high above the smog in the Cameron Highlands. Waving ornate palm fans over their stressed brows.

Ach! My head is swelling. I can feel the rage building and this is not a good thing. I watch my hands and the veins turn through blue to purple and swell and throb. My spectacles are misting over and sweat is collecting on my forehead, beads of betrayal, that threaten to run down my cheeks and into my collar. I must close the shop for the first time ever. Even when I had influenza three years ago I slept in a camp bed in the tiny alcove at the back overseeing Hung Ling and his friend. So ill that even the cockroaches that ran over my face and hands couldn't distract me from how many times the till was rung or the shop door jangled.

But today is different. My birds are in danger and they are too silent and still. There is no joy coming from their tiny bodies – just a silent quivering of fear and possibly death.

There are four cows queueing at the counter but I ignore them in my quest to close the shop against the smog. I wasn't planning on shutting the shop for ever. Just enough hours to wait out the poison and see if it settles. As I bolt the doors I see a scrawny little brown hand plucking at my sleeve and I turn and there is a skinny farm girl, num- . ber 20 maid, with tears in her eyes, begging me to open the doors. Snot is running down her face and her eyes are puking tears. She is disgusting and I shrug her off. Unsteady on her feet already she falls to the ground and lies there.

Then one of my regulars, number 35 maid but not maid, shouting in my face. Her pale, bovine cheeks redden as she lows into my face. How I detest these western cows. This one has rolls of fat and huge udders straining against the flimsy material of a cheap royal blue sarong with small golden elephants dotted all over it. I do find those breasts faintly erotic but the overall demeanour of her repulses me. How dare she shout in my face? I place my hands over my ears and start to hum loudly. This technique used to work with my ex-wife. Shouting over her I explain that it's not for ever and if they could just calm down.

I didn't notice the little western boy until now – the really beautiful one with the smile like sun-drenched jasmine. I have always liked him because he is so polite and has such a sweet smile. Also his western cocksucker parents pay their bills on time and their maid is the most beautiful in the area. But she turns me down every time. Politely, sure. But every time? Who the fuck does she think she is? Some Filipina tart who would be working the Manila casas or KTVs if she wasn't here. I think maybe this anger shows in my face because when I look up she flinches and hugs the boy close to her. Why won't these stupid women understand that I'm trying to help them? Trying to save them from terrible things outside. And all I'm getting is snot and shouting. And then two things happen almost simultaneously.

The Chinese woman who resembles a mad *xiǎochǒu* has begun wailing and scratching violently at her face. Blood begins to creep out from beneath her broken nails and I think to myself that this is a woman possessed. That a demon is inside her or nearby, and fear starts to boil in my stomach and my legs feel unsteady. I find myself staring helplessly at them all completely at a loss. They don't seem willing to listen or even understand how helpful I'm being.

A banging starts on the outside of the shop door. A relentless thudding and kicking at the door. I can hear a muffled male western voice shouting and swearing outside and as I think about his fists pounding on the doors and how he might, enraged as he is, use those fists on my body, one of my Chinese statues comes flying through the large window that faces onto the green and catches the light particularly well to show off my bargain bins.

A huge, bearded fellow, the Sir of the Filipina maid and papa to the beautiful western boy comes stepping through the smashed glass and broken goods wielding a golf club. It is the raving Scottish teacher and I hold my hands above my head in a placatory gesture. After all, we Asian men know that red-bearded westerners are to be avoided at all costs. They have a fearsome reputation and their anger knows no limits. I care nothing for my shop window but I do care for my life. He spits and swears into my face, towering over me, and I think about cutting his head off with a machete and that makes me feel a little better. My face feels hot and my eyes film over with what I hope is sweat but believe to be tears.

Then the huge, furious *ang moh* gathers up the women and herds them out of my shop and I watch as they pick their way through the hostile fragments of glass and wood. My statue is gone, shattered into thousands of cheap replica pieces, and I can only hear the thunder of blood in my ears competing with the hysterical shrieks from my birds. I stare at the wreckage and shake my head in dismay. How has this gone so horribly wrong? How did this day become so destructive?

I take my time and cover each cage with its individual coloured cloth and then begin the big sweep up, coughing and choking as I go, marvelling in my sacrifice and its consequences. I feel elevated by my own goodness and under my breath tell all of them to fuck their mothers as I wait for the glazier who is charging double because of the haze. I open up a bottle of Johnnie Walker to sip from, and contemplate this burden that is my life with a slight smile on my face and a hum in my heart.

After all, for a few moments, my dismal whore of a shop was a place of strange power. The power that is outside in the choking, burning, poisonous wind that fills lungs with dust and hearts with fear, and the power that is here in my mind because of who I know I am and because of what I see. For once, I was able to give those westerners and those whores a very big fright indeed.

LUCILLA

19 Sabre Green

Today Ma'am visited her head doctor for a check up. She travels once a month up to Orchard to see Dr Pauline at Mount Elizabeth Hospital. Ma'am does not like travelling in Singapore and the family has no car allowance so we take taxis everywhere.

Ma'am says she feels imprisoned without a car and if she had one here she would be driving to Malaysia on the weekend for the experience. Ma'am is an adventurer, a nomad. Her childhood was spent everywhere and nowhere. I think her Papa was an oil man and Ma'am says she dodged some bullets during her childhood and then laughs nervously. She speaks a little about her early childhood in Nigeria, just after it had become a bit safer and just before it got much more dangerous.

It sound like the Philippines except Ma'am says the people there have midnight skin, almost blue-black in its beauty. Her nanny had soft, kinked hair with fiery lights that she would roll into seashell shapes and tie with brightly coloured twine. She would rock and croon Ma'am and put her dry-palmed hand on the little girl's face, gazing in wonder at the whiteness and smallness of her charge. And Ma'am loved her with all the passion of a small child and still talks about her to this day. She says that I remind her of Imari the way I tend to Rory and she says how lucky her son is to have a woman like me in his life. Ma'am says because of me Rory will love and respect women.

Sometimes, he calls me Mummy, and sometimes, Ma'am Lulu. And she chuckles and says I'm his second mother. Some western Ma'ams get very angry when their children call the helper 'Mummy'. But if that woman is caring for the child fourteen hours of the day then it is natural that a bond will form. Guilt makes these women angry, snapping at the little ones and helper alike. They should remember that children love the little things. Grand gestures mean nothing to them. They would rather you build a town out of blocks with them than organise a complicated outing somewhere. Children really don't need very much. Just some good attention, love and consistency.

I hope I have my own children. I worry that I have left it too late and for a Filipina I am positively ancient. Most of us give birth during our twenties. I am thirty-seven and still have no child. Ma'am says I'm a spring chicken and that she had Rory when she was forty-three. You have years, Lulubell! Better to get it right, my darling. Nothing wrong with being an older mum. I pray that Ma'am is right and that God will grant me a child one day. I know I will make a good mother. Sometimes the longing is so great I have to breathe in and out quickly to shoulder the pain. How can you feel the loss of something you've never had? I'm not greedy. I'm not asking for three or even two. Just one beautiful brown-eyed baby with my smile and my lover's shining eyes.

A part of me, a legacy, and someone I could pour this passion and dedication into. Sometimes the baby's eyes change to blue or green if my dreaming has lassooed a western man. Would his family take to me like a lost daughter or would they shun me, turning from my brown skin and soft-lipped smile in tight circles of shame?

My last boyfriend, he was Singaporean, and took me all the way to Malaysia to meet his parents. They treated me stiffly, without courtesy, and I ended up cooking and serving along with the other helper to make life easier for everybody. I never forgave him for that. He must have known what was in store for me. Perhaps he didn't care or maybe he thought I would be the one to change their attitudes. I found out later that their stiffness had nothing to do with my nationality and everything to do with him being married still.

It's difficult to trust when so much of life is based on trust. And so much is betrayed in the name of trust. When I confronted the man about his marriage he shrunk before me – almost grateful that I had found out. It cleared the air, he thought, a fresh start.

Well, I may be bottom of the heap in this dung trench but I'm still strong enough to understand my worth. My parents were very careful to nurture my self-esteem and honour. My mother has such dignity and grace that is not easy for a poor woman. But she always keeps her head up high and refrains from bad words. This sets her apart a little from the other women in the village. It inspires jealousy and bad blood. One time a neighbour came into their shack on the pretext of borrowing their kettle but stole a hand mirror, something personal. She gave it to the local voodoo woman to torment my mother. At the same time my mother's diabetes flared up worryingly. It was touch and go for her for a time.

My Ma'am says to put mirrors facing outwards on every side of the house to reflect back evil intention. She has also mentioned salt to keep out demons. Ma'am is happy to talk about ghouls and witches and has natural oils and herbs for all sorts of ailments. I think the haze was frightening for her but Sir came like a hero and that strange moment in the shop is like a bad dream now. Perhaps my Ma'am would be at home in the village. I can see her sitting there with my mother, making bread and chatting using hand signals and my translations. I think I would be proud to have her there. Maybe. Maybe. I will think on it. Maybe next year.

MA'AM LESLEY

35 Sabre Green

Some suited men came by the house today. If they thought it odd that
I showed them up to Jocelyn they didn't reveal it. No shadows passed
over their faces, no twitch of shock registered. They spent a very short
time up there with Jocelyn and then returned and cornered me in the
kitchen.

Ralph has disappeared with some rather sensitive documents. Do I
know anything about this? No, no, of course not. Am I aware that
Ralph has not returned for some time? Has there been some trouble
with the marriage? So sorry to ask such sensitive questions, but they
have to be asked.

I am standing facing these unwelcome men, my back against the
fridge – my bottom and shoulders are becoming cold but I don't
feel safe standing any closer to them and need some physical distance
between us to think. I explain that things are complicated at the
moment and that as far as I am concerned Ralph is on a business trip.
This prompts another flurry of unconcerned questions. Do I know
where? Have I found any stubs or receipts? Would I please look out
for any in the next few days, and, of course, if Ralph were to contact
me, I must encourage him to call into his department. It's probably
all a misunderstanding; these things do happen. This is said in a tone
that leaves me in no doubt that they believe Ralph guilty of something heinous and unforgivable and they don't want the little woman
to give him the heads up.

As Her Majesty's representatives drone on about my husband and
his very delicately implied treason I study their faces. They are both
wearing suits but the differences in material and cost are startling.
The older man, Mr Norfolk, created from centuries of aristocratic
breeding, exudes a hypnotic charm. His suit is cut from navy blue

linen. The expensive sort that hardly ever creases. Free from sweat he lounges against the opposite wall observing me with a detached amusement. I can imagine him leading the charge over the trenches or facing down the proud Zulus in Africa but I don't trust him in the least. Mr Suffolk, who is younger, gives the impression of being totally out of his depth. His suit is cheap and fashioned from a man-made fabric that is absolutely the wrong thing to wear in the tropics. It positively encourages sweating. He is puffy, red faced and carries his anger and class insecurity like a tatty battle standard. The foreign office, if that is where they hail from, are an odd bunch. Still bound by Oxford conventions, contemporary pressure has forced them into accepting an eclectic crop of officers, and I believe the British security services are in a similar position.

Mr Suffolk is not comfortable and every glance and sharp retort makes me realise that he has already decided my guilt. Some British just don't do well in the tropics. It heats their cool island blood and promotes drinking and inappropriate behaviour. Maddened by the lack of a soothing chilliness, they drink to forget their homesickness and memories of the club in London. Others turn into monsters. Bullying house boys and waiters with fists and words. This, I believe, is Mr Suffolk's future. He is being rude to me in my own kitchen and as every woman knows that is most insulting. A kitchen is the hearth and the heart of home. Historically, a woman's domain, where she cooks and cleans and provides for her family. The chamber that most represents the womb – the essence of feminine influence.

'You've not been here long, have you?' I enquire waspishly. Mr Norfolk tries to suppress a chuckle but is unsuccessful.

'I arrived last week,' he snaps.

I nod. 'Yes, I thought so.'

Norfolk intervenes at this point and asks Suffolk to wait outside. It is my turn to suppress a smile at the thought of the spiteful boy sweltering in the heat. Suffolk looks furious, but it is clear who is in charge and so he obliges.

'Sorry about that. He's new. Have to break them in somehow. Not a sophisticated bone in his body I'm afraid. As subtle as a North Korean general.'

I smile as Norfolk hands me his card.

'Look Mrs B. I don't know the set up here. But as you say, it looks complicated. Your husband could be in trouble. I hope against hope it is not what I think it might be. Ralph's always been a good chap. We were together from the start, you know. But his undoing is his love of beautiful things.'

I blush at this. I think he knows exactly what is going on and is trying to get me on side. I feel more embarrassed than gratified, although Norfolk looks genuine. But that is when the British are at their most dangerous. When they are bumbling around and the world stops taking notice.

'Have you been here long?' And then I feel ridiculous for asking. Do I even care?

'Yes, a long time. In and about Asia for thirty-odd years.'

'Don't you miss England?'

'Not often. That landscape has become pretty uninhabitable for chaps like me. Dinosaurs and relics.'

'Are you married?' I blurt out. What the hell is happening here? Norfolk considers me.

'No, but you are.'

I blush again, humiliated that he has misunderstood my intentions. But has he? There is something about this man. A connection wavers between us like the hum of bees.

'Please. Contact me if you hear from him or about him. It's vital.'

I nod my understanding and he smiles for a final time before leaving to relieve an angry Suffolk. I watch through the hallway window as they have a brief conversation. Suffolk blustery and lobster-like and Norfolk Arctic-fresh and smooth. I watch the car drive off and think it's all rather obvious for a clandestine visit, but then I realise there is nothing secret about this. The foreign office is simply demonstrating its belief that Ralph is scrumping apples. I am just a chess piece and truth matters little if the outcome is satisfactory. I have no idea where Ralph is and am unsure of how long he has been away this time.

I look at the stairs and think it is time to speak to Jocelyn candidly. I push open the door gently and can see she has been crying. Pregnancy does not suit her at all. She looks sallow and insipid as if the baby is leaching the colours away from her. Her skin looks gritty and dull, her eyes red-rimmed and a sickly yellow. Her stomach has swelled quickly because of the heat and her small bones. It stretches tightly and rather obscenely under the form-fitting dress. I sit on the bed and to my surprise she doesn't react.

'Do you know where Ralph is? Any idea at all? Those men, they were from the British government and they think Ralph might be in trouble.'

At first there is no reaction and I think perhaps she has either not heard or is just ignoring me. In this state Jocelyn might be more volatile than ever and I need her to stay calm.

'Jocelyn?'

She pushes over her mobile phone.

'I haven't heard from him in three days. Not even to ask how baby doing. I think he not coming back.' She looks so sorrowful I feel pity for her. I really do. The circle of fate has turned and pointed me back towards harbour.

'Can I look?' I ask, indicating the phone. Nothing. Just the same dull, desperate stare.

And then. 'I don't want baby. Please will you take baby, Ma'am. I just want to go home.'

The use of Ma'am is not lost on me. In her frightened, beleaguered state Jocelyn has fallen back into old patterns and now she needs me. I might expect to feel more powerful and victorious but mostly there is a sense of disbelief in the quite extraordinary way life is unfolding. I know Jocelyn doesn't want the child. Every fibre of her body is trying to reject it but Ralph's genes, though treasonous, are strong from rugby and cold showers. I know that she will go to full term and I know, in those swollen seconds, with absolute certainty, that I will take the baby.

SHAMMI

112 Sabre Green

Today, I have been shopping with Madam in the wet-market. I had thought the smell of fresh fish would remind me of my Ebu, but not today. Today, the slime, scales and eyes make me retch. It is like the poison of decay or meat left in the sun for too many days. Rotted and sticky, making every breath a difficulty. Madam enjoys haggling with the market traders. She is proud that they call her a 'hard bargainer'. She crows about it to me on the journey home. I suspect they have a very different name for her when she is absent. Madam haggles and whittles the price down to a fine point. So sharp you have to watch yourself. I hope they give her the older fish and fowl that is not at its best or is beginning to turn. It gives me small comfort that the family may be eating putrid food. But Madam is so full of the devil perhaps it will not harm her. Perhaps it will make her stronger and she will turn her true face to me and rise up on six black legs, high, high above the apartment blocks, to visit her fury and hatred upon the earth.

As we pick our way through the slippery wet-market, we pass other Madams with other maids. Some I recognise as Indonesian girls and we pass a secret smile between each other. More a twitch of the lips but a little something for us. I breathe in and hold my breath as Madam enters into a violent bartering with the spice seller. I only half-listen. My eyes are bewitched by the earthy powders racked up in lines above us. I can see saffron, the queen of spices, very costly and difficult to grow, its mustard glow casting an arrogant stain on the wall behind it. Cinnamon, nutmeg, allspice, ginger – all compete in a dance of muddy warmth. I inhale and surrender to my dusty memories. I am transported through the bus stops of my life in quick succession. Images flash and my stomach clenches with the hurt. A clicking of fingers brings me back to the present. Come on! Come on! Always dreaming. These village girls always dreaming. Madam looks to the spice seller for confirmation and receives none. The woman is of Malay descent and her hair is covered by a burnt-orange hijab. Once she has received the money she ignores Madam and speaks directly to me. *As-Salaamu Alaykum*. I nod my thanks. I recognise it as a blessing and receive it gratefully although I will pay for it later. Madam does not like to be thwarted. I can feel the cold worm of doubt burrowing into my mind. Then, when we have walked maybe twenty paces away, Madam tuts and orders me back to collect one forgotten package. As the woman hands it over she winks and says, I sold her the cheap saffron and the damp cinnamon, the ugly nutmeg and the stale cloves. And then she winks at me before turning away to tend her wares, whistling an innocent tune. Everywhere there are surprises today. A half-smile here, a conspiratorial wink there, proving that I'm not so transparent after all. I hold this knowledge close and allow myself the luxury of a brief inner glow and quicken my step to catch up with Madam.

We cross the street and enter the large shopping mall. It is bright and airy with a very vigorous air conditioning system. I am regretting that I have not brought my warm top. The icy air drums onto my skin until the little hairs stand up to be counted. My teeth begin to chatter and I hug myself to keep the last bits of warmth in my body. I trail after Madam, holding the basket as she throws things in, muttering to herself, never acknowledging the counter or checkout girls. I don't know how someone can live with such stone inside them. I think of gushing rivers that move so quickly and the flat slabs of rocks that lie immobile being etched and slowly reduced by the relentless shaping of the water, and I think that Madam is the same way. Perhaps her mother love will save her because that is the only light I see in the darkness of her heart.

I am cursed for dreaming but it is more remembering. I need to commit this shabby, sad life to memory. I can't forget it because my fear is that if I do then I will forget myself. My sense of Shammi will dissolve slowly and I will have no legacy except perhaps a smudged imprint on my Madam's mind. And I want more than that. I can't become a figment, some erstwhile smoke in the background of a life more distant already than most.

Following Madam out of the door my skin is greeted with a cheery burst of sun. Caressing and comforting. The warmth is important to me and I turn my face to the brightness, soaking up as much as I can. Clouds are swirling towards a big storm I think. Soon the sky will be slashed with lightning and the thunder so loud it can make you yelp. I wonder if the other countries have such vivid storms. Other thunderous realities where lightning sirens whine themselves into a hysterical pitch and mopeds stop on the expressway under purpose-made bridges to wait out its threat.

We Asians take mother nature seriously. When the sirens blare the children rush to take cover while teachers and mothers cluck round efficiently, sweeping the last errant child out of harm's way. The taxi drivers take cover and refuse to take calls. Driving is erratic and, during the intense rainstorms, can become lethal. Even the birds congregate to witness its power. Worms dive beneath the soil's surface and snails make their way to the dome-leafed plants for cover. Everything dips and plunges, races and leaps to avoid the machine-gun blasts of rain. Singapore shuts down for a little. And the crack and cry of industry recedes, leaving nature a short time on stage to explode in its wake.

The taxi home takes a little time. Madam sits in the front and I am relegated to the back. If it was legal to stow me on the top of the vehicle I'm sure she would do that. Any prolonged contact with me in a tight space leaves her feeling acutely uncomfortable. I wonder how she would cope if we were stuck in a lift together. I smile involuntarily. Is this a kind of happiness? I can't remember what it feels like and I can't afford to relax into it. So I stuff it back down to my toes and curl them tight to keep it there. Madam goes for a rest when we get back. This means I unpack everything myself and it is a dangerous job. Madam is very particular about where things go. Certain items go in certain places and if I don't get it right or lose concentration for a minute she punishes me. I breathe slowly through my mouth and out through my nose as I stack and line up cans and packets. Trying to remember what shelf in the fridge the pak choi goes and where the spices are put exactly. Sadness is an easier emotion to embrace.

It numbs you and makes you sensitive simultaneously. But the long periods of blankness allow for better concentration. I find myself slipping back to the Indo girls' smiles and the spice seller's wink and reliving them like tiny film clips. I bite my lip until it bleeds while I finish my task. I can't take much more physical punishment. It eats away at me like a pestilence and I have become weak and fearful. I will do almost anything to avoid Madam's anger.

Sitting down outside with my back to the wall I take five minutes to shovel in the noodles that I've been given to eat and watch the butterflies dance. There are some cold carrots waiting to be thrown out and I stuff them in my back pocket for later.

Later I find some freshly baked biscuits in a secret place between the fences that divide the properties. The Ebony Ma'am must have left them there for me. She had wrapped up the sweet rounds in a plastic bag to keep the ants out. I haven't got the courage to remove them yet but I will later. I will smuggle them into a little spot I've made under the sinks outside. My Madam never goes there unless it is to inspect my handwashing and to criticise the quality of it. And so I will take this gift of more than food, this gift of love and acknowledgement, and I will hug it to me, like Sara Crewe's crumpets dripping with butter. The emerging comprehension like a lemony dawn that somebody else sees me in this place. Somebody sees me.

MADAM EUNICE

134 Sabre Green

It has taken me a long time to actually speak to Little Ping. She has clearly been enjoying her short power trip and I have allowed her to have it. I have left several messages that became quite satisfyingly bleating by the final one. She will have found satisfaction in that, I think. Eventually, I received a call. It was short and unfriendly. She asked exactly what I wanted and why. I responded in kind and said I would be so grateful if she could give me the address of the fortune teller so I could go and see him in person. I could almost sense the pause from down the wire. A slight hesitation as Little Ping wondered if she could eke out my punishment just a little longer. She has been waiting for years, hasn't she? Quietly biding her time until I have an obvious need. Something she could help with and something where she could hold a little back. Then she said she would email it to me.

I was used to these games, having played them hundreds of times with countless acquaintances. Keeping everybody on their toes. Sowing tiny amounts of discord, just enough to keep a slightly bitter taste in everyone's mouth, and spreading a light dusting of paranoia, just enough to keep friendships from becoming too close. I was quite majestic in my instincts. I had ruled the roost for a long time and been knocked off by a woman whom I had never really considered at all.

Little Ping was tolerated. Her barrenness kept her low in the rankings and out of harm's way. I had never really considered her at all. But thinking about her now several notions cross my mind. She is very attractive, probably the most attractive of our circle, and that gives her a currency. She also has a law degree from Shanghai University so she is bright, in a professional, not an academic, way. That means she might well outsmart me in the short term. But not in the long run.

Enjoy it while it lasts, Little Ping, I think, as I wait patiently for the address to come through. A few minutes later it does, along with a short note informing me that Little Ping sees our friendship as dissolved and she will not be communicating with me again. I don't bother to reply, just answer with an amused snort. I have barely been aware of her friendship – the loss of it means very little. It might be awkward at some social functions – a polite but embarrassed shuffling of name cards and a staggering of appearances. But I also know, as Little Ping does, that my social worth far outweighs hers. Even though I might be shadowed by rumours of demons and possession by a spirit, the old guard would never turn their backs. I have too many pictures of too many closets. My husband has taught me very well about storing information about everybody. I practise this on a much smaller scale than my husband, who uses it to protect his political interests. That is politics I suppose, and no different from the guile and machinations that women perfect during the fan dance of acquaintance.

I have a beautifully lacquered cabinet with a secret drop that I can push things through, and they will be completely invisible to even the most practised of thieves. In here I have photocopies, and indeed originals, of passionate and slanderous letters, printouts of emails, photographs of all kinds of people *in flagrante delicto*. You would be surprised at the lengths people will go to just to be near their heart's desire. The risks they will take, the indiscretions they will perform, the three-act kisses in the alleyway just lit enough for a grainy but well-defined image. But I have nothing on Little Ping. I have never thought to bother. She has always seemed so insubstantial. Perhaps I have underestimated her.

I squint into the sun that is flaring behind the new build beginning to thrust its way upwards towards the gods. It is ugly and utilitarian. Created for rentals and profit. The paintwork is grey and the landscaped and terraced flowers are wilting already as if announcing their sadness over the whole affair. The artists' impressions are almost unrecognisable if you compare the actual site with the pictures. They should remove those soon otherwise complaints will start flooding in.

So much money to be made here in Singapore, but for hard work.

The agents are out in the roads, waving down cars like western pros-titutes and cold-calling houses. A reasonably pretty girl with an eye-wateringly short skirt is sashaying down the road, a trickle of cars following in her wake. I see her stop and look astonished. Then she smiles sweetly (what an actress) and hands out the developer's partic-ulars to each car granting them a little bow. I see her return to the end of the street and start the whole process again. She is young but she has a very cool head on her shoulders. Two older men in suit trousers and shirts watch in dismay as she collars almost the entire neighbour-hood with one jiggle of her hips.

I glance back at the address Little Ping has sent and I resolve to go tonight. Why wait? I would just be pacing and irritable and I don't want to take it out on the children or even Lisa for that matter. She may be a total fool but she tries hard and is of a sunny disposition unlike some of the more ill-disposed maids around this neighbour-hood. It occurs to me that I haven't pushed for a move lately. I think my husband's position deserves one, further into the city. Sabre Green is a good area for the suburbs, but not a prestigious one. It's comfort-able, safe and has a few well-regarded shops, but it is not lux by any means. I need to see this man as soon as possible to dispel any ideas he might have and to task him with getting rid of the damn thing if that's possible. I'm not thinking too deeply about my actions or what I propose to do. There is very little point. I have to rectify this situation if I am going to rid myself of this spectre and I have no idea how to do it. But the address is a start and Little Ping's abasement will have to wait.

My next anxiety is how I look. I have these scratches on my face. I don't know how they got there. I can only assume that in the mad-ness of that episode in Mr Lim's shop one of those panic-crazed maids went for me. They have healed enough now for me to cover them with concealer and make-up and a good layer of powder. And what to wear? I suppose a casual outfit is called for and not one that will draw attention to me in any way. I disrobe and lay my silk and lace and good cotton garments across a chair in my dressing room. I pull on a pair of jeans I haven't worn for years and a hooded sweatshirt that I used to exercise in. A pair of slippers will do for my feet. In the garden I roll around on the grass, hoping nobody happens to be peering out of their windows, and endeavour to make the clothes look older. And then I call a taxi.

I give the address to Uncle expecting him to roll his eyes or perhaps mutter under his breath, but he just shrugs and asks which way I want to go. The reasoning is that if the fare chooses the way the driver cannot be held accountable for any traffic snarls or jams. Chinese people expect fast and excellent service. I tell him to take the East Coast highway and go from there. Uncle mutters something under his breath but I couldn't care less about his thoughts or opinions. Just shut up and drive, I think to myself. I watch the sky darkening as it does every night at around 7.15 in the evening. I give thanks to Taisui for my beautiful babies and the life I have had so far. I am determined to hold on to it but I'm not counting on Taisui to help me accomplish that. No, I'm on my own here and that is a state I am very comfortable with.

The traffic lessens as the very short rush hour dismisses the cars into filter roads and driveways. The taxi drivers have started to calm down and there are fewer exclamations and shakings of fists and heads. Lurching to a stop he taps the meter and holds his hand out. I slap ten dollars into his hand and get out quickly. The HBD winks in the blackness. It looks like a self-appointed beacon of knowledge, and the thrill of it, the anticipation, and even the concrete path leading up to the block, excite me. Then the temperature drops suddenly around my head and the back of my neck explodes with raised follicles. Is he coming? I can feel the same sensation of the air being sucked out of the world and time standing still. I make a run for the first block, concentrating on getting to the safety of the doorway, refusing to look around me.

Like a small child I believe in that moment that if the ghoul can't see me he can't hurt me. I have committed the address to memory and can see I am at the wrong block. The atmosphere is still being squeezed by a supernatural vice and I am getting more breathless. The block I need is about 100 metres away and the apartment is on the tenth floor. I shudder as something flickers in my peripheral vision – a silent horror movie. My knees buckle and I sprint for the next block. I stagger into the doorway and try to climb the stairs but the feeling of there being no oxygen makes me giddy and I have to pause, checking the stairwell. The light bulb begins to fade in and out and my fear propels me up those stairs for ten floors until I burst out of the stairwell into a darkened corridor. Eighteen pairs of eyes at least turn in my direction noting perhaps my ashen face and my flustered appearance. I ignore them, quite used to my fellow Asians' inclination towards the interested stare. Glancing about for something to sit on, I feel I might be too late. Boxes, crates, piles of newspapers and a couple of deckchairs are occupied by the devotees of the fortune teller. Everybody looks preoccupied and serious, holding their offerings tightly. Some have brought money, others spirits and fruit. This man is held in deep regard.

And so we wait for our turn. For the moment there is a kind of calmness in me. Whoever was with me on the stairs is quiet for now. I know I am in for a long wait because I seem to be the last person to have arrived. I am patient. Asian women understand patience and we practise it with ease. Our faces start to relax and our eyes become heavy lidded. Limbs and joints stretch out or in and heartbeats slow.

Time becomes irrelevant and the waiting is everything. I try to empty my mind. The fear, the worry, the bemusement and the nagging voice of reason that keeps asking me what the hell I am doing here in a rag-tag building with a group of people with whom I have nothing in common but a shared need. This I suspect brings us together like any crisis would. Cataclysmic or otherworldly events tend to bring out the best and worst in humanity. Some stretch themselves between their conscience and their God, rising above the devastation and becoming the better woman, seeking the good in people and in the events past and still to come. Others just throw their moral compass out of a speeding car and don't even give it a backwards glance as it bounces and then settles, slightly battered, in the desert ground, companion only to sidewinders and crickets.

And then, very suddenly, it is my turn. There doesn't seem to be an order. A stooped figure appears, dusty and indistinct in the gloom, and beckons at one of the petitioners. The sequence of appointments appears to be arbitrary and even though there are a number of us crouched or sitting in the cramped corridor we know exactly whom the figure is pointing to. I feel a distinct chill and stand shakily, gently shifting the feeling back into my legs. They protest only a little before the blood begins to tingle my nerves back to life. I wonder as I step over feet and bird-cages if anybody else can see the spirit that is haunting me. Do they seem to withdraw slightly as I pass or is it just polite considerateness? I feel tainted. An indistinct malaise that seems to engulf my spirit. Is this madness, or the reality of a haunting by a perfidious spirit? I shake my head in amazement at these strange thoughts and pick my way down the hall and into the darkened room at the end of it.

LUCILLA

19 Sabre Green

Tonight I lie with Rory in Ma'am and Sir's bed waiting for him to sleep. We both feel languid and happy. Curled and cuddled he tells me a child-sweet story. A little girl is captured by a dragon who steals her away to its cave full of gold and huge gems the size of Scotland. There are weapons from warriors long devoured, and maps to forgotten places. The dragon, Rory confides, is very hungry and pops the little girl into his mouth but, she being intrepid (and Scottish, so Rory tells me), her bright red hair bursts into flames and scorches the dragon's mouth. The dragon is used to hot things but unused to flaming hair so spits the little girl out and she grabs a sword and slices through the dragon's neck before he can react. And everybody lives happily ever after. So Rory says.

That was a lovely story, darling, I tell him but his eyes are already fluttering as sleep nips encouragingly at his lids and his breathing slows. We lie together with his little legs hooked over mine to keep the chill of the air conditioning out. Like me he is a product of the tropics and catches the cold easily. This is a strange expression for me. If you catch a cold then why not release it so you don't get sick? Rory chuckles in his sleep and twitches. I think what a very happy boy and maternal love soars upwards and then dives into his sleeping form.

My Sir has taken Ma'am out on their date night. Nearly every Saturday they dress up and go for dinner. When they return they are giggling and flushed with wine and love but the first thing Ma'am does is go upstairs and kiss her child.

She told me once that it's like being in love. The depth of it, the strength of it, the sheer weight of it consumes you, and you are overwhelmed by this child you love so much. That you never sleep properly again or feel completely relaxed because the emotional investment is so absolute. And Ma'am looks radiant when she tells me this. I think this love must crown the world.

I brush silky strands from his face and watch his chest rising and falling and I think about my own childhood. It was very happy. Poor but so happy. My parents showered me with love and taught me the importance of goodness and faith in God. Being Catholic is a badge of honour for me. It raises me up and gives me both hope and strength. Prayer costs nothing and is part of my armour against this world. And I am happy here, caught in the sparkling brilliance of a child sleeping and a woman that calls me her heart sister.

When I have brushed those few strands of hair away and checked the covers are lightly covering his body and delivered an impassioned kiss on his cotton-soft brow I return downstairs. There is a little more ironing to do or I could watch a film. My boyfriend is picking me up later and we are going to Little India. I check the time on my watch that Ma'am brought back from one her trips. They will be back soon, so perhaps it is time to get ready. I pull on a pair of tight jeans and a pretty flowered top. The birthday shoes I was given will be perfect. The soft leather moulds round my feet and the block colours are eye-catching. I don't like to wear short skirts any more. The attention I receive is not flattering and I don't want to be mistaken for a bar-girl. I don't enjoy being 'devoured' on the street by predatory men who make me feel like cheap material in the seconds basket. I don't want to be hissed at or nipped by fingers as I walk past.

I notice my hair has grown past my waist now. It seems thinner but shines with life like a cascade of dusk shadow. Slicking it with a touch of oil I smile involuntarily. Are women of my age allowed such vanity? I think in the privacy of my own room it is acceptable. I have my working clothes and my party clothes. If Ma'am sees me dressed up she always compliments me and tells me I look beautiful. I always feel very shy but I'm screwed up with delight inside. Every woman likes a compliment and from another woman – they are even richer.

My mind flits back to that lunch with Ma'am and Rory in the hotel. So many pictures of Singapore life right there. I remember seeing the western man with his three girls, and Ma'am and I laughing about the beautiful *bakla*boy with the Adam's apple, and the man too drunk with lust to care. But as I picture again the girl nearest the man, her face is anxious and feverish. Her hand is clasped possessively to his leg which is stretched out before him. She keeps one eye and one ear on the man making sure she laughs loud and hard at his jokes while looking as sexy as possible and the other eye and ear on the other 'girls'. Making sure they don't advance too far towards the man and oust her from the position she has probably worked all today, and last night, to achieve. There is a visible aura of fatigue about her. The same feverish cast that affects victims of a terrible event. The man shifts and dislodges her hand from his leg, leans over the table and laps up the dirty flirts that float towards him from the *bakla*. Snow spoiled by oil. The girl slumps in her chair and surrenders. She sips on her drink and scowls. The man remains unmoved, or is just unaware of her. I try to smile at her and she scowls even harder. I shrug.

Sisterhood is not what it was or perhaps what it has never been. In a world like this, unchanged through centuries of cultural and political upheaval, where sex still reigns supreme and lithe lust is able to bring down governments and powerful men, women will always be competitive with each other. And shame travels with us like a heavy, unlikeable relative. Quietly leaching our strength and reinforcing our weaknesses, unlikely to change.

My boyfriend would like a beer tonight so we have arranged to meet at Orchard MRT. He lives up in the north and hates walking. The Singaporean influence has rubbed off on him and he would drive three minutes to the corner shop if possible. The Chinese don't understand walking for the sake of it. Why walk like a peasant when you can ride like an important man? A car is a symbol of wealth and prestige in all countries I think but particularly in poor ones where even the most battered and rust-punched wrecks are celebrated and praised. Any form of private transport raises status because it is still unafford-able to most. Transport being a deliberate route to freedom and a way to get away from your mundane life and embrace the novelty and excitement of elsewhere.

We eat at a little restaurant called Bare Foot Dining on Upper Dickson Street. It is modest and cheap but the food is so tasty. We sit downstairs at wooden tables surrounded by graffiti from travellers who have found themselves in this place. Hearts and lyrics from Inga, Berlin and Rachel, Australia. Cheeky words from Connor, Ireland, and some enchanting Japanese script surrounded by smiley faces from Kio. I am amazed at the travelling the western children can do by working very small jobs for so much money. I long to see the world and the women who look like me in South America. I wonder if I would feel a connection to them. Would it be like glimpsing family with their full lips and Aztec noses and poker-straight black hair? And for my heart would there be much in common apart from a distant bloodline to an abandoned race?

I don't like too much heat so I have the butter chicken accompanied by rice so fragrant with spices that I have an urge to capture it and keep it under my pillow. The mango *lassi* is delicious. Frothy with spun yoghurt and dizzy juice. My boyfriend has a hotter dish, his Malay taste buds immune to the hot-coal pain of chilli. We eat and we sip our drinks and we touch hands and smile. This is a place for intimacy. The owners wander through making random comments and asking questions as if you are well known to them and they have no airs about whom they serve. All are welcome at Bare Foot.

My boyfriend talks about his day and I half-listen, studying his ripe lips and the bones that grace his shoulders. He does not have the bravado other Chinese Malay men do. He is more delicate and sensitive, his body thin and brittle from the long hours of navigating the highways and expressways of Singapore. He has no swagger and no testosterone-fuelled activities. He makes for a good companion now that the jealousy has subsided. And the incident with my Sir that my Ma'am is still cross about.

A year or so ago my relationship was going through scrubland, stones and other obstacles fighting in a harsh landscape. I confided in my Ma'am who let me have time off to cry with friends and soothe myself with food from home. My Ma'am told Sir that I was sad and my boyfriend was being a bit difficult. One night, Sir comes out to the car where I am sitting quietly with him and we are fine and chatting nonsense and enjoying the peace. Sir is a bit drunk, his hair is damp with sweat, and he is holding a bottle of spirits.

Sir raps on the window hard and my boyfriend makes to open it and I warn him no, no, Sir has bad temper. You stay, I will get out. And Sir is shouting and swearing and I get out and say, Sir what is it? and he takes me by the hand and is trying to tell me how much the family care and that he won't stand for this man hurting me. And as I stand there, the fumes of his evening blowing gently past me on the wind and his wild eyes darting from night sky to black road and back again, I keep my head down and my distance. This Sir is frightening to me. And then my Ma'am appears and draws me behind her and tells Sir quietly that it is not his business and that I am a grown woman and he is never to do this again. And she takes me inside and leans her forehead on the cool wall and apologises for long time. Next day she doesn't speak to Sir until the evening. And this withdrawal of her warmth and love, of her spirit and life spark, is enough to drive Sir to penitence. He becomes withdrawn and pale but has the courage to apologise to me too. He says that his actions, however wrong, came from a good place. Came from his heart, and he felt that he had to protect me as a member of the family. I am truly embarrassed and stutter that it is fine and not to worry, that I understand and I do. But my Ma'am has never forgotten and still mentions it from time to time. She never laughs about it or minimises it for her own piece of mind. She takes it seriously like a judge's verdict.

Some people have clarity of conscience. A very definite idea of what is right and wrong. And they practise their lives accordingly. As I walk through the colour and thrum that is Little India I find myself soothed by the humanity here. The throngs, the families who are replicas of each other in different sizes. The gaudy cloth and the gold bright trim. The truth of stale sweat and clothes imbued with food stains and smells. This happy natural soiling is a signpost to nirvana.

MA'AM LESLEY

35 Sabre Green

Still no sign of Ralph. Jocelyn and I have been living side by side in the first tiny bubbles of harmony. She relies on me for everything. The pregnancy has sapped her energy and she already appears consumed by it. I make soups and bake bread from scratch. Using nourishing seeds and wholemeal flours. She sits sullenly staring into space taking tiny bite after tiny bite like an absent squirrel.

I read to her for hours. Dipping into volumes trying to find things she might like. Jocelyn has regressed back to a childlike dependency. Grasping my sturdy English marrow and sucking at it like a greedy infant. It is an odd reversal of roles albeit a strangely comforting one. I have found to my delight that she loves *Pride and Prejudice*. Although the language is difficult the universal fairy story is not.

Curiously, Enid Blyton's *Mallory Towers* is also a hit. I have racked my brains trying to work out why a Filipina like Jocelyn would feel an affinity with the girls of the jolly hockey sticks variety, and it struck me that it just doesn't matter what Jocelyn likes as long as it keeps her quiet and calm during the scant month left of her confinement.

Without the toxic influence of Ralph we are settling quietly into each other. I have contacted the family lawyer and asked him to draw up adoption papers. An expatriate lawyer working in the tropics doesn't bat an eyelid at my request. Asking only for passport numbers and independently witnessed statements of intent.

It is the first time I have seen any light in Jocelyn's eyes for months. She signs all the papers with a flourish, desperate to end her purgatory. What had she been thinking, I wonder, when she set out to seduce Ralph? Because it had been a deliberate and calculated move. I believe she is the type of woman who doesn't think much beyond the excitement stage. The planning and execution are independent of each other. The pregnancy a ghastly mistake. I wasn't sure what the current rate for surrogacy was but I knew I'd overcompensate. Both for the guilt and the happiness.

Where will I be in a year? A mother surely, but still a wife? I am sure now that Ralph is either dead or on the run. Appallingly, I would rather he was found to be a traitor than a child pornographer. It's not the shame factor, more the idea that I once shared space with a man capable of such duplicity and filth.

Norfolk and Suffolk have not returned, but I received an interesting parcel three days after their visit. DHL delivered an iPhone, courtesy of H M Government, from Norfolk. *Dear Mrs B*, he wrote, *just to keep in touch. Sincerely, David.* I enjoyed that touch of intimacy and rolled his name around my tongue like a schoolgirl practising her married name. I have never called him but often wonder about him and his daily life. The usual mundane life-stuff questions have crossed my mind, but the librarian's instinct for history and knowledge is stronger, and even though Norfolk is probably not his name at all I am fascinated to learn more about this line of strong, historically corrupt and ambitious men.

Traditionally, a Norfolk is the king's man second and his own man first. I suspect that when the stakes were so high (beheading and loss of lands) the ambition would be bloody. What is the point of risking everything for little? My favourite Norfolk is the fourth duke. Aristocratic and terminally ambitious while he was alive, he refused to play Elizabeth's divisive court games and eventually paid for it in blood. I admire a man who can resist a woman's charms; Elizabeth recognised this as a personal affront. Hell hath no fury like a woman scorned.

I will miss Jocelyn, I think, when she leaves. It won't be a difficult parting for her, more the end of a nine-month sabbatical from her normal life. She is young enough to have many more children if she wants and I envy her that luxury. I suspect I have been tolerated during this time only because she has felt feeble and the hormones have been playing havoc with her natural brusqueness. I have little doubt that Jocelyn will leave us both behind without a second glance or thought when the time comes. And we will resume our lives in very different ways. But for now she needs me and I even receive the odd thank you and I catch her smiling during the telling of Mr Darcy and Elizabeth's story.

While we wait in the humidity for her due date I read extensively about pregnancy on the internet and even conduct a few antenatal classes in the bedroom. I now sleep beside her at night in the big bed. Ostensibly to help her get to the bathroom if she needs it or to wipe her face if she is sweaty and uncomfortable. But in my heart it is to live vicariously, every moment that's possible, through another woman's pregnancy. I place my hand on her stomach during the dark hours and the dawn hours and feel my baby kick and press towards me and if I listen intently I can hear a whisper: *I'm coming, Mummy, I'm coming.* I continue to cook and clean and wash but with a sense of purpose and a clarity that has previously been withheld from me.

I don't think any woman can live with the supremest cruelty day in and day out without coming adrift in some way. Isolated from reason and physically vulnerable, we start to petrify under the steady flow of abuse and eventually shatter. Afterwards, we carry on as a fragment of our former selves. It takes a long time for the body and mind to heal; sometimes it's impossible. But the heart's edges may start to feel less ragged. The eye begins to look up more and the brain starts to process information from different viewpoints. Is this healing? I suppose it is, but I'm not an expert. The violence I experienced, the casual SS brutality, the random acts of humiliation are still tight inside me. My skin remembers it all even if the bruises and cuts have faded almost out of sight. And my psyche reminds me each time a thunderclap makes me stagger with fear.

Then one day I receive a text message from Norfolk. I am surprised and, irritatingly, excited.

Mrs B. I've been asked to search Ralph's private papers. This may or may not be distressing for you, but if you wish to be present then you are most welcome. I will also need access to his home computer. Shall I bring cake? Norfolk.

Cake? How extraordinary this man is. I text back slowly, handicapped by lack of experience.

When? Not really. OK. No – I will bake something.

His reply beeped back swiftly.

Tomorrow @ 3.30. I am a fiend for Madeira cake.

And I smile properly, enjoying this stunted flirtation for what it is. Safe. After checking on Jocelyn and finding her much the same, morose, whiney, fed up like a teenager with the measles, I go downstairs to bake a Madeira cake that, in tropical heat, is a feat of resolve. I have hardly started mixing when the sweat begins to trickle down my back and the insides of my legs. I use my sarong as a towel as I cream and fold and beat, taking huge gulps of icy water every few minutes. I add plump, rum-addled sultanas, and a sugar crust, and feel it is a job well done.

Afterwards, I wander into the atrium and stand in the doorway of Ralph's study. This is his territory and I wouldn't have dared go anywhere near it before. But he isn't here now and even though I lock the front door as a precaution, I walk in and stand there for a whole ten seconds before leaving quickly. Maybe it will feel different with Norfolk there taking command. I suppose I should have been through those papers but Ralph's wages are still being paid into the joint account.

Although really, my financial needs are basic, and Jocelyn's easy. She has absolutely refused to go to the midwife all along, or to leave the house at all, so I summoned our family doctor saying that a family friend was pregnant and possibly suffering from some sort of pre-baby blues. He dutifully came. Tutted a few times, measured, palpated and took some blood quite heroically from the shrieking and swooning patient. His opinion was that she was in good health and the baby had a strong heartbeat. He urged us to get a scan and I nodded and promised, knowing it would never happen.

Jocelyn is biding her time and every extra day she carries the baby she feels more chained by her pregnancy. Angry red stretch marks have appeared across her stomach and I feel both sad and irritated for her because the one aspect of her pregnancy she has become really involved with is all about vanity. She oils and smoothes and creams and nourishes and still her genetics are too strong. She is marked, as her mother and grandmother and great grandmother have been.

Our views are so different. She sees parasite, and I see new beginning. I sit downstairs and contemplate my future. Hugging the possibilities to myself like the precious things they are. A hint of hibiscus is in the air thick with other perfumes. They open up so rarely that to catch them blooming and showing off like a Mardi Gras parade is a secret pleasure for me.

I close my eyes and carry on with my plans.

SHAMMI

112 Sabre Green

I don't find a present in my secret place every day but I always look. Sometimes, my Ebony Ma'am puts sweet things or vitamins or a pretty hair slide. I don't care what they are, it's what they represent that is so important. Each time I find something I start to heal and I have hope. I feel better physically and my hair begins to half-shine. She has even given me an Indo–English phrasebook which I study nightly. Trying to memorise words and sentences.

For the first time in months I feel as if there is an answer and God has not forsaken me. I feel less weary and start to sing again while I work. This seems to irritate my Madam and she becomes extra harsh. I think she prefers it when I am dog weary and colourless. She doesn't trust this new girl. This emergent woman. What tricks might I be getting up to if I have too much energy or too much time to think? And so she cracks the whip and invents more jobs, more chores that I fail at. But even as I apologise in the force of her displeasure I am glowing and feel a wriggle of pleasure at the new blush in my cheeks and the softer angles of my face.

I watch the Ebony Ma'am and her family leaving for a holiday. The maid is going with them. I don't know where they are going because strictly speaking I'm forbidden to talk to them. It has only happened once in a while and in secret. But they see me peeking through the fence slats and wave and smile. The Ebony Ma'am approaches me and holds my hand. She whispers to me in low, soothing tones. I under-stand the tone of her voice if not the words. I stammer a thank you in English and pull her hand to my forehead.

It doesn't reach entirely but I'm trying to tell her how much she means to me. This woman whom I have never hugged, laughed or eaten with and I don't even know her given name or her favourite book or if she likes crumpets. But I know she sees me and, for that, I worship her. Ebony Ma'am's husband comes over and smiles at me. His teeth gleam in his smooth umber face. He doesn't touch me but performs a short, respectful bow. I have never been shown such consideration in this country. I bring the knuckle of my hand to my mouth and breathe heavily into it. They look so beautiful. Such organised beauty. Happy, smiling and confident. What sort of goodness have their ancestors had to make this life so good for them? And that goodness exists like the bee, the rainbow, and the tropical storm. Fleeting but recurrent. A sliver of light in my small life.

Tonight, the children stay with their grandparents and I am to remain at the house because my Madam and Sir will be back much later as they have been delayed on a day trip to Malaysia. The children go straight from school and so I find myself alone in my gilded prison and no one has locked the patio doors.

I open them and step carefully, slowly, silent as a sea snake, onto the crisp grass. It is dew-damp and comforting to my feet. I plant them firmly on the ground and scrunch my toes up around the soft, fat blades. The smell of hibiscus and frangipani is heady and the moon shines high above the city, buttery and luminous like a clear light in a fog-bound sea. I would not dare to step out this way if it were day except to clean car, but in this soft darkness the sense of excitement is too much for me. I creep carefully around the garden touching the leaves and buds and trailing my fingers over scrubby branches and lush foliage. I feel freedom here camouflaged by the dark and hidden by the night. This is the first time I have been properly alone for what feels like a long time. I know that my employers will not be back for hours and an idea occurs to me. I think back to the day of the haze. Then that small escape felt desperate and the fear choking and not just because of the poisoned air. Now the forbidden idea is, oh! so sweet like a stolen fruit. I move silently round the side of the house, stepping over the garden tools, and turn over rusty buckets, placed in line with a government directive to help to keep dengue fever at bay.

I haven't put my shoes on and the path is still warm beneath my feet although the sun set some hours ago. I put my hands on the bar of the security gate and stare out. Do I dare? What would be the consequences? Dismissal, perhaps, a beating certainly. With a burst of courage I find I don't care.

This moment is too important to ignore. I must grab it. I must be brave and so I am. I hold my breath and climb over, landing cat-like on the other side. I use only my eyes to search the blackness of the night for figures. I need to work out if they are employers or maids. Two middle-aged Singaporean women walk quickly past, pumping their arms and matching strides. I shrink back into the shadows, willing them to walk even faster.

I bolt towards the park opposite. Finding my legs I begin to run around the path, swinging my arms and listening to my lungs becoming breathless and raw. The park is small, no more than a kilometre square, but for me it's the race-track of the world. I begin to jump and whoop, quickly stuffing my fingers in my mouth to stop my giggling.

Evening-off maids emerge from the shadows and steamy alcoves, phones clamped to their ears, while Bangla men hover uncertainly. Eventually, I have to slow down. Lack of good food means that I tire quickly so I wander through the grass and touch the leaves and trace the parched bark of the rain trees. The moon seems to shine harder here as if freedom enhances its beauty and the air is sultry and thick with moisture.

And then a man steps into the path and stares at me. I don't recognise him. Why would I? Never much leaving the house – but I recognise his intent. In the darkness his eyes glow red with fatigue and I can smell stale onion sweat from his body.

We stare at each other for a few seconds and then when he lunges towards me I side-step, and then I run for the house. His footsteps pound after me but stop abruptly as I leap onto the gate like a dancer and climb over it. Heart hammering and pounding, and grabbing huge lungfuls of air, I retreat to the darkest shadows and watch from safety behind the big main gates. Could he climb over? He stops on the pavement and I can see the battle between lust and fear. Those frightening red-rimmed eyes search the darkness of the car porch over and over. I stay still because he can't hear my breathing from where he stands. A crack of thunder, horribly loud, and a flicker of lightning up the street leaves this man exposed. He backs away quickly and disappears into the undergrowth. For a moment I see his eyes, still searching, and then they disappear.

My breath whooshes out but I'm smiling. Huge, happy smiling. I have risked so much tonight and I have passed my own test with flying colours. My colours are rust red, lemon yellow and verdant green. The colours of earth, sun and life. They are everywhere tonight, even in the darkness. I see them brushed by the moon, I see them in the woody bark and terracotta pots, I see them in the honeyed mangoes and damp, lime-green leaves of the hibiscus. These colours represent my life and my blood.

I run for the kitchen quarters. My feet are caked in dirt, in freedom, and I feel a brief sadness as I wash them quickly with the outside hose. The water feels unusually cool from a tap in the tropics and my skin bounces with the shock.

Then I hear the gates groaning open and hurry to dry my feet in time to greet my Madam as she returns.

MADAM EUNICE

134 Sabre Green

The room is thick with rancid food, old sweat and incense. It feels bloated, too full for anything else, and on the edge of sickness. I squint and cough trying to orientate myself. Through the gloom I can see a figure at the end of the cramped room, cross-legged and slightly bent. Two red lanterns beam a weak glow around him, and as he looks up they inadvertently cast a strange shadow over his thick glasses, making his eyes glow demon red for an instant. I draw a sharp breath and take a step backwards. The man, at least I think it is a man, beckons me forward and down and I comply gratefully, feeling dizzy from the intense smoky perfume and thick fug of concentrated humanity.

The fortune teller is not imposing. Slender, of middle age, but with that particular brand of ageing that confuses between young and old, and a disastrous combover. But something reverberates around him. Not shimmers, nothing as delicate or as weak as that, but a definite actual vibration. I find myself drawn undeniably to this man. Perhaps the incense is a narcotic and is intended to make supplicants weak and suggestible, but I don't care at this point. Sinking to my knees I face the man. For a long time he stares at me. Not in a lascivious way but as if he wants to understand me. And I am held rapt by his gaze. Trapped by the theatre of it all.

At last he speaks. Just a fragment of a sentence to start with. 'Your demon is awake.'

'Why me? What did I do?' I ask.

'Not you. Someone close asked this of me. To wake your demon.'

'You did this?' I snap.

The man shrugs as if it matters little to him. 'I do many things for many people.'

'And you do it for money?'

187

'Of course.'

I am not particularly shocked at the bland honesty but I am anxious. My heartbeat is gathering speed and my breathing is becoming laboured and difficult. 'How do I get rid of it?'

'I can do that for you.'

'How much?'

The man leans back and examines my face. 'You are a rich woman, I think. But I always ask for something that is difficult to give. Impossible even.'

I hesitate as the icy fingers return to plague my spine. 'What do you want?'

'Your firstborn child.'

I smother a giggle. He must be toying with me, testing my limits. 'Don't be ridiculous.'

The man cocks his head to one side, eyes glowing crimson. 'There is another way. Perhaps the most concrete way. Chop off the poison at the source.'

'I don't understand.'

'I think you do.'

'Please, stop talking in riddles. I don't feel well.'

'You must end the life of the person who asked for this curse. And do it fast. Bad spirits attract other bad spirits. Yes, you must do this thing quickly.'

'Who? Who asked for this wretched thing?' A silence follows my question that stretches out as it gathers weight and power.

Finally, the man speaks. 'You know her as Little Ping.'

I sag against the wall. This is unexpected. I am far more shocked that Little Ping has such cunning in her than by the fortune teller suggesting murder to me. After all, I am still not convinced that the demon actually exists. I refuse to analyse it at all. Pushing the possibility away whenever it pokes through my conscious mind. In the way that children pretend things don't exist to stop them existing.

Barely aware of the people crowded in the corridor like refugees awaiting placement I push my way to the lift and stand there feeling absolutely lost. The lights in the hallway begin to flicker oddly and the air grows very still, but I refuse to be cowed by this fear.

I am the formidable Eunice Tan.

I will find another way to rid myself of this madness. Tomorrow I will make an appointment with Dr Chan and together we will make sense of this. Disassemble the past few weeks into what it is. An episode of some kind. And take practical steps to make it disappear.

This planning helps me feel better. Being practical by nature, for me details are always important. The 'big picture' makes me wary and I much prefer starting at the beginning and plotting a course without the distractions of creativity or genius. Yes, tomorrow Dr Chan, and putting this nonsense to bed. I draw myself up and set my jaw firmly in the tradition of burdened Asian women. These are just interesting times. *My* interesting times.

And then the door of the lift opens and standing in the flickering, spoiled-egg light stands the most exquisite little girl that I've ever seen. Her braided hair gleams like polished obsidian and her complexion is strawberries and cream. Only her eyes seem faded and lacklustre as if sadness is a disease that has taken root in her young body and death is not far away. Her mouth opens and closes as if she is trying to say something, and tears form at the corners of her eyes and spill heavily onto her cheeks.

'What, little one? What?'

The child can't or won't speak but raises her arm and points into the space behind me, and I notice something is terribly wrong with her arms. The veins in the crook of each arm and at each wrist are distended and almost black. And then the air stills once more and I know the other creature is behind me. Despite my shaking hands and the real fear pounding in my chest I turn because I have to, and there stands the cowled thing. Mocking me from the doorway of the room I have just left, dragging the fortune teller's limp body in one hand and holding his still-beating, bleeding heart in the other.

I back up to the lift doors, determined to protect the child but the girl, if that is what she is, is laughing so hard that her mouth has begun to change shape. Her teeth have become elongated and fang-like, her dark eyes shine with corruption and as she reaches towards me the lift doors close abruptly and the hall bulbs resume their half-light glow.

I spin round to see if anybody else has seen the foul girl-like thing in the lift or the spectre in the corridor, but nothing has changed at all. People are still sitting side by side hunched with anxiety, waiting for the young–old man to bestow his particular brand of commercial evil on them, the man whom I had just now seen, or thought I had seen, being pulled along, half-alive, minus his heart, by my hooded figure.

Our superstitions and our regard for diviners and soothsayers are as old as civilization. Asia is certainly not alone in its groping through the murky waters of the esoteric. But what I can understand now, whether I am experiencing a savage psychosis or am plagued by an actual haunting, is that I am in a very dangerous place. *Dr Chan, Dr Chan*, softly chanting his name like a protective talisman, and I don't stop as I flee the building, blindly taking the stairs down two at a time, not caring about the twisting of my ankle or the muttered obscenities from an old couple that I push past as if the devil himself is behind me.

Because maybe he is.

LUCILLA

19 Sabre Green

I have the biggest news. Today my Ma'am told me that her Sir is not renewing his contract with the school so next year they will be leaving and going to a different country in Europe. And Ma'am has asked me if I want to go with them. Not just to work, Lulubell, but to study and learn to drive. Lots of things, Lulubell. You are so capable and clever. So wasted here washing our clothes and cleaning our bathrooms.

I see that my life will change and it frightens me. After all, I am a village girl from Leyte. I will be far away from my parents and family. And even though I'm not convinced my boyfriend is the way to my happiness he is all I've got. And I do love him in my way. He may not be the most rich or the most handsome but he is mine and if I leave to go to Europe I will be leaving behind certain things.

Ma'am has said that I can return home at any time. But what do I know of European contracts? It might be worth as much as Filipino contract in Singapore. And will ignite like a hot kindling in the dry winter. I trust my Ma'am but I don't trust the world. It's not for trusting. Too much has happened in my life. Too many knocks and stings. Too many cuts and bruises.

I'm leaving the house early today to send money home. I have to get to Lucky Plaza before 7pm. The queues are hours long at the weekends so I try to go in the week and I have a Western Union Gold Card that makes the process quicker. I often see someone I know. But it's not all smiles and ice cream. Even with the large sisterhood, we still get the snake and scorpion girls. The ones with too much damage, lah! Too much at stake for them to be soft again. They carry chips of ice in their hearts and I stay out of their way if I can. My contentment is obvious and it earns jealousy. Best to keep it quiet and low. I know the girls think I'm *suplada*, unfriendly, but I'm just being careful. You need to know how to move carefully in prison. Put one foot in front of the other and breathe. Keep your head down and hope for the best.

If I go abroad how will I start again? Friendships are worth everything and nothing here. Without our shaky sisterhood it would be very lonely. The exchange of language, food, memories and experiences keeps us sane. I love my Ma'am but we can never be equal. It is a sugar confection in her head. She will always be my queen. To my Ma'am, I will always be Lucilla, her heart sister, but the place of the lighter-skinned woman in the world and the place of her darker-skinned sister are very different. Some call it privilege, I call it history. Ma'am says we are both women and the same red blood runs through our veins. But her skin is that bit lighter and mine is darker and our world has very definite ideas about the colour of a woman's skin and her worth. Sometimes, she will pick a frangipani blossom and tuck it behind my ear and kiss my cheek. Always, I worry about my smell and the fact that I've sweated. I don't want to get my stink on Ma'am. And when I protest she just holds me tighter and whispers, I don't care, Lulu. It is nothing to me; and just like that my feelings are dismissed. And sometimes she will look forlorn as if her heart is bending in a strong wind like broken rushes by the river and will ask for a cuddle. She holds me tight as if I am family. As if she is trying to remember being held by her mother and I might hear a stifled sob in my ear and my heart hurts for her.

So I would be safe in Europe with my Ma'am but the idea is too difficult. It is a dream and I have never thought it would be achievable, and now here it is laid on a wooden platter for me and that makes it more frightening.

I have another concern, a secret really. My auntie in Manila has adopted a wonderful boy called Peter. He is a good boy, devout and clever at his lessons. Auntie is getting old and frail now and worries about how Peter will live when she is gone. I agreed to be his legal guardian so how can I leave and go to the other side of the world? What if Auntie dies soon and Peter needs me? So many worries and questions. I will have to speak to my Ma'am about this. I always feel so anxious before I ask her something important. It is an echo of my past employers who made such requests feel like murder. And drew them out until they were stretched to breaking point. And my nerves would squeak like unoiled chain and my mind would flare with the bruises of one thousand fresh hurts.

We are on this earth for a short time and I try to turn my mind from the inequality of the world. From comparisons between pampered, honey-fed children with lazy, complacent smiles and scarecrow children from Tondo slums in Manila, thin and rickety but wearing the cleanest clothes because of a mother's pride. Happiness can be found anywhere. Even under rocks where a tiny lizard has hidden successfully from a hungry owl. Even in Tondo where a newborn is cradled and proclaimed the most beautiful and baptised into God's love.

Maybe it is possible. Maybe.

MA'AM LESLEY

35 Sabre Green

I find myself looking forward to Norfolk's visit more than is absolutely necessary. I haven't had the opportunity or the inclination to flirt with a man for so many years. Cowed by Ralph and stunted self-esteem I ate and gorged my way to oblivion in a land where physical beauty is a common currency. But Norfolk seems uninhibited by the usual rules and seems to think nothing at all about my scruffy appearance. I have experimented, disastrously, in the mirror with a pair of kitchen scissors and now my hair sticks up in questioning tufts and ridges. It looks ridiculous but has a certain gamine quality that when I was fat I could never have pulled off.

My Madeira cake sits fat and smug and preparing to share itself at teatime. I won't let Jocelyn have any until Norfolk has been served. I feel proprietorial towards this cake. A ridiculous feeling but it is all I have to offer him.

I hear Jocelyn calling, a different, more timid, tone to her voice, and take the stairs two at a time. I have boundless energy today despite being bemused by my middle-aged infatuation. I have no thought of what might happen past enjoying this fleeting, random visit. I've shuddered at the thought of older women who fly to the Gambia and believe they are being genuinely seduced by young and nubile Gambian men. In a country where land can be bought for the price of a dinner for four in a decent restaurant in the west these woman are genuinely respected, but they are 'used'. Poverty brings with it a barter system and you must give if you want to receive. The attentions of these young black men are not free. They do not have that luxury and fighting for crumbs and self-respect is a dirty business.

The door to my old bedroom is only half open but I can hear her laboured breathing from outside the door. Not now, not now, I whisper. You are only eight months. Just stay a while. A few more weeks. Please, my darling.

I find Jocelyn sitting at the end of the bed with her legs splayed in a parody of the grotesque. Her belly, distended and ripe, looks ugly against her tiny frame.

'It hurts, Ma'am. Oh! It hurts. You think the baby comes now?'

The truth is I have no idea. I'm not a midwife and have never given birth. I do remember that contractions called Braxton Hicks are quite common during the later months as a dress rehearsal for the real thing.

I hum and haw a bit and feel her belly. Certainly the baby is very active, pushing, shoving and kicking. I watch with some delight as a tiny foot imprints itself against the tight drum of Jocelyn's stomach. That must hurt, I think.

'I don't think this is actual labour. What you need to do is try to relax. Walk around a bit to relieve the pressure. I can rub your back. Would you like that?'

'Yes, Ma'am, yes. Thank you, Ma'am.'

We walk a bit and I talk to Jocelyn. Not about the baby because she dislikes talking about the baby. So we discuss magazine gossip and talk about her travel plans in the future. It is a strange relationship, with both of us knowing that we'll never meet again after the baby is born, and yet I am taking as much care of her as I would my own daughter. I don't even like her particularly. She has a hard and atavistic quality that I suppose has been engineered by living and working in Singapore. I try hard not to judge by my limited western standards. What do I know about growing up in a slum in Manila or being used cruelly by a first-world country so emotionally deformed that some foreign domestic workers still toil through seven-day weeks? I keep it light and empty my mind of her previous hurts and insults. I feel I am being paid in full for those indiscretions.

I go downstairs and make lemonade. The old-fashioned way with juice and water. Jocelyn loves hers very sweet. I like mine tart and friendless. I eye the wall clock and time is dragging its heels. I check my new phone and the screen is untroubled by flashing icons. Technology has this tiresome habit of keeping you completely up to date.

Even if you want to lean backwards into more restful times there will be a beeping or a flashing that will tear you sharply from your dreams.

The pastoral epics of Wordsworth and that particular type of agony that Owen's poetry describes in the grip of war would be impossible now. There is more to fear in the world, more to hunger for, and the stakes are higher. Our triumphs and disasters are spot-lit for the world to rake through and to comment on and they are wearing thin.

I once hoped for a better world but worked out that you make the best of what you have. Keep your circle small and raise your head only when it's vital. The papers might be signed and Jocelyn absolutely adamant that she will not change her mind, but I know that until the baby is in my arms I won't believe it. So much relies on human capriciousness and so much on patience. I glance at the clock face again and curse how time creeps when there is something to look forward to. I am becoming an expert at waiting.

Wherever Ralph was, above or below the ground, he will appear again in my life somehow. And Jocelyn will give birth when the time is right. And Norfolk, curse him, will trip up to my door at precisely 3.30pm with his laconic smile and air of absolute capability.

I hum with happiness.

I am dusting the same spot near the door where I can see the gate but not be obvious about it when the sleek black saloon draws up smoothly at precisely 3.29 and Norfolk stares at the house a minute before he steps out from the car. I watch him smooth his hair back, not through nerves but through habit, and adjust his cuffs. I wonder if there is a woman in his life who notices these things. A woman should notice these things. The scent at the nape of his neck. The strength in his hands. The twitch in his jaw when under duress.

I move to the door and open it and true to style Norfolk shows no surprise that I have anticipated his arrival, just, Mrs B. How lovely to see you.

He expresses no interest in Jocelyn and accepts a glass of lemonade and three slices of Madeira, exclaiming in the tempered way of an Englishman how very delicious it is. I feel pleased with myself, watching as he eats heartily but not indelicately. This is a man of many talents and I suspect some are not as legal as others. A good man to have on your side. Probably a lethal one to have as an enemy.

He watches me with interest and no apparent guile. Asking the odd question about my life and how I am coping without Ralph, and then, gently, after a lengthy pause, 'Shall we?'

I take rather a ragged breath and stand up shakily.

'Gently does it, old girl, gently does it,' Norfolk murmurs.

I can feel him behind me as I lead the way to Ralph's study. His presence is reassuring and he has substance and solidity, something that is surely comforting in a man. This man in particular.

'Would you like to stay or leave me to it?'

I glance sharply at Norfolk. Does he want me to go? 'Can I do both?'

Norfolk smiles gently. 'Absolutely.'

So I stay a while and watch as Norfolk takes great care searching Ralph's papers and drawers. I have no idea what he is looking for but still find myself flabbergasted when he finds a secret button that when pushed reveals a deep double drawer behind a false one.

I close my eyes briefly. Please let it be treason, please let it be secrets, I beg the universe.

Norfolk pauses and pulls out a high-resolution black-and-white photograph. He glances at it but says nothing. I shake my head and leave the room. He finds me kneeling underneath my beloved frangipani rubbing dropped petals as soft as angora between my fingers like worry beads. He lays a gentle hand on my shoulder and squeezes very gently communicating only compassion.

'I had no idea, you know. He was very violent. It distracted me from engaging with his life at all. I would never betray my country.' I still can't look at him.

'Mrs B? I have to ask you a question of some delicacy. May I proceed?'

I nod.

'Did you know that your husband was bisexual?'

This time I look at Norfolk. 'What do you mean?' I ask stupidly.

He hands me the picture that he has taken from the hidden safe. 'I

suspect your husband was being blackmailed because of his relationship with this young man.'

I glance at the photograph. I can see Ralph sitting in a booth in
a bar looking incredibly happy and relaxed. He has his arm flung
round a young man, a boy really, of Asian origin who has his hand on
Ralph's thigh. There is no mistaking the intent of the photographer
or the subject matter he has captured.

It makes so much sense. The anger, the cruelty, the lack of sex. The
child with Jocelyn probably some sort of smokescreen.

I bury my head in my hands and sob for a long time. Norfolk kneels
down and holds me, murmuring quietly the sort of things one would
say to comfort a child, and after a while I begin to relax. I am happy
to stay that way until the sun drops and the inky black night of Singapore drapes itself around our shoulders.

SHAMMI

110 Sabre Green

Ebony Ma'am is back with her family and I am glad. Like herons to storm clouds and black pigs in mud glad.

I am handwashing as I do this every day and there is a never-ending pile of clothes to wash carefully. When Madam wants to punish me I sometimes must wash all sheets, pillowcases and bedcovers by hand too. I don't mind too much today because the water is cool on my chapped hands. I would like to use a soft detergent that I've seen in Fair Price but I don't think there is much point. This cheap liquid shreds my skin like the razor-sharp blue coral in the shallows back home. But none of that matters because Ebony Ma'am is back and she is my good luck talisman.

Her kindness heals every little thing and I missed her sorely when they went on holiday. A tiny space in between my ribs ached on the days she wasn't here, but when I checked the place where she leaves things there was a box with a tiny crystal fish through a leather thong, a packet of sweets, 150 dollars and a card with a name and address on it in black ink. The money didn't interest me much. Where would I spend it? How could I send it home without time off? So I squirrelled it between my legs and kept the card for later.

I think I hear Madam moving in the house so I move out of the sun's glare and back into the shelter of the back porch. Cheeky Asian blackbirds hop about on the lawn pecking indiscriminately. The casual rainfall attracts them with its steady tapping. Move quickly, little birds, my Madam doesn't like you on her grass. She doesn't like free things. Quick. Quick! But nature doesn't care about my Madam and why should it, having existed for so much longer than she has, and the birds eye me with cold, yellow stares and continue to hop and peck at will. I enjoy their wilfulness and envy it.

I gaze at Ebony Ma'am's house. Yesterday, when I saw her dreaming in the garden, even the flowers seemed to bloom more fragrantly. I often compare her to Our Lady because she has a light that I can't see but always feel its warmth. Sometimes, I feel ill with love for her. Wanting to be near her, just touching the hem of her soft skirt or the sun-loved leather of her sandals would be enough. I could sleep at the end of her bed or in the kitchen serving her during the day with loyalty and love.

She is the kind baker who gives Sara Crewe sugar buns to eat. Like her, I gave my last biscuits to the more needy. In her case younger children, and in mine skeletal, stray cats, abandoned early on in the Asian quest for perfection. And she is my Ram Dass although I can't speak Hindustani. I don't speak anything really, any more. Just an attempt at human. These thoughts I have are easy enough to frame in my mind but impossible to voice. Who would I tell them to? Abandoned in my 'attic', frozen with loneliness and need. Sara and I have much in common. And suddenly I crave my Ebu and her gentle voice and the way that story unfolded in a different tone each time.

I push my hair behind my ears, squat near the bowl of soapy water and look again at the card. I have smudged the first two lines a little but can still make out the letters. I think it is a name and address with 'Switzerland' in bold letters at the bottom. And a stamp at the top that reads, 'We are moving!' in happy letters. Who is moving? I feel confused and a very real sense of dread rises up from the depths of me. No, no, no. Please don't let it be her. Please, God, Father, Jesus, Oh! My mother! No, no, no.

I duck my head beneath my arm and rock and sob. If they leave I will be alone. Abandoned again without hope or any daily kindnesses. I will become thin and ill again. My new hard-won sleekness will disappear along with the flesh on my bones. My eyes will dim like the forest at dusk and I will become invisible. No more running in the park or stepping outside to feel the crispy earth between my toes. No more presents and no more Ebony Ma'am. I run to the fence not caring about consequence and hook my fingers through the slats. I shake it in fury and fever and howl like a wild dog in a bamboo trap. And no one comes. Because my cries are silenced by grief and my strength

202

evaporates quickly and I sink to the ground and rest my feeble head against the fencing. Eyes closed against the glare of the sun and the heaviness of loss. I stay in the same place, willing the sun to bleach my bones to dust and my soul to return to a place of love and light, but then I hear the click click of my Madam's shoes on the path and start.

'What you do? What you do? Why you not finish the washing?' Slap. 'My silk ruined!' Slap. 'No wages.' Slap. 'No food. Ungrateful, lazy, filthy!' Slap.

I have no energy or will to protect myself but from practice, I curl into a ball and cover my head with my arms. Madam never kicks my face. Her violence is quick to rise and quick to stop and she will pause soon, panting and spent with froth spilling from the corners of her mouth. Then I will crawl to the back porch and, like the injured dog she believes I am, I will lick my wounds and keen softly and hope that my life ends soon.

I'm sorry Ebu. I'm so sorry, Bapa. I am not the daughter you deserve. I am not the strong, bronze-limbed, stout-hearted woman in God's grace any more. I am a shadow. The leavings of a whole person after they have been filed down by disappointment. I sit and stare at the sky. Please forgive me. Please forgive me. I don't know what to do any more. Forgive me, Father, for I have sinned. Forgive me, Mother, for I am nothing.

The water in the handwashing pot is tepid now. I fill it with the hottest water I can boil. And lift the sheets and delicates and the 'white as snows' and push them down under the surface until they are twisted together. A few suds make it to the water surface and pop in surprise. A tiny slice of sharp and then blood starts to flow into the water and drips onto the ground. The copper-red water will stain the clothes and as I fall sideways the water tips and flows into the parched grass. And I watch as my blood and ashes meander towards Ebony Ma'am's fence.

I am not afraid as my eyes become heavy. The sun begins to blaze my trail, tiny snippets of shine dusting my vision, and day turns to night and I feel colder than I've ever felt but I'm travelling to a better place and leaving hell behind.

MADAM EUNICE

134 Sabre Green

It is very early morning and I find myself outside Dr Chan's consulting rooms before the staff have arrived. My night was plagued by visitations and earnest recommendations from dark shadows that I dispatch Little Ping without losing another moment of sanity.

But who am I to trust? My belief system lies broken on the floor and the voices that I've been hearing for days now are just getting more insistent. I can't decide if I'm mad, bad or dangerous, or even if I am real.

Dr Chan will probably prescribe more drugs and a nice holiday in Bintan. I'm looking pretty shabby and when the noises in my head pause I hear sirens blaring in the background and I wonder if they are for me. I remember that one of the signs of breakdown is deteriorating physical appearance. I researched psychosis in minute detail after my first illness, so I know what I'm looking for. My skin smells odd too. Sulphurous and tainted. They say madness has a stink of its own. Maybe a haunting does too. Fretful and anxious I feel myself slump to the floor and in a cold daze watch the early shop-workers take a wide route around me. Today I am not a wealthy, vibrant and high-achieving Asian woman. I am dusty inside and out from exhaustion, and this heavy fear deep rooted like a truffle in the earth. I hear the work-shy jingle of keys and turn my face slightly to see one of the receptionists staring at me, mouth agape. I'm not aware that my appearance is so distressing and I feel anger suddenly coursing through my veins as venomous as a Chang Mai centipede. I start to stand, and my legs buckle.

I get doctor, the girl mutters as she furiously drives the key into the office door. After a moment's struggle she darts inside and locks the door on me. On me! I crawl towards the door and start to batter on it.

Through the glass I can make out the receptionist retreating further into the darkened room on the other side. I hear her on the phone, garbled and stuttering with fear.

This is ridiculous, I think to myself. I just need to get in and explain to her that I'm perfectly safe, but I've had no sleep, and am struggling a bit. I glance around and the only thing I can see is a heavy wooden chair, lacquered to perfection, outside the newly opened osteopath's opposite. I bang on the door one more time to allow her to be reasonable. From the other side of the door she shakes her dark-skinned Malay moon-face at me and hunkers down behind the desk. I realise there is only one thing for me to do and I get to my feet, walk shakily to the door of the osteopath and hoist the wooden chair above my head. I stagger back towards the glass door and with my last gram of physical strength hurl the chair at the doorway.

I hadn't really expected the door to collapse as dramatically as it does. I rather thought it would bounce off like in films, in secret labs and spaceships. Dr Chan clearly had not invested in expensive glass, preferring, instead, the cheap shattering version that explodes on contact with something hard and shoots pointy icicles in all directions. It is loud. It is noisy. It is very messy. I start to giggle slightly hysterically at the mess and at the girl hiding behind the desk and realise I had better pacify her quickly. Walking as steadily as I can towards the reception desk I hold my hands out in a placatory gesture, unconcerned about the blood streaming from my left palm down my clothes.

Why did this silly girl look so frightened? I am feeling angry again. My emotions are everywhere. A disorganised haystack.

And then, in the corner of my eye, I see the little ghost again, distorted by the half-shadow of the office but framed in a halo of oily light. I can taste that light on my tongue. It's coating it thickly with a viscous bile. I feel myself gagging. I turn helplessly to the moon-faced cow standing staring at me and try to warn her, and then I hear a whisper in my ear.

'Madam Eunice?' And as I turn I see Dr Chan with a puzzled look on his usually inscrutable face. Pale, unlined and slug-like.

'Don't touch me!' I warn him and push him away with my right hand. The shard I still hold slashes his face and tears a deep gouge.

I hear, to my satisfaction, Dr Chan scream and watch him drop to his knees. The cow starts to low behind the desk and for a second I have absolute clarity. There is blood and glass. People screaming. And the little ghost girl just keeps pointing at the door, her mouth a silent scream, and I do the only sane thing possible. I gather up my crumpling body and my strength and I run.

Gleneagles Medical Centre is bustling and that is usual. I push through the patients and visitors, taking the stairs because I don't want to encourage questions about my bloodied hand in the lift. I have already caught sight of myself in a window, and my own reflection shocked me, but I have no time to dwell on how I look. I have a limited amount of time to do a certain thing. And do it I must. I back into the ladies' bathroom and wipe the blood from my palm. I have a deep cut through it that is bleeding steadily so I wadge some towels together and grip them in a fist. I brush my hair back from my face with water and dab the night's dirt and recent tears from my cheeks. Brushing down my clothes I feel that a taxi will take me now.

I must have dropped my handbag somewhere at the HBD after the terrible fright of the child-spectre in the lift, but I find a fifty-dollar note in my jeans pocket. Don't run, don't cause alarm, I chant softly to myself. And so with all the presence and the iciness of a debutante at her first ball I stride swiftly through the lobby to the taxi queue and wait patiently. I refuse to meet anybody else's eyes and stare stoically ahead.

The Uncle driving gives me 'the' look but doesn't refuse my fare. I give him directions and assure him I don't care how he gets there. 'Take the AYE, the PIE, Alexander, Holland Road, I don't care. Just get there.'

Uncle raises his eyebrows at that but centuries of smooth face and miànzi prevents him from commenting. The blue cab swings out of the hospital grounds and onto Napier Road. I start to giggle again. Mirth rising up in my gullet. An unwanted bubble in a jar of pickled plums. Not a flicker from Uncle. I keep the fifty-dollar note in between two fingers so he can see it at all times. The traffic around surges forward with as much motivation as a sun-baked lizard. Constant beeping, sighing, muttering and hand gestures accompany

Uncle's driving. I begin to feel listless and pull myself up straight in the seat. I haven't bothered with a seat belt. Why would I? I am so disengaged from the world. It is impossible to be caught up in the here and now when I am straddling madness or worse.

I am hopeful that after I've rid myself of the 'debt' my life will be transformed. I think it will possibly be easier and safer to let myself descend into the maw. I can hear it roaring on the edge of my psyche and it would not take much to allow myself to swallow-dive to oblivion. I am very tired. My cheeks feel hollow and I sense my complexion yellowing like rancid oil. I know I must stay lucid for a while longer. Uncle pulls up in the street I know so well and yet it feels completely alien today. Strange how a familiar stretch of tarmac lined with trees and detached houses can feel so odd. That odd sulphurous smell envelops me as I open the door. I try to hand Uncle the fare but he pushes me off and stares at me in the rear-view mirror.

'Get out. Get out. *Mogui!*'

The taxi screeches off and I watch the dust rise in its speedy wake. Suddenly I long for the cool of some lake water. Where the cranes pick their way elegantly through the reeds, those dignified assassins of the waterways. Just to rest my head on the mossy ground and let the *yinghua* carpet me with their sugar pink blossoms. Maybe, after this is over, I will travel with the boys to the countryside again. Perhaps home-school them for a while with hugs and kisses. Remove their glasses and let them hop about naked in the eager sun as it tickles the brown into their little boy-skin. Yes, that is what we will do.

I adjust my eyes to the harsh sunlight. Even at this mid-morning hour the glare is unforgiving and makes my nerves wince. I edge towards Little Ping's house. Soon to be dead Little Ping's house. I can't help but giggle again. It's terribly funny really. There I am edging towards my nemesis about to take membership of a very élite club and all I can do is giggle. In fact, I laugh so much I have to wipe saliva away from my mouth to prevent it dripping onto my chin. I receive a couple of odd looks from a maid but nothing that makes me particularly anxious. Why would I worry about a maid's opinion? The day that happens is the day I know I've really lost sight of myself.

The house looks empty but then it usually does. Little Ping enjoys quiet, such an odd thing for an Asian woman, and she lets her maids have a free hand, allowing them to watch television on their breaks and use their cellphones indiscriminately. Still at least that means there won't be too many eyes on me. I don't bother with the front door and instead crouch and run through the heavy undergrowth around the periphery of the garden until I arrive at the back of the house. I take time to appreciate the beautiful space that has been created, then step through to the kitchen. It is empty and I select a large butcher's knife from the block conveniently located for me on the nearest surface.

Gripping the knife I totter through the house. Fizzy flashbacks erode my concentration as echoes of parties and laughter flow past me. I head for the living room where I can hear Haydn, no, Bach, it is definitely Bach. I catch myself wondering if Bach is a good composer to die to. I push the door open and find Little Ping sitting alone, eyes half-closed, paying rapt attention to the music. She starts up when she sees me and looks of horror and confusion battle on her face.

It is over very quickly but there is so much more blood that I thought there would be. It decorates the walls with a Rothko intensity and the colour is majestic, ranging from scarlet to ruby and then into streaks of a deep jam-colour. I drop the knife and walk out of the front door.

There is no memory of travelling back to Sabre Green. I do not know if I walked, ran or hailed a taxi. But I when I come to a young, ill-looking Indonesian helper is shaking me gently.

'Madam? Madam? Are you all right? Are you hurt?'

Her hair is very odd as if someone has hacked at it with hedge shears and suddenly she frightens me. I push her away and notice some of the blood from my hands has smeared itself onto her cheek and pock-marked her white shirt. The girl backs away from me slowly and disappears like a ghost into the air. Perhaps she is one. I'm learning that the world has turned on its head. Attempting to stand is a fruitless exercise and as my legs sag under me I manage to sit cross-legged outside the front gate on the pavement. I'll just rest a bit, I think, hearing the hysterical drones of sirens but not feeling involved with them at all.

I can feel myself falling asleep.

MA'AM LESLEY

35 Sabre Green

Days have passed after I crumpled in front of Norfolk and evidence of Ralph's infidelity. I have experienced an odd sense of relief. After years of guilt and emotional self-flagellation I feel vindicated. I look at myself in the cracked and dirty mirror in the room I now sleep in and exactly the same image is reflected back at me as the one in the Venetian mirror that steals attention in the master bedroom. For the first time in many tear-stained and darkly shadowed days I realise that who I am is based on the recurring image I see in the present and not the ever-changing, ugly self-portrait that I harbour in the attic of my mind.

Norfolk had been conciliatory and anxious. He wouldn't leave until he was sure that I was quite recovered. But my infatuation with this man had halted abruptly. Loyalty to his country and his job far outweighed any muted affection he might have felt or demonstrated for me. His dramatic revelation of those pictures had been a purposeful device intended to shock me into an honest reaction. I wonder how disappointed he is that I have proved myself an innocent party. Is this what healing feels like? A profound but gentle sense of recovery? I am invigorated by this idea, and find myself relaxing into the old rocking chair in the garden. I had always imagined breastfeeding in this chair and letting time wash over us, and the idea that I would be feeding my child here in the future excited a smile of plenty.

Ralph is never far from my mind but he exists only as a construct from my past. Even if he returns he can never be present in my life again. I was beaten by a fallacy of a man. A deceit so unworthy of my tears and pain I don't think I will ever grieve again.

I sigh and think about juicing some fruit for Jocelyn. I am beginning to find her presence really tedious and ache for the time when it will just be the baby and me and I can begin my journey of motherhood. The lack of milk in my breasts is nothing when I think of the breathless yet fluid love that rolls from my pores and threatens to overwhelm me. I am so crazy for labour to start I find myself watching Jocelyn carefully, determined to leap on the first twitch of her body beginning to move through into the birth. It should start any day now. I have been warned, though Jocelyn is not in the least bit interested, that because of her diminutive size the baby could be premature. This doesn't pose any immediate health problems but I should be watchful.

And as these things generally play out in this world full of realities and coincidences, Jocelyn goes into labour at 2.09am. One of the worst hours of the night for me is the battle between two and three. There is usually an agonising hunger for the light of morning and yet the demons caper on through the darkness. But when I first hear Jocelyn groan and shift her position in the bed I wake quickly. I have been sleeping next to her for the last few weeks and my sleep has become light. Yowling toms, insensitive drivers and the Singapore haze have all contributed to a lack of rest. But I feel ready for anything and adrenaline lasts a surprisingly long time in the body.

Jocelyn wakes up as her waters break and she panics. I murmur nonsensical calm things to her and encourage her to get off the sodden sheets. We need to get to the hospital, I tell her, but then as she sinks to the ground I see it is far too late for that. Her hair is already matted with sweat, strands clinging to her perspiring face.

'Ma'am, Ma'am,' she pants.

'It's okay, love, it's okay.' But is it? Despite all my anticipation, I have no real idea at all how to birth a baby. The only fact I can remember from books is that in all cases, whether it be Anne Boleyn's or Mrs H's from 'Ackney, towels and hot water are mandatory.

The poor girl is crawling around the floor screaming every few minutes. I grab some towels and a bowl of hot water from the bathroom.

'I've got to push, Ma'am! Aye! It hurts, it damn hurts!'

I hunkered down beside her and shouted, 'Well, just bloody do it then!'

So my baby comes into this world brown-skinned, bloody and the most glorious thing I have ever seen. Jocelyn is exhausted, panting and desperate. She glances at the baby once and wrinkles her face. 'Why are they so ugly? You can't change your mind, Ma'am, you signed the papers!'

I laugh at the absurdity. Not ugly at all. Absolutely beautiful. Jocelyn relaxes visibly, reassured that I won't be giving the baby back because it is unappealing. 'Do you think you can breastfeed? For a little bit? It's so good for the baby.' I know it is unfair to ask but a mother's selfishness for her child is upon me and I want Lily – because that's what I will name her – to have the very best start. I have considered the chance that Jocelyn might re-bond with the child but this doesn't happen.

'I won't. The idea make me feel sick. I don't want my *suso* getting old and saggy.' So I sigh gently and lay Lily on the bed carefully before making Jocelyn comfortable. Lily watches me with an intense stare and I realise that her eyes are as green as a Cornish rockpool. I had supposed they would turn brown, but then Ralph's eyes are an extraordinary olive colour. Perhaps his genes will be strong enough.

Gathering Lily from the bed I move downstairs and put the kettle on, humming to myself. My daughter, how wonderful that sounds, needs a bath and bottle. But feeding first. I make up the bottle with little grace. A measured, easy routine is out of my reach at the moment, but I do my best and Lily seems to like it. Sucking away contentedly, a rosy glow appearing on her cheeks. I pick a bottle of water for Jocelyn and shove some fruit, biscuits and crisps into a plastic bag and climb carefully back upstairs.

Unfairly, I begin to resent Jocelyn imposing on my time with Lily. I have fallen in love irrevocably, finally. All I want is to hold her near to me and breathe in the wonder of my child. I find Jocelyn's behaviour odd but reassuring. Her lack of interest in the baby and her desire to leave quickly clearly mean she has not bonded with the child. I have been unwilling to admit to myself how much I have feared her reaction. I am weary from the weight of recent struggles and would have had little spark left to defend our agreement if pushed.

I am grateful that Jocelyn seems intent on leaving our lives as soon as possible accompanied only by her shabby Hello Kitty suitcase, my gratitude and a large cheque. Ralph I now hardly give a real thought to. Do traitors have parental rights? I wonder briefly if he will pursue us if he is still alive. It is unlikely because of Lily's gender. A boy would have been far more interesting and useful to my husband. A baby 'beard' to demonstrate to the world his masculinity and vigour. Poor Ralph. He wouldn't be the first closeted gay man to have had children. Children tend to distract from a person's sexuality unequivocally.

And so I bide my time and wait for Jocelyn to heal and take her baggage, emotional and physical, to faraway climes where she can maintain a well-fed life and, no doubt, find other men to entice and enrapture. And her departure doesn't sound with trumpets or fanfare. There is no proclamation with the dawn. Just a blue cab for a brown girl. Eager and fulfilled, with money and an escape.

And our goodbye is faltered and awkward. Jocelyn hesitates at the taxi door and turns to look at me and then for a second longer, at Lily.

'*Ingat*, Ma'am.'

Then she ends and Lily and I begin.

SHAMMI

112 Sabre Green

I wake to white. And I think with great peace that I am in heaven. And then the light becomes too bright and I can hear voices pushing at the sides of my head. I feel woolly and insubstantial like a shabby duck feather that has absconded to a muddy river. The intensity of the light increases, becomes whiter and forces my eyes open to acknowledge it. I can see faces moving around me and I'm hopeful that they might be angels. I am totally at ease with where I am. It will be the end of distress, pain and endless wondering about the sanctity of my life and the mortal sin I might have committed.

But these feelings of peace start to recede as pain engulfs my body and I cry. Sharply and quietly like a bloodied mouse. A cool hand soothes my forehead and I ask that my sins be forgiven. And then white beckons again through that angelic voice.

Later, I wake to a hospital room. It is more than I have ever had. I am lying on a bed with a mattress that is soft. I hear machines and when I bring my hand up to my eyes I feel a snag in my hand where the tubes enter. I feel panicked and try to shout my fear but only a cracked memory of voice remains in my throat. Bandages cover my wrists and I am swamped with shame and a disconsolate sadness that sits heavily on my shoulders, an iron shawl embroidered with tears and ribbons of grief. Lying rigid with my self-disgust I await my fate passively. I will not protest or excuse myself but talk to God truthfully. I will say that I will do better and that I fear I have failed him most miserably and take whatever judgement he pronounces.

I hear the door opening and close my eyes tight like a child expecting pain. I hear her calling me but I can't quite believe this is real. Perhaps I am hallucinating.

'Shammi, Shammi, darling, dear one. Please come back to me.

Babu? You are safe now.' I open one eye slightly unwilling to commit myself to the mockery of an illusion. And there she is. My Ebony Ma'am. Her blueberry-black hair in an industrious plait and her face tight with worry. 'Can you sit up, little one. Look, see the things we have brought you.'

My Ebony Ma'am helps me shuffle up the pillows. I grimace with stiffness and disbelief. 'Are you real?'

'Yes, *Babu*, I am real. Look, feel.' And she puts my hand very gently onto her face. I trace the lines of her bones like a blind woman imprinting the planes and inconsistencies into my memory.

'I did a terrible thing. A mortal sin. You shouldn't touch me. I'm bad.' I withdraw my hand and turn my head away to face the wall.

Ebony Ma'am walks to the other side and faces me again. 'Not bad, darling girl, never bad. Sad and abused and badly done by. It is I who should feel guilty. I didn't save you hard enough and for that I am deeply sorry.'

I realise she is asking me for forgiveness. An incomprehensible idea swims towards me. This woman who is so much more than I can ever be is humbling herself. I nod because I'm unable to do more. She acknowledges this and a trickle of her sincerity, a sign of her goodness runs down her cheek. I feel myself warming in her sun shadow. A place of greater safety. And as quickly I remember my Madam and suddenly I am very frightened. I tense and swallow. 'I can't stay here. My Madam will be very angry. I must let her know.'

Ebony Ma'am draws a breath in sharply. 'Your Ma'am is being questioned by the police, *Babu*. You have many old wounds and two ribs are fractured. Your eye is black and your face is swollen. She faces prison for what she has done.'

I am shocked to silence. 'But what will happen to me? I need money for my parents! The agency will ask for more money.' My chest starts to constrict and I can feel myself panting a desperate beat. My hands claw at the bedding.

'*Babu*, *Babu*. Everything is taken care of. You won't have to work here again if you don't want to. You could come with us. Work for us. Or I will pay for you to take a course. Massage or beauty, maybe. You could work in a big hotel. A luxury chain.'

Ebony Ma'am is hopeful for me. I barely hear what she says, enjoying just looking at her face. Her beautiful, calm face that is for the moment racked by worry.

A nurse enters and I cringe away reflexively. Drawing my knees to my chest with my chin down. Eyes down. Everything low and submissive. I hear her whispering to Ebony Ma'am but still I can't open my eyes. There is too much at risk. I'm still not convinced that this isn't a figment of the devil's imagination. As I lie, as tightly drawn as a viola's strings, I start to see the room in focus.

Flowers in vases everywhere, beautiful, painted with God colours. Some leap from the vase like shadow puppets daring you to look away. Others are more demure like nuns lining up for Mass. And then the details of the room begin to emerge. I see an impossibly beautiful silk robe thrown casually over a chair. There are clothes hanging in a cupboard. I see three soft toys, a rabbit, a dragon and a bear, sitting, happy with their status, ready to love. There Ma'am sits, watching me take in her efforts and waiting patiently for my satisfaction.

We are quiet for a time. The rain has begun again but the prevailing winds have been kind to some of us. A feeling of quiet and calm, quite unfamiliar to me, is present in the room. I realise that for the first time since arriving in Singapore I have time for myself. Time to think, time to cry, time to live. From now on I will never let myself be compromised again. I will never sell myself for a pittance, or clean another woman's house, or betray myself to such dark self-esteem, or lie bruised for a night, or allow a man to place hands on me.

I gaze at the blue robe, the sunburst in the corner of the room, the pattern of lethargic dust, the dove flying high, and now these things can be meaningful for me. I can be red and green and brown. I can be rose, lemon and grey. All these colours contain me and tiny fingers dusted with pigment beckon towards freedom, towards a dusty road to my past or a carpeted corridor to my future.

'Shammi, Shammi?' Ebony Ma'am questions. I am overcome with my possibilities. I am overcome by Shammi. An inelegant girl poised for life. The grace and state of my rose-chipped future in place like mosaic.

MADAM EUNICE

There are so many ghosts here. That is my first impression. Hazy, desiccated husks that move around stickily, slightly out of focus like an eye with a displaced lens. They haunt the corridors and bedrooms, the recreation room and the doctors' offices. And they visit me in my room to try to mock me. But I know their stories now and these ghosts have colourful, murderous pasts. We aren't here for kicking the dog. Ours are beastly, dreadful, *Straits Times* front-page deeds. And yet, in this house of shame, in this warren of lies and badness, I feel safe. I don't have to pretend to be the slicked-back, capable, glacial Asian warrior, a terracotta mother crumbling from the inside. I am a monument to blessed relief.

I have a pair of pyjamas. They are lilac with tiny jade flowers, homage to the jade figurine that I became when I stopped listening. Once you remove yourself from the aural world it all simplifies. Turn off the chatter, the voices, and the agony of the hum. Only a true introvert or the mad will appreciate the pain of noise. And am I mad? Possibly. It is certainly the consensus. A psychotic break of some sort brought on by a hormonal imbalance. I toss my head at the allusion to the menopause. That is more insulting to me, as a woman, than the brooch of madness they have pinned to my chest. I believe most conscientiously in my haunting.

And I won't betray it just to be able to leave here. I refuse to simper like the old trout in the next ward. Chun Tao is a peach past her sell-by date, but she's still game. Her face is an ornamental koi pond. Generally murky with vivid slashes of colour. She wears a deep red, waxy lipstick that seeps into the lines around her mouth like blood poisoning. But her eyes glitter blackly from sockets that are shrinking into death.

This is different from the last time, certainly more serious. Last time was baby blues and now it's murder. But they can dress it up how they like; it was self-defense when all is said and done. Of course, I have repeatedly told them this. There was no trial so I was unable to defend myself. I was diagnosed and sectioned back into the care of the Woodbridge Hospital in Buangkok which is now the much more formal 'Insititute of Mental Health'. This hospital was founded in the nineteenth century, and in true Asian style, because we don't do over-embellishment. A cow is a cow. A lunatic is a lunatic. It was named the Insane Hospital and then changed to Lunatic Asylum, which I respect more. Why dress up this place with woods and bridges? Most of us are never getting out. Most of us don't want to.

I've stopped my children coming here for obvious reasons. That is all I want to say about them.

There is a smell that pervades these corridors. They reek quietly of abandonment, shame, disease and days-old Bok Choi. The food is foolish and inept, mush for sloppy minds. They should feed us hard edges to make us crisper. The drugs are making my brain feel like a trampoline. The regime or protocol they have chosen performs a dance of death in my head. I resist atrophy. I refuse to concede. The mice that squeak about at night might very well work for the ministry of state security. A lot of the ghosts think that. There is more para-noia here than in a Korean general's medal tally. I laugh at that but it is an ugly sound as if I have forgotten how to externalise myself. I don't want to be noticed like Chun Tao, her tragic skin leaving a trail of crumbs in her wake. Don't follow the crumbs. Bad things happen when you follow the trail. Just ask Chun Tao's maid. She can tell you stories of needles and acid. Except she can't.

Or Ying Ying. I've no idea about the authenticity of her name but everybody calls her that. It's soft, gentle and sounds like a female panda. Except her favourite trick is to smear shit on her hands and then wipe them on the faces of as many people as possible. Something bad happened to Ying Ying. Rumours and legends abound in here. Some say she was a North Vietnamese spy and was tortured by the Americans, others that she was gang-raped by some border drug-mules caught in a heavy rainstorm and sheltering in a cave that Ying Ying stumbled upon in the dark. All I know is that she doesn't like to be touched and it's not good to look her fully in the eye. Like all wounded animals she reacts with shocking violence.

I nurture the climate of avoidance in here. Although you get used, shockingly quickly, to the grunts and screams of this monkey house, I would still rather have isolation. I find the doctors incredibly frustrating. They have no variation on a 1960s model of treatment, which is very drugs-based. Group therapy is pointless but they push it relentlessly. Even I pretended catatonia from time to time to give myself some breathing space. The less people believe my story the more sharp edges I develop.

To aid the recovery I'm not the least interested in, my doctor has painstakingly told me that the fortune teller never existed. That he went personally to the HBD I described and interviewed the taxi driver that I had ridden with. The taxi driver completely denied ever seeing me after studying my picture minutely for three minutes. What would a stupid pig-faced man from farmer stock understand about the machinations of my mind?

I'm cultured, educated and a delight in social circles. I will not have the last twenty years stripped away from me over the demise of that useless woman. Soiling my soul with my efforts to support my husband. If I could just pop home I could use my secret papers and pictures as leverage. Not that I want to.

But that *pantu*! Not a word from him, and the only letter containing notices of impending divorce. The irony is metal on my tongue. It is a bride's scold, it is bound feet, and it is she-*ganado xiuchi*. When I think of him I ask the little girl to seek him out with her black eyes and maw for a mouth. Sometimes I ask her to move something in the house. Sometimes I ask far worse. So far she has refused.

There is a Japanese cast to her eye and I wonder where she goes and whom she tortures when I can't see her. What keeps her here close to me? At first I was relieved that the child turned up. I asked questions, demanded answers and eventually threw things at her. Now I just gain a subtle comfort. I like to think that she is perhaps an ancestor come to advise and protect. But the malice in her eyes and the twist of her mouth make me doubt it.

I still have my jade figurine. I found it in my hand when the police roused me. And slipped it into my crotch for safekeeping. It is only three inches tall but, as our culture dictates, gold is valuable and *yŏu*

is invaluable. My little sculpture is an heirloom from my grandmother. A lotus flower, from the Quing dynasty and carved by a delicate hand. The top half is a vivid green but the bottom is a milky
white. When I was a child I liked to imagine who had carved it and
to whom it had been given. My grandmother would tell me the story
of its inception, when I was ill, to soothe me.

A young craftsman had been commissioned to make the treasure
for a very rich man. A mandarin who was as powerful as he was
wealthy. His cruelty was legendary and celebrated. Many peasants
worked hard on his land and, for sport, he would ride through the
fields picking out young women for his sadistic pleasure. On this particular day a plain young woman whose demure and diffident pos-
ture inflamed his lust caught his eye. He sent a message to her parents
to expect a cart to collect their daughter the next night. The parents were distraught but too frightened of the merchant to refuse.
The mother counselled her daughter to be obedient and stay silent
on all matters of pain and she would survive the night. The daughter had a secret love, the young craftsman who had been commissioned to make the jade figurine for the merchant. When he heard
of the merchant's plans he carved the means of escape in tiny detail
deep into the leaves of the lotus and sent it to his love via a crane that
he had tamed. The young woman obeyed his instructions before the
merchant's henchmen could collect her and they were able to run far
away to safety.

In retribution the merchant murdered the girl's parents and nailed
their bodies to planks that remained there until even the carrion birds
turned their beaks away in disgust. When the girl heard the news, her
heart tore into tiny pieces and her tears filled with pain that turned
the jade white at the bottom of the figurine as a symbol of her lack of
filial obedience and her selfishness. Distraught and racked with guilt,
she threw herself from the highest mountain she could find to atone
for her sin.

I revelled in the beauty of this tragedy when I was younger. Snug-
gling into my grandmother's bony frame I swore to myself I would
be obedient to my parents and my future husband. And I kept that
promise.

We Chinese are very keen on paying blood with blood. Sometimes it is the only way to get closure on a difficult situation and our stoicism as individuals is deemed a cultural virtue. In the face of hardship and lean times the China man will work his fields harder and eat smaller portions. Shortage and need are very familiar figures to the farmer peasant; without them they do not thrive. I have always admired this desire for hunger and restraint. Like the stick girls in Ward Three, it takes a very real discipline to train yourself to refuse nurture. I haven't eaten enough for twenty-five years and I've come to realise that I also thrive on less.

My environment is not ideal or aesthetically pleasing but it provides a cradle of safety. There are no obstacles. No acts of revenge. Time actually passes smoothly. There are no choices and no responsibilities. It is restful, in the main, and my only frustration is the child and my inability to engage her. I've ceased mentioning the girl to the doctors who raise eyebrows and talk about breaking through my psychosis. Sanity is hard work and thinking too much makes me anxious.

I clutch my figurine and repeat my grandmother's story until I self-soothe enough to stop rocking.

Of the robed figure I have neither seen nor heard anything, and the air still streams around me and the clattering mass still belches and curses. The acute and unbearable beauty of feeling time stop has never returned. I am bereft without its truth. Sometimes I think he was a motif of my life. The jealousy of Little Ping in corporeal form, or my traitor husband's lust, perhaps.

It is strangely relaxing not to have a plan. I am not puzzled about my future. Futures in places like Woodbridge are precarious, mercurial things. They are best not tackled too often. The doctors never mention them and we don't think to. Why would we where the present is permanent and psychotropic drugs contain us so masterfully?

Best to avoid bloody images from a past that are blurred and water damaged. Staying in the present is safer.

A ghost wanders in to gibber at me. A nurse to advise that group is starting. And I take my time. Consider my options.

And the day she returns is a day of ambiguity. The snow falls heavily outside my window and the palm trees are coated like iced macaroons. I see a deer grazing in the grounds, eyes alert and gleaming with cold, each breath released in a plume of chilled smoke. Nostrils snort angrily against the ice that threatens to form there. Jade statues have appeared overnight and glow with cold, suggestive of seaweed sculptures in the depths of a northern ocean. I haven't felt weather cold for many years and am entranced. My pyjamas are scant comfort against the chill but I am beyond caring and barely feel it. Even my little ghoul seems friendlier today. Perhaps it is because I am compliant and happy to follow where she leads.

Up, up, up we go – ascending an intricate spiral staircase that I was unaware existed before now. The higher we get the colder it becomes and my body starts to feel sluggish. I notice piles of snow heaped in the corners of the staircase as we ascend, and icicles of differing sizes hang dagger-like from the cornices and ceilings. A large wooden door appears around the next corner and the little golem pushes it open to reveal a snow garden, high above the hospital. It is a replica of what I could see from my cell window and I hobble forward, my legs becoming blue and useless in the freezing temperatures, towards a statue of a sea monster. It is magnificent and I turn to include the little girl, but can't see her through the snow that is being whipped up by a wind that has never seen the Arctic.

I stagger sideways and find myself nearer to the ledge than I had thought. My poor feet are mottled ice colours and marbled with freezing blood. And the gale howls with malice, pushing and shoving me nearer to the edge of the roof.

It is how I imagine drowning to be. When a wave sucks you under and traps you on the seabed. Every time I try to suck in a breath it is snatched away from me by the cruel wind. I am exhausted and unable to do anything but shove feebly back at a force I can't see or fathom.

When the push comes it is almost gentle. A tiny hand in the small of my back forces my balance and quite suddenly I am in the air. Flying like Yuki-Onna, the snow woman, my hair streaming behind me and my skin glowing like alabaster and for seconds I am flush with love. For this ice world and my children. I hope they will remember me in their dreams and when they travel to frozen places, and keep my death warm in their hearts when they drown their own children in love.

And that my memory will be more than just of a brittle woman who failed to understand her fragile nature and who will perhaps be thought of with some kindness when darkness falls and the cicadas begin their choral works.

No pain. No pain at all. A blinding cold and heavy eyelids defeat me and my last, tiny smile is for a child with bleak eyes and terror for a mouth who stands beside me like a sentinel.

LUCILLA

19 Sabre Green

I'm walking the dog in the little park opposite the house tonight. Rory is with me on his blue scooter. He hurtles towards hard surfaces with no fear. A smile of the thrill of it plastered on his little face. I nod and *kumasta* other helpers. Some can talk, others motion with their eyes that Chinese employers are nearby. It is the way of things. Rory scampers towards the slides and swings. Look, Lully, look! my darling boy shouts as he attempts a grand gesture of a leap or bound. The other children look so pale in comparison to his ruddy, western complexion. If I took him home to my village he would be adopted by every mother there. I think Rory would like the mountains and streams. We have fish there and they nip and dart in the moonlight. We could waggle our feet in the cold mountain water and squeal. Eat bananas from the trees and name all the new goats. I think my darling would really enjoy that.

I sit by the other helpers and nod to the moans and groans about employers. I have nothing to add and instead fix my gaze on Rory. Some of the Chinese children are refusing to play with him and I feel my hackles rise. It's a good thing Ma'am isn't here. She doesn't stand for that sort of behaviour and strides towards the children, eyes blazing and skin flushed and talks quietly to them until they leave ashamed and sheepish.

She is a warrior when it comes to her child. Rory shrugs it off. He is secure in the love of his parents and the innocent assumption that the world adores him too. It is a good way to grow up. He is kind for his age, gentle even with insects, but brutal with his Lego bricks.

I will miss this park. I will miss this routine. If you have very little control in your life then routine is comforting. I will miss the rain trees and the Asian doves. And I will miss my Ma'am and Rory the most. I don't want another employer but I'm unsure about Europe. I don't feel it is right in my heart. One might call it instinct. I must talk to my Ma'am about it. She will know what to do and give me options. There is freedom to be had in choices if you are lucky enough to be given them. Most maids are unable to even trace the word let alone benefit from its meaning. They are unused to liberty and are anxious about the larger boundaries. I suppose I am just like them, really.

Afraid of the larger boundaries.

Rory is charming the other helpers. They adore him because he makes exaggerated gestures of chivalry. He will bow slightly and say in a loud voice, after you! And the Filipinas giggle and pinch him gently. Sometimes Ma'am comes to the park with delicious treats that she has baked herself. Brownies oozing richness or shortbread, sweet and melt in the mouth.

The Indonesian and Myanmar maids sit apart usually. They are not encouraged to mix or socialise and usually their employers circle them like hyenas, alert for any weakness or infringement. These girls are hollow-eyed and listless. They watch the children play with faces devoid of expression from months of hard work and lack of food. Their employers, the ones who choose village girls precisely for their naivety and circumstances, take advantage of their willingness. They come to Singapore warm-skinned and light of mind and leave raped by poverty and ill-treatment.

I always try a tentative smile at them. Sometimes, the delight at receiving some positive attention imbues the faces with the most wonderful light. Gold and green suffuse their round, beautiful faces and their eyes close with joy and I get a glimpse of the village girl surrounded by family and love and I'm filled with a bitter sweetness. Not like eating chocolate and salted nuts together. But the sour–sweet taste of pickled plums, cloying and sharp with no respite. Other times, they just stare or drop their faces. Sadness haunts their eyes and hopelessness turns their bodies into elderly versions of themselves. Lack of hope ages them more surely than time could ever hope to.

I shake my head to rid myself of this malaise that seems to sink into my pores. I try a smile out on my face and search for Rory. There he is, balancing, on high, arms thrown wide, face to the sky. My darling is exhilarated by his life, the moments, the possibilities, the genuine joy of being five and free. I hope I have children. Filipina women make wonderful mothers. It is our gift from God, a talent as important as being able to paint or speak well to a crowd. We are changing the future within our wombs. The life we bear grows and shapes and directly impacts the universe. Nothing is really more important. Perhaps men have always been jealous of this gift. What other reason could they possibly have to treat women with so much hate and suspicion throughout history? We have paid for their collective guilt for centuries. And we have paid in blood and pain and disgrace. We have picked ourselves up time and time again and succeeded in surviving.

But I admire men. I do. Their strength and passion and how fatherhood bends them into compliance as bamboo in a moderate wind. How they stay childlike until their death, terrified and adoring of us in varying degrees. Will we always be blamed for the Original Sin I wonder? Is it fair to be held accountable for an act so many years ago? And Eve so new and in love, at her most vulnerable and only wanting to share something delicious with the love of her life. Why wasn't Adam tested in the same way? Surely, he would have bent under temptation's wicked stare.

A scream tears through the air. I turn blindly in panic searching, searching. Where is he? I run to the play area and push past the children gathered at the foot of the slide. And there he sits, face as white as untreated silk and screwed up with sobs and fear as he clutches his ankle.

I drop to the ground and snarl at the children to back away. I feel along his slender, greenstick bones and sigh with relief. There is no breakage that I can feel but I will not take any chances. I ring for the ambulance as I soothe him the way Ma'am has instructed in any Rory-related emergency, and I text my Ma'am with the news but try to be as positive as possible.

Rory moans into my arms. 'I thought I could fly, Lulu, I thought I could fly.' You will, I think to myself. One day, my darling, you will.

And as I hold my wounded boy close I think that maybe freedom is enough to fly. That self-respect is enough to fly.

I don't think it has to be complicated.

Just invested in.

Like the business of breadfruit.

Or a meander of tears.

Or me.

Helpers' Song

(rough English translation from Burmese – the maid who wrote this
would like to keep her anonymity)

We come from the Land of Smiles and villages of shacks and laughter,
from Burmese firelands and the memory of Pol Pot's slaughter.
We arrive in cities of neon and glass that are hard-edged and very fast.
Full of hope, us women who clean and mop and tidy
surrounded by suspicion and people who despise us.

We care for and nurture your most precious children.
And daily we feed and hug and keen for our own babies left behind
remembered in tattered photos rarely seen.
We try to smile for you every day,
heads held high even when forced to keep four steps behind.
An unpaid packhorse and slave in a supposed free land.
I am strong and vibrant. I have stories to tell.

I am wise and beautiful and deserve freedom, not a cell.
And still you fail to notice the smudges beneath my eyes.
My rail-like thinness beneath cheap cotton ties.
Your eyes gloss over me; I'm simply not there.
I am a woman just like you, my Ma'am.
But I am a woman who cares.

Glossary

Akar Saga – highly poisonous seeds

Andaliman pepper – hot Indonesian spice

Ang moh – westerner (literal translation: red-haired)

As-Salaamu Alaykum – peace be upon you (Arabic greeting)

Aswang – ghoul/evil spirit

Bakla boy – gay

Bapa – father (Indonesian)

Bloody Banglas – unkind term for Bangladeshi men

Bojing and Peacock emperor – a very vain man, who thinks he is much more attractive than he is

Bubur candil – Indonesian sweet porridge

Dian Masalanta – Pinoy goddess of love

Ebu – mother (Indonesian)

Fajr – dawn, one of the five daily prayers offered by practising Muslims

Ganado xiuchi – livestock

HBD – Housing Development Board

Hokkien – people inhabiting South Eastern China

Hungry Ghost – Chinese festival to honour dead ancestors

Ingat – take care

Karanji stray – wild dog from the Karanji part of Singapore

Kumasta ka – how are you?

Longan – fruit from Southern Asia, also known as Dragon Eye

Mahal kita – I love you

Mahal din kita – I love you too

Maganda – beautiful

Meihua – plum blossom (term of endearment)

Miànzi – reputation, 'face'

Mogui – ghost/evil spirit

MRT – Singapore underground railway

Multo – ghost

Pabango – perfume

Pàntú – traitor (Chinese)

Pinoy – relating to the Philippines or Filipinos

Rajah – king or prince of India

Rangda – demon queen of Leyaks

Sabi – idiot

Salamat po! – thank you

Suplada – unfriendly

Suso – bust

Taisui – Chinese deity

Tembusu tree – large evergreen tree native to Southeast Asia

Tristesse – sadness (French)

Uncle – Singapore taxi driver

Wah piang eh – Hokkien phrase meaning surprise or disappointment

Wakwak – vampire

Xiào – filial piety, a virtue in Chinese culture

Xiǎochǒu – clown (chinese)

Yībān shāngdiàn – small shop

Yīnghuā – cherry blossom (Chinese)

Yǒu – being (Chinese)

Yuki Onna – Snow Woman spirit

Patrons

Jane Anderson
John Auckland
Ross Barnes
Simon Barrett
Alan Bebb-Lambie
Sandy Bennett-Haber
BJH
Druva Black
Helen Bolt
Lisa Brideau
Leigh Broom
Katy Bruce-Jones
Niamh Bryan
Dominic Burke
Ria-Jane Cann
Stuart Carter
Cazzikstan Cazzikstan
CharlotteAsh CharlotteAsh
Glennis Chung
Gail Cleare
Stevyn Colgan
Auntie Colin
Patti Collins
Russell Cruse
Harriet Cunningham
Edward Davis
Diane M Dickson
Al Dingwall
Euan Downie
Jennie Ensor
J F
M.J. Fahy

Ann Forster
Dan Forster
Frankie & (the mysterious) Em Saxx
Laura Freeman
Corinna Gallop
Ben Glanton
Roberta Gordon
Nicki Hambleton
Henrietta Heald
Paul Holbrook
Gary Holden
William Horwood
Elie Howe
Jason Howell
Karen Hunter
Polly Johnson
C Reg Jones
Ray Jones
Elena Kaufman
Patrick Kincaid
Shona Kinsella
Linda Knowles
Bradley Kornish
Werner Krotz
Ewan Lawrie
Ellie Lee
Jack Lenox
M E Lucas
Paul Lucas
Fran Macilvey
Neil MacKinnon
Yvonne Maddox
Richard Maitland
Tonia Marlowe
Sharlene Matharu
Melanie McAinsh

BobnSheila McGoran
Stuart McGougan
Aidan McQuade
Monique Metelerkamp
Evelyn Mitchell
John Mitchinson
Boff Moatman
Virginia Moffatt
Arif Moghal
Kali Napier
Tina Nixon
C Of
Scott Pack
Lev Parikian
Jonathan Partington
Poppy Peacock
Claire Picken
Jennifer Pierce
Dan Pullen
Lynn Quinn
Tina Rath
Andrew Ritchie
Guy Robarts
Jacqueline Robinson
Paul & Jean Robinson
Angelika Rust
Sebnem Sanders
Julie Shaw
Ian Skewis
Gen Soledad
Cindra Spencer
Georgiana Stirling
Teddy Stirling
Darius Stransky
Kerry Symington
Helen Taylor

Natalie Tett
Linda and John Thom
Lesley Tither
Solitaire Townsend
Liz Tranter
James Turner
Karien Van Ditzhuijzen
Veep
Gavin Vickery
Damon L. Wakes
Raphaela Weissman
Richard Wellings-Thomas
Laura Woods
Jacob Wright